THE
◆ BOOKS ◆
OF
The KeePeRS

BOOKS BY ANN DOWNER

The Spellkey
The Glass Salamander
The Books of the Keepers

THE BOOKS OF

The KeePeRS

ANN DOWNER

Atheneum 1993 New York

Maxwell Macmillan Canada
Toronto

Maxwell Macmillan International
New York Oxford Singapore Sydney

Atheneum
Macmillan Publishing Company
866 Third Avenue
New York, NY 10022

Maxwell Macmillan Canada, Inc.
1200 Eglinton Avenue East
Suite 200
Don Mills, Ontario M3C 3N1

Macmillan Publishing Company is part of the Maxwell Communication
Group of Companies.

First edition

Printed in the United States of America

10   9   8   7   6   5   4   3   2   1

The text of this book is set in Weiss.
Book design by Claire Naylon Vaccaro

Library of Congress Cataloging-in-Publication Data

Downer, Ann, 1960–
The Books of the Keepers / by Ann Downer. —1st ed.
p.   cm.
Summary: Bram, kidnapped to an underground kingdom to be consort
to the Elf Queen, escapes with the help of the Goblin Pretender and
returns to his mother Caitlin, who is seeking the Books of ancient
magic from the Elder Age. Sequel to "The Spellkey" and "The Glass
Salamander."
ISBN 0–689–31519–8
[1. Fantasy.]   I. Title.
PZ7.D7575Bo   1993
[Fic.]—dc20   92–30131

To the Keepers of the Books—
Barbara Lucas, Marcia Marshall, Ruth Mortimer, and Irene Rouse—
this book is affectionately dedicated.

Contents

1.

The Consort Pending

✦

The Consort Royal and Most High, Pending Examination, woke long before Morag was due to rouse him and lay in bed studying the ceiling of his room. This was vaulted, plaster over solid rock, painted with a cracked and much-faded map of the known world.

From Ylfcwen's palace in the center, tunnels and canals in gold and silver leaf wound past gemfields and pomegranate groves to the outlands held by the Goblin Pretender. The border of the ceiling where it met the four walls was a pale blue void, an arid home to wingless monsters. This was the world beyond the elvish kingdom, the mortal realm known simply as Above.

In the schoolroom there was an anatomy book with colored woodblocks of elves and goblins. Of these he saw living examples around him every day. Elves had wings and six-chambered hearts that pumped pale violet blood beneath their nearly colorless skin.

Their bones were long and hollow, like a bird's. Goblins were by contrast more feline, with peaked ears and yellow eyes. They were wingless, their hearts had five chambers, and their blood was not purple but red. It gave them a ruddy complexion. Their bones were solid. This made them strong and well suited to work in the gemfields.

The anatomy did not devote a colored woodblock to humans, so the boy was forced to study himself in the looking glass. He felt his shoulder blades nightly for signs of fledging—did he only imagine an itching there? His own blood was a puzzle. When he held his hand up to the light, the blood beneath his skin seemed blue; but when he pricked his finger, it welled up in little ruby beads.

If he stared at the map for a long time without blinking and then closed his eyes, the Consort Pending could see a ghost of it on the backs of his eyelids. Before the image faded, he would try to see what lay beyond the void. But, try as he might, he could never make out a thing.

❦ ❦ ❦ He only realized that Morag had come into the room when the golden light of a daylamp slowly spread across the ceiling. The goblin nurse went around the room extinguishing the nightlamps.

The stronger light of the daylamp showed a familiar crease of worry in one corner of Morag's mouth. She sat on the edge of the bed and mussed the boy's hair.

"Pending, I wish you wouldn't brood over that old ceiling."

The boy held his arms straight above his head. "Why?"

She pulled off his nightshirt and folded it carefully, shaking her head. "It should have been painted over long ago."

He laughed. "I'm glad it wasn't! How bored poor Tomus would be then, when he's sent to my room without dinner." Tomus was the goblin whipping boy whose lot it was to receive the royal punishments. As often as not, the Consort Pending sneaked in to serve the punishment with him, and they would lie on their backs and gaze at the ceiling, taking turns making up stories about the wonders to be found Above.

"The monsters will give you nightmares."

"They don't frighten me. Besides, I'm quite certain there aren't any monsters Above."

"And what makes you so sure?" she asked, smiling.

He had opened his mouth to answer when Morag suddenly stood and twitched smooth her smock, her eyes darting to the door.

Vervain swept into the room, her silks crackling as if with displeasure. "In future, Morag, please see that His Most Highness is not in a draft when he is being relieved of his nightclothes." She turned to the boy, her annoyed expression replaced by one of practiced inoffensiveness. "Most High, your bath awaits."

The boy pulled on his robe as he ran and they presently heard the slap of water against the side of the bath as he got in.

Morag made as if to pass with an armload of bed linen when Vervain's fingers closed on her arm. "Must we have another talk about overfamiliarity?"

If she shook inwardly, Morag preserved an outward calm. The goblin nurse looked the elvish governess in the eye. "No."

"Then don't let me catch you sitting on the edge of his bed again. Remember, he is the Consort Pending."

Morag lifted her chin a fraction of an inch. "But a boy, just the same!"

Vervain shook her head. "No—not to you, not even to me. He is the Consort-in-Waiting."

Being goblin, Morag could not cry, and her eyes glittered with a hot grief they could not shed. She turned and went into the adjoining bath to see that the Consort Pending washed behind his ears and did not splash more water on the floor than was seemly. Being a relatively recent addition to that section of the palace, the bath had no decoration, on the ceiling or otherwise, that could present any danger to a young imagination.

Vervain went into the schoolroom and began laying out pens and ink and parchment. Taking the Chronicles down from the shelf, she opened the massive volume to that morning's history lesson—the Goblin Revolt and Schism. Vervain shook her head; they would never get to the next lesson if the Consort did not memorize his Goblin Pretenders.

Vervain was worried. Someone had been telling the boy tales of Above, and she was unpleasantly certain who it must be. Even if Morag were capable of such foolhardiness, she had never ventured beyond the palace itself and so could not have told the boy anything. No, the boy had been sneaking off to the mines again. He'd heard those stories at Ethold's very knee. It was brash and unpardonable and could not go on.

Above all, Ylfcwen must never learn of it.

The Consort Pending came into the room, dressed in his everyday robes of dark blue damask with silver buttons. His dark hair, damp and carefully brushed by Morag, was already beginning to rise up in a cowlick. Sliding into his seat, the boy saw that the Chronicles lay open and made a face.

"Most High, I must risk an impertinence and ask you a question, and you must do your best to answer me candidly. I know you would never tell an untruth, but omitting to tell me the truth could have grave consequences."

The boy blinked and, sensing something more was wanted, slowly nodded.

"Have you been down to the mines? No"—she held up a hand—"it was wrong of me to ask. You need not answer. Only let me say this: If you were to go down to the mines, and if the queen should hear of it, it would not go well with Morag. It would be thought that she had encouraged you to go. You would not want Morag to get into trouble on your account, would you, Most High?"

4

The boy frowned, staring at the list of Goblin Pretenders. "No, Vervain."

"Then the next time you want a diversion, you must tell me. We'll pack a lunch and go on an excursion. Would that please you?"

The boy had been staring at the chart of the Goblin Pretenders without really seeing it. Now he raised eyes clouded with worry. "Yes. But, Vervain—"

"Yes, Most High. What is it?"

"Can't we begin with the rune tables today, instead of the Goblin Pretenders?"

🦋🦋🦋 Ylfcwen reclined on her silver grasshopper lounge and sighed as her dresser laid out wing case after wing case on the end of the bed.

"One would never guess that elves were supposed to be known for their needlework," said the queen. "Is this *all*?"

The dresser was that rarest of creatures, the elf given to plumpness, and she was pink and panting from the exertion of climbing up and down the ladders of the queen's closets. She gazed down at the dozens of wing cases ranged over the bed and upon velvets spread over all the tables and the floor. There were wing cases made of gilded parchment, wing cases encrusted with powdered dragonflies' wings, wing cases of cloth of gold stuck with beads of glittering jet. There were wing cases of spun silver and hammered pearl, of jeweled damask and hummingbird feathers. There were wing cases of cobwebby silk stiffened with a sizing of crushed opal and varnish. None of them would do, and there were no wing cases left to show the queen.

"No, madam," lied the dresser. "There is one more." And she disappeared into the maze of closets as if to fetch it. Returning from the closet empty-handed, she had caught up a wing case neatly as she passed the foot of the bed.

It was old, worked in a style long passed from favor. Midnight-blue silk was embroidered with pearls in a pattern of lilies of the valley. The pearls were only second-best, and at the corners the silk covering was worn shiny with age.

"It's perfect. Absolutely perfect," said the queen with a sigh. "Honestly, you are such a pea brain! Why by all Below didn't you show me this one first?"

The dresser had. She merely murmured an apology as she laced the queen into the wing case.

🐛🐛🐛 The queen's morning promised to pass in the usual tedium. Over breakfast her numerologist determined that it was not an auspicious day to visit the shrine of her ancestors at the center of the sacred underground lake.

Ylfcwen was disappointed. She loved visiting the shrine; it was a rare opportunity to use her silver barge. The ceremony itself was especially pretty: the relighting of the ether torches and the dedication of the gifts. And a feast to follow, involving many courses and the pandemonium of the right-of-seat, a ritual form of musical chairs.

She dragged her attention back to her numerologist, only to discover that he had left and that it was now her rune caster who sat beside her, advising her on the unlucky words she should avoid that day.

"Oh, by Above and Below and All-in-Between!" she snapped. "I might as well stay in bed!"

Since the Royal Household Agency had conducted the last purge of goblin spies, there had been no one interesting to talk to. There were no ambassadors or envoys to receive. She had all day to amuse herself before anything really entertaining could be counted on to happen. Her orchid arrangements and her watercolor scrolls had become tedious. The book she had been reading was being repaired, her pet mole having chewed out the binding.

She could always rearrange the tapestries in the Great Hall or, rather, have the stewards rearrange them while she sat by eating pistachio cake soaked in rootwine. But the queen was too restless to do even that.

Ylfcwen stopped picking at the silver embroidery on her gossamer robe and looked up.

"Where is the child?"

One of her myriad attendants, indistinguishable from all the rest, answered. "With Vervain, madam, in the northwest schoolroom."

"Let him be summoned. No, stop. I shall go myself."

She took one of the dilapidated corridors, part of an extensive network that was under constant repair. It had been years since she had come this way. Didn't it turn here? Yes, it did. Then you went down the corridor and made—a left?—yes, a left. It all came back to her. And suddenly there it was, as clean and tidy as if it had been waiting for her—the spy hole with its shutter, the folding stool with its worn tapestry cushion.

Ylfcwen settled herself and put her hand into her pocket for the cake she had taken from the secret store in her night table. It was nursery food—a marmalade tart from the boy's schoolroom tray—and she was ashamed at having taken it. Morag alone knew of the habit and deliberately left the Consort Pending's tray unattended to give Ylfcwen the chance to lift a few sweets. The cook would never have insulted the queen by preparing such a childish treat.

In the reign of an ancestral queen, when the palace had been much smaller, what was at present the northwest schoolroom had been a council chamber. Then the spy hole had given many an elvish queen a chance to find out what her trusted advisers said about her behind her back. At least one Goblin Pretender had met his end because of it. Through it Ylfcwen had spied on her own son, her Aethyr. It had been a young mother's only chance to see her child out from under the watchful eyes of his keepers, the ever-present instruments of the Royal Household Agency. The queen's interest in the present young scholar scowling over his Goblin Pretenders was altogether different. Ylfcwen pressed her eye to the spy hole.

The boy had worked one foot free from his slipper. With his stocking toes he was fiddling with a loose rung on his chair. The governess was intoning a list of names, pausing now and then to prompt her pupil and getting no response.

At last Vervain shook her head. "That's enough for today. But you must promise me, Most High, that you will at least *look* at the lesson before we begin. The sooner you learn the Goblin Pretenders, the faster we can move on to something else."

"But Vervain, *why* must I know all the Goblin Pretenders?"

The elvish governess considered this rather treasonous question a moment before she answered. "Tell me your full name, Most High."

"The Consort Royal and Most High, Pending Examination."

"Can you tell me what the last part means?"

"It means that I am the Consort Pending."

Vervain folded her hands over her grey smock. "It means, Most High, that you *will* be the consort once you are examined. You will not be examined until your seventh birthday. If the result is satisfactory, you will become the queen's Consort Apparent. And, when you are old enough, you will be crowned Consort Royal."

The boy drew in his bottom lip and considered this. "But, Vervain—"

"Yes, Most High?"

"What if I don't pass the examination?"

"Then you will have to study six years more and take it again on your thirteenth birthday."

The boy's eyes widened so that the whites were visible all the way around the amber irises in the middle.

Vervain bit her lower lip to suppress a smile. "With your

8

permission, Most High, I will withdraw. Morag has your lunch ready. We will take your afternoon lessons in the orchid nursery. Bring your brushes and colors, and make sure Morag has your painting smock for you."

The boy slid off his chair and ran from the room.

❦ ❦ ❦ Ylfcwen closed the shutter over the spy hole. She suspected the goblin nurse of feeding the boy the same meals the miners had. She frowned, thinking of coarse goblin food flavored with things that grew in the outlands, hard by the borders with Above: cavern figs, cave swift smoked with cloves and roasted with the stunted onions that grew in the dark. The queen sighed and thought of her own likely lunch: some mossy salad, pale hothouse fruit, pistachio cake, and wine. The queen brooded on this a moment, then lifted her chin. A headache was in order. Yes, she was quite sure she felt a headache coming on. She would retire to her bed, where there were at least two marmalade tarts in the drawer of the nightstand.

But it was not to be. She was accosted by the director of the Royal Household Agency. She was too near him to pretend to be out of earshot. In the moment that she hesitated, considering whether to duck behind a tapestry, he was upon her. There was no escaping.

"Madam, there are still some matters that need to be decided for the Consort's examination."

"Surely not. The preparations began four years ago. What by all Below can be left to do?"

"The examination clothes for yourself and the Consort Pending remain to be commissioned. And there *are* still a few legal difficulties that must be resolved favorably before all can proceed."

"These legal difficulties," she said in her cold, smooth, silver voice, "tell me, exactly how—*difficult*—are they?"

The director paled; she could see him trying to think of the most inoffensive words in which to couch the unpleasantness. "There has never before been a case of a consort being examined when the mortal mother was yet living and retained memory of her child."

Ylfcwen's face was as seamless as a mirror. Her enormous eyes studied the director as though he were a moth found among her precious silks. She was assessing the potential damage. At last she said only, "I am not unfamiliar with the particulars of the case." The goblin sent to replace the human child had not "taken." When discovered, the changeling had not been exposed to the elements, but named and, worse, loved. "I suppose you want me in a room somewhere, to sign things. Tell my dresser to fetch the signet ring."

"If you will pardon the liberty, madam, I have brought the necessary papers with me." He held out a sheaf of large, limp, closely written pages. "The Authorization of Royal Commission for the Consort's examination suit."

Ylfcwen took the papers and scanned them. "Is it not irregular? He must be at least seven to sit for the examination."

"That is so. But, as it happens, the terms of his indenture expire when he turns seven years and seven hours old. We have looked over the regulations most carefully and have found a most fortunate exception. He may begin the exam while he is six, so long as he *turns* seven years old before he finishes it. It is possible for him to be examined a few hours before his indenture ends; in that case, he then forfeits his birthright to return Above. Of course, it will not be put to him that way." The director of the Royal Household Agency cleared his throat. "If madam will sign . . ."

Ylfcwen paid him no heed. She was remembering her son on his seventh birthday. Nothing had been spared in the lavish preparations and gifts, the most fantastic of which had been a revolving kaleidoscope room. When the time came for him to make a wish over the cinder cake before it was cast into the fire, the boy was nowhere to be found. He turned up at last under a couch, playing with a wooden top a goblin nurse had given him.

🌿🌿🌿 Vervain waited until Pending was twenty minutes late before dispatching servants to find him and remind him of the drawing lesson. The search proved futile. Morag reported the boy had bolted his lunch and beat from the room like a bat from Above.

"Boys will be boys," she said, biting off a thread from her mending, "even if they are Consorts-in-Waiting."

Vervain swallowed her chagrin. "Well, he's nowhere to be found. For all anyone can tell, he's turned into a mole and disappeared down a tunnel."

She was not far wrong.

🌿🌿🌿 It had all started several months earlier with a game of hide-and-go-seek. His goblin whipping boy, Tomus, had been the seeker and, even with the consort's head start to offset goblin intuition, Tomus had found him six times running. Determined not to be found again, Pending had hidden himself in one of the old dumbwaiters left over from another regime when, afraid of being poisoned, the queen of the time had dinner laid in dozens of decoy dining rooms to outwit the Pretender of her day.

He had been congratulating himself on his latest hiding place when the dumbwaiter began a rapid descent, plummeting past all the inhabited levels of the palace, past unseen basement storerooms and armories and kennels, so that he thought he must be moving toward the very middle of the world itself. This, everyone knew, was filled with the Ether of Life and molten gold. The boy bit his lip and prepared to be gilded alive.

The dumbwaiter had come to a rusty halt, and someone on the other side—some creature of the ethereal interior, impervious to the temperature of molten gold—had cursed the dumbwaiter doors while trying to open them. When they opened at last, the boy looked with astonishment upon a broad face grimed with soot. Recovering from his own astonishment, the goblin yelled to the others.

"That Alma! Come look at what she's sent for our supper! If it isn't the Consort Pending's whipping boy!"

The tallest of the other miners came over.

"Whipping boy, nothing. That's the Consort Pending himself. No mistaking Vervain's handiwork." He threw back his head and laughed. "And he's sat on Alma's best pie."

That was how he first met Ethold. At the miners' insistence, he had joined them in a lunch of flattened mole pie. Contrary to Ylfcwen's suspicions, the miners ate food from the queen's own larders, prepared in the palace kitchens by the queen's own second sauce cook, a goblin lass by the name of Alma.

Hours later, after singing many goblin songs whose words were cleaned up for his benefit, and drinking much strong tea with a slug of rootwine in it, he had tiptoed through the palace to find Morag had fed his dinner to Tomus and put Tomus to bed in his place so that Vervain would not guess he was gone.

"Pending, I won't give you Tomus's whipping, but you do deserve it, you know you do! They'd flay me alive for speaking to you so, but mercy, someone has to tell you. If Vervain had discovered Tomus, do you have any idea what would have happened to him?" And she had fed him Tomus's dinner, and put him to bed on Tomus's pallet, and Vervain was never the wiser.

🌿🌿🌿 This day, while Vervain waited for him in the orchid nursery, Pending found the miners engrossed in a game of cat's eye, a drinking game played with somersault tumblers. Instead of a pedestal, these tumblers ended in a metal cage that enclosed a pair of dice. When the glass was filled the player emptied it in a swallow and set the glass upside down in front of him; the dice sealed in the cage showed a number or a "wild" rune. One miner, no doubt losing, accused another of having weighted his glass so that the dice always came up elevens.

A fight seemed about to break out. Ethold looked up and caught the boy's eye.

"That's enough, boys. Here, Pinch; take over my hand." With that he got up and came over to Pending.

"Well, it's been some time since you've paid a visit. Vervain must have been holding your nose to the whetstone." Ethold put out a hand and felt the boy's nose. "Yes, it's noticeably sharper." Then he felt the back of the boy's head. "She *is* cramming you full of wisdom. Here, feel it yourself."

Pending laughed and knocked Ethold's hand away. "Not so crammed as all that!" He related his problems with the Goblin Pretenders.

"Just remember, That Which Is Required Is Forbidden," Ethold said. At the boy's blank look, he repeated himself. "That Which Is Required Is Forbidden. It's a memory device: Each word begins with the first letter of one of the goblin kings, in order from the first king to the last."

A light dawned and Pending broke into a grin. "Tabardyr, Waerleg, Irlkin, Roleg, Ivo, Fustaugh!"

"Ah, we'll make a goblin of you yet!" muttered Ethold under his breath.

"But, Ethold—"

"Yes, Pending?"

"You called them kings, but Vervain calls them the Goblin Pretenders. Who is right?"

Ethold shook his head. "For as long as anyone can remember, the elvish queens have been fighting the goblin kings."

"What are they fighting about?"

"It's very complicated, Pending. The elvish queens say they have ever and always been fighting to defend the throne, while the goblins claim only to be fighting for their freedom. But listen: When you are with Vervain or anyone else from the palace, you must call them the Goblin Pretenders and nothing else, understand? Much hangs on your learning that lesson."

🌸 🌸 🌸 Ethold waited at the appointed place. The person he was meeting was late. It would have been nice to have a pipe while he waited, but he could not chance it. The queen's spies were everywhere, and clove smoke was a giveaway. No one in Ylfcwen's court would smoke anything so goblin. So Ethold stood in the half-light of a dimmed miner's torch and waited.

If he had so desired, Ethold might have lived at court with all the rank and privilege due a noble, even one of goblin blood. Ethold could pass for a full elf: he was uncommonly tall and lithe, lacking the florid complexion and stocky build of most goblins. His complexion had, in the poetic phrase of the court, "the kiss of the pomegranate" with none of its stain. His eyes, catlike only in their slant and intensity, were a mutable violet. Like all goblins, he possessed great physical grace and stamina as well as strategic intuition. These qualities made him a formidable opponent at wrestling and chess—and war.

Ethold had been at war with the queen for eleven years. To mention his name at court was an offense punishable by banishment; he had gone over to the side of the Goblin Pretender.

At some point, one of them must falter and bring the confrontation to an end. But it would not be soon; a similar blood feud several dynasties back had lasted nearly two centuries. There was plenty of time for Ethold and his followers to lard the queen's treasuries with counterfeit gems and set cave-ins at certain key tunnels in the gemfields. The rebels had allies within the palace itself. It was such a one that he awaited now, in the hour before the lighting of the daylamps.

The darkness of the tunnel gave up the form of a woman.

They greeted one another with the secret sign of their cause. Even when safely in the shadows, she did not push back the hood of her cloak.

"I am suspected," she said.

He darted a glance down the tunnel behind her. "Followed?"

"No, I am almost certain I was not. But suspected, yes."

"Have they any proof?"

"No, but you and I both know that with Ylfcwen, suspicion is as good as fact—or better. Ethold . . . I have been thinking. I had better not come anymore."

His laugh was full of affection. "You've been thinking too hard."

Her voice shook and she tried to steady it, speaking clear and low. "No, hear me! Someone else could serve in my place. The risk is too great—"

"And you are too valuable to us." He slipped his hands inside the hood on either side of her face. "And you're quite indispensable to *me*."

It was an uncomradely kiss. She turned her head and mumbled into his shoulder.

"I should go. They will miss me. . . ."

"As I will." His eyes glowed amethyst in the dark.

"Before you make me forget, here's this." She drew a linen-bound notebook from her cloak.

He slipped the notebook inside his shirt. "You're right about one thing, sweet. We'll have to be more careful. We'll change the place and time we meet. I won't send word to you for a while, for safety's sake. In the meantime, my thoughts are with you."

"And mine with you." She took a different tunnel, slipping back into the darkness. She did not look back, and soon had disappeared from his sight.

When he was safe in his bunk in the miners' barracks, Ethold drew out the notebook. It was full of elvish runes in a child's hand—not any child's hand, but the schoolboy script of the

Consort Pending himself. Handwriting exercises, nonsense sentences, maxims of an arcane schoolroom etiquette. The boy had struggled to shape the court script, with its clawed feet and hooked tails. The assignment had been constructed to force the boy to work on the most troublesome characters:

◆ Crimp the crusts and cut the crinkled cakes.
◆ Weave wet willow wands for weary wasps.
◆ Quiz the queen about the quick, queer quest.
◆ Bury the busy, bright blossoms, bumblebee. . . .

Ethold took out a small wheel fashioned from two circles of stiff paper, one large and one small, pinned together in the middle. A crescent-shaped window had been cut in the smaller circle. He turned the wheel so that a certain number showed through the window. Now, each goblin rune on the outer wheel was aligned with an elvish rune on the inner one. Ethold glanced at the first page of the notebook, then at the wheel, and began to fill a blank sheet of paper.

The palace is busy with preparations for the examination of the Consort. Ylfcwen has commanded the Mistress of the Stones and the Woman of the Rings to lay out all the royal jewels so that they may be sent out to be cleaned and mended in preparation for the ceremony. In addition, the queen has sent a servant Above to engage a tailor to make the examination suit for the Consort Pending. This presents us with an excellent opportunity to strike. . . .

2.

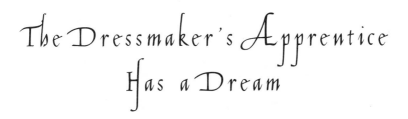

The Dressmaker's Apprentice Has a Dream

✦

The dressmaker's apprentice rarely dreamed anymore of her former life among the wolves.

At first, the memories had padded tirelessly after her. Not the recent past, with the circus troupe, or even the years at court before that, but her very earliest recollections—of the den; the warm, solid body of the old she-wolf; her first sight of winter trees silvered by an ice storm.

Seven years since, Ulfra had left Folderol's troupe and settled in Moorsedge, coming to live with Tansy over the dressmaker's shop at the sign of the Cat's Face, named for the curious appearance of its owner, a former attraction with the same circus. She had been the leopard-woman, and her countenance had about it all that the name implied: Coarse black hair covered her face except for the tip of her small, flat nose, which was white and pink. Her prominent upper jaw formed a kind of muzzle; because of it she spoke with a soft lisp. "All I lack to make the illusion complete are whiskers and a tail," she once told Ulfra, "and that old rogue Folderol tried to make me put them on, too."

Ulfra came to her new living at the age of twelve, more than a little rough around the edges. Before she could be entrusted with the shears or the heavy tailor's iron called a goose, Ulfra had to master the rudiments of acceptable behavior. Tansy taught her apprentice not to take meat from the spit before it had been carved at table, not to bare her teeth whenever a strange man came into the room, and, most difficult of all, to submit as meekly as she could to the indignities of soap and hot water, and the hated hair comb and nailbrush.

None of these things had come easily. Ulfra's snarl had driven more than one customer from the premises, and before she learned the rules of the house, Tansy would come down to supper to find the joint had been divided among Ulfra and the neighborhood dogs.

Ulfra was now nearly twenty-one. Looking at her, with her hair smoothed back, dressed in her spotless blue smock, few guessed her strange beginnings. But even now, when being introduced to a stranger, she pressed her lips together to suppress a wolfish grimace.

Tansy and Ulfra's conversation had about it an understated affection not found in many families, let alone between master and apprentice. Ulfra had a bedchamber of her own tucked up beneath the eaves. When her work was done she had the run of the house until Tansy called her to supper by the fire in their common sitting room. The leopard-woman took delight in being read to; many an evening in bitter weather Ulfra would oblige, with a traveler's tale, if it were a book of her choosing, or something with a good heroine, if Tansy's.

On a fine evening Tansy would take up her heavy walking stick and Ulfra would fetch their cloaks and they would walk along the lamplit streets and out of town, far enough down the road for the darkness to close in and show them the teeming stars.

Sometimes on these walks Ulfra's contentment would swell without warning into the keenest joy. Afterward she would crawl late to bed and sleep a bottomless sleep. If she dreamed a dream, wolves figured in it not at all.

❦ ❦ ❦ Tansy's old friend and confidante Lady Twixtwain came one evening to sup with them in their rooms above the Cat's Face. Ulfra helped her out of her cloak and hat. Lady Twixtwain's person was very large and exquisitely dressed, her humor unfailingly good, her tongue and wits sharp, her face reckoned among the two or three most beautiful in the thirteen kingdoms.

"Ulfra, my sweet, will you kindly take Opaline along to the kitchen for her tisane?"

"Have a peek at dinner, too, will you?" said Tansy. "If it's ready, you can just dish it up."

Opaline was Lady Twixtwain's aging and adored greyhound, who carried around her neck a purse containing her mistress's smelling salts and snuff, rouge and brandy. Ulfra unbuckled the purse and led the dog to the kitchen, where a bowl of chamomile steeped in milk was keeping warm.

Lady Twixtwain watched Ulfra go. When she was out of earshot, her ladyship began to peel the snowy kid gloves from her hands.

"She is much improved, my dear, very much improved. I commend you."

Tansy protested. "I have only tried to show her the advantages of mastering a craft and of sharpening the mind."

Lady Twixtwain considered this, her head tipped to one side. "In some cases, the only way to accomplish one's end is through a slow bringing along. But really, Tansy, you have succeeded admirably. She is lovely and natural without being at all false or coarse."

"I should hope she is still her own person."

"Oh, my, yes. That she is and will always be, have no fear of *that*."

Tansy shook her head. "I am afraid this is a hermitish life for a young woman. I go out so little, myself; my friends come to me. Our circle is small—outside of our patrons and one or two servants, I am her sole companion. It's a pity she should spend her youth making gowns for the daughters of merchants and councilmen without enjoying the same advantages. Though, to tell the truth, she never seems to envy them. She might be nine, not twenty, for all the interest she shows in the opposite sex."

Lady Twixtwain nodded thoughtfully. "Perhaps she is a winter's rose and will blossom when all hope of it has been given up. It's only natural, considering what her life had been. Think how much further she had to come than most young girls. When she *does* lose her heart, I think it will be wholeheartedly, with the same quiet passion she brings to everything."

"I hope you're right." The leopard-woman rose and went to the fire, taking and lighting a taper from the mantelpiece. She touched the taper to the wicks of the tall candles in the center of a card table laid for three. "I can't abide the thought of her breaking her heart," she said, shaking her head. "After all, I stripped away all the wildness that protected her. I made it possible for her to be terribly wounded."

Lady Twixtwain smiled. "But how else is love possible?"

Tansy rose and went to the hearth, where three plates were keeping warm. Wrapping her hand in the folds of her skirt, she transferred the hot plates to the table. "May I tell you something?"

"You mean, will I keep a secret?" Lady Twixtwain heaved a sigh. "It goes against my grain, but I shall."

20

Tansy first went and listened at the door. Ulfra's voice carried faintly, answered by Opaline's happy yelp. Taking her seat again, the leopard-woman began her tale.

"It was market day a few weeks past. We went out walking. I had bought her a hat, her first. Though she protested fiercely at the expense, I could tell she was quite pleased. It was very becoming, but with it on, she suddenly became unlike herself—coy and giddy.

"Well, we stopped at a stall where a farm woman was selling her wares. Ulfra said she was sick of partridge, why didn't we have sausages. It was a joke: Actually, business had been slower than usual, and we'd been dining on nothing but beans for a month. I began to barter with the woman and Ulfra asked the boy about the jam."

"Wait. Whose boy?"

"The farm woman's son, I supposed. I only glanced over for a second. I was wearing my veil, but I could still see him. He was about twelve or thirteen, small, wiry, brown as a nut, with strange, white hair."

"Wait. My feeble brain begins to stir. Wasn't there a mute with her in the circus? An albino, if my memory serves me?"

Tansy nodded. "Though, from what Ulfra has told me, he was neither mute nor albino. His name was Nix. And that is all she has told me of him in seven years."

"Did she speak to him?"

"Only what she had to, to buy the jam. It was plain to me she knew him. His face was a terrible thing to see. She smiled and thanked him; he handed her the jam; we left. And do you know, she hasn't worn the hat since, nor will she touch the jam. We never speak of it."

"Small seams," Lady Twixtwain said under her breath. This was a signal used by tailors to mean: The person you are talking about is coming into the room.

Tansy busied herself with the saltcellar.

21

Ulfra entered the room carrying the supper on a tray. Lady Twixtwain smiled.

"You had better hold that tray a little higher, or Opaline will have those chops out from under your nose."

❦ ❦ ❦ Ulfra awakened the following morning to find Opaline asleep at the foot of her bed. When the game of spoilfive ran on after dinner, the old dog would follow Ulfra up to bed and nap until Lady Twixtwain went home. The game must have gone on very late indeed.

Opaline opened her eyes, licked Ulfra's hand, and yawned. Watching her made Ulfra yawn, too, and she laughed.

"Good morning," she said, scratching the dog behind the ears. Opaline beat her tail on the coverlet politely, but her plaintive look said, It is past my breakfast time.

They padded downstairs together, where they found plum cake and hot wine keeping warm, and a note from Tansy.

Hope you both slept well. Opaline looked so sweet we didn't have the heart to wake her. I've taken the court gowns to Lady Alders in Blackswan Street for the final fitting. Please pick up the order at the button maker and then drop Opaline off at Lady T.'s—she has gone to the baths for the rest of the morning to lick her wounds. (Ha!)

Ulfra smiled; Lady Twixtwain always retreated to the public baths when Tansy had beaten her badly at cards.

They went out into the street. Moorsedge had been in decline for many years, a rough town on the border of the downs. Then one year the king's only son had come to hunt and stayed. He had reopened the long-closed palace built by an earlier king as a refuge for his queen during a drawn-out civil war. The prince's set had flocked to Moorsedge, and the merchants had followed them. Biding his time until the crown should be his, the prince indulged his tastes for the theater and other amusements.

It was the last market day before a holiday, and the streets were thronged with merchants selling tinware, live ducks, bottles and corks, melons, sausages, ribbons, flour, copper saucepans, cheeses, and hothouse grapes. One could have scissors sharpened, chickens plucked, boots mended, teeth pulled, keys made, curses removed. The air was filled with the fragrant steam and smoke from a stall where you could buy a paper cone filled with tiny, sweet crabs, dipped in batter and fried whole.

Ulfra had to drag Opaline away from the crab stall, where the dog was in danger of being nipped on the nose. They made their way to the button maker's, where Ulfra picked up the parcel. When that account was settled, she went from case to case in the tiny shop, looking for some buttons for the bodice she was making as a surprise for Tansy. At last she bought some of jet and amber in the shape of bees.

She had spent more time deciding on her buttons than she meant and hurried through the streets, with Opaline casting anxious looks up at her, as if to ask why they were in such a hurry.

As they turned into Lady Twixtwain's street, Opaline pulled up short, so frantic with fear that she tried to clamber up into Ulfra's arms.

In the cobbled yard, a slight, weasely man was baiting a wolf. If the wolf had not been muzzled and hobbled, it would not have been much of a match. A crowd of well-dressed onlookers watched from balconies and doorways, drinking wine and cheering the man on.

The wolf was too spent to resist as the man poked it in the ribs with a sharp stick. It lay glaring up at its tormentor. Then it caught sight of Ulfra and began a strange, high keening, a mingled greeting and plea.

Ulfra rushed up and struck the stick from the man's hand. The crowd roared. Scarlet with anger, the man grabbed her shoulder. She seized his thumb smartly and bent it backward so that he shrieked and let her go.

Ulfra knelt by the wolf and started to loosen the hobble. The crowd saw what she was about and their shouts faded quickly to a nervous murmuring. The courtyard quickly emptied, echoing with the clatter of many doors and shutters being fastened at once.

The animal was but half-grown, rope-sore and frightened, but Ulfra found no open wounds. She ran her hands over the wolf to reassure it, speaking to it low in her throat, in the whines and growls of wolf speech.

Keeping a safe distance, the man clutched his thumb and protested. "That's our wolf. There's a gold bounty on it! It's as good as stealing, what you're doing! My master will have you flogged for thievery—and for breaking my thumb!"

"Be careful what you say, William," said a new voice. "She looks capable of doing a little flogging herself."

Ulfra turned to see the newcomer. In the doorway of the inn stood a man of blunt, bearlike features and build, with a weather-roughened face above a grizzled beard. He held a goblet in one hand and a napkin was tucked under his chin, draped incongruously over the iron-studded leather breastplate of a professional hunter.

He was, in fact, the king's own huntsman. Seeing her there, her ice blue eyes the match of the wolf's, the animal calm and trusting in her arms, he was not about to tell her so.

"She's broken my thumb," the first man complained again.

"It's the least you deserved," Ulfra snapped.

"Yes, William, it is the least you deserved. Never tease a wolf. You had no way of telling if the muzzle would hold."

Ulfra stared blue daggers at him. "Is that his wrongdoing? Carelessness, and not cruelty?"

"Madam, that is my wolf. I intend to collect the bounty on it, in the name of the king. If you have some argument with that, then come with me, and we shall let the king decide the matter."

24

The huntsman smiled and held out his hands. The wolf curled its lip and growled low in its throat. Ulfra spoke to it in wolf speech; the animal flattened its ears in submission.

"This is a Direwolf," Ulfra said. "It is untouchable under the king's or any other law. If you harm it, you will answer to the Direwolves."

The huntsman frowned and considered. He had eaten a large meal; he wanted to finish his wine and have a pipe and a nap. He did not want to stand here arguing with a wolf-eyed girl.

"It is asking me to let it go so that it can kill you," she added. "It says you killed its mother with a trap."

"Tell it," he replied, carefully biting off each word, "that its mother and her kind have been killing the king's deer."

"It is the wolves' wood and their deer."

He saw that she would not be moved. "Take it. Take it back to the damned wood. But I promise you this: If I catch it again, I will skin it myself on the spot."

Ulfra nodded, coaxed Opaline from her hiding place under a stairway, and left, carrying the wolf in her arms.

The huntsman watched her go. "William, never interrupt my meal in this manner again," he said, and went back in to his repast. But his venison had lost its savor, and his hand, when he reached for the wine, trembled.

One spectator had not fled when Ulfra untied the wolf. He stood now as he had when the scene first unfolded, leaning against a rainspout in rumpled clothes the color of earth, a strange green hat perched on his head. He waited until the huntsman and his kennel master had left. Then the odd spectator bent and retrieved something from the ground, a parcel no bigger than a loaf of bread: the buttons, forgotten in the scuffle. The parcel was labeled in ink:

✦ T. Panter, Dressmaker
✦ At the sign of the Cat's Face
✦ Everlasting Lane

"Oh, my heavens!"

Tansy stood in the doorway to the sitting room and gazed in dismay at the scene before her. A half-grown wolf lay on the sofa, its paws bandaged, taking bits of raw liver from Ulfra's hand.

"It's all right," said Ulfra. "I've put down a cloth to catch anything he drops."

"Oh, Ulfra!"

"He's not strong enough to travel. He would never make it back to the wood on his own."

"Oh, my." Tansy ventured into the room and gingerly took a seat. "But who will take him there? No—you cannot think of going."

Ulfra shook her head. "I won't need to. When he is well, the others will come for him."

Tansy stared. The wolf stared back, then rested its head on the sofa cushion and grinned at her, tongue lolling.

"All right," she said, "but please make it—make *him* understand the rules of the house. And I think it best that our customers do not make his acquaintance."

🐾 🐾 🐾 The next day there came to the Cat's Face an odd customer. They were in the workroom when the bell rang; Ulfra set down the hissing iron goose and went into the outer room.

The person on the other side of the counter was remarkable even by the standards of the Cat's Face, a man of birdlike slightness and grace, dressed all in brown. He held in one hand a hat of ivy green. His face was outwardly stoic, with the merest hint of mirth about the eyes. These Ulfra took at first to be blue, but then realized that they were in fact silver and were only casting back the color of her work smock.

"May I be of some service?"

"I require a suit of clothes for a boy of not quite seven years."

26

The silver eyes roamed over the room, changing hue as they settled on various garments on display, drinking in a brilliant court dress in cloth of gold before turning on Ulfra a gaze as full of liquid fire as a cat's. "I am prepared to pay handsomely." One birdlike hand disappeared into a pocket and reappeared with a purse. Five-sided silver coins spilled onto the counter with a musical clatter. It was a currency unfamiliar to Ulfra, but in her circus days she had learned never to turn up her nose at other people's money.

"For such a sum you could have something handsome indeed. What is the occasion?"

"An examination."

Ulfra thought that odd, but held her tongue. She knew there was nothing of the kind in stock; among all their youngest patrons, there were no boys of seven. Then she remembered a commission recently completed for an old friend from Tansy's circus days. Ulfra fetched the suit and slipped it onto the smallest wooden form in the shop. She did not mention that it had been made for a dwarf.

It was black velvet, faced with cream silk and lavishly trimmed with lace and pearls.

"So heavy!" marveled the stranger.

"Yes. There are over one hundred pearls on it. Will something like this do?"

The odd customer smiled. "Something like it will answer our requirements most admirably."

Ulfra reached to get the heavy pattern register down from the shelf behind her. When she turned back to the counter she was alone, and the suit had vanished.

Ulfra returned to the workroom and took up the hissing goose.

"Who was it?" Tansy asked.

Ulfra started to say "A thief," but heard herself say instead, "The strangest person."

✿✿✿ That night Ulfra was roused from sleep by a loud rapping noise. She lay in bed, breathing as though still asleep, listening intently. The sound seemed to be coming from the heavy, dark wardrobe on the other side of the room. Easing off the blankets, Ulfra rolled out of bed, landing softly on the floor. Still in a crouch, she crept noiselessly across the room.

The wardrobe had stood in a neglected corner of the workroom until recently, when Tansy had decided Ulfra required a wardrobe of her own. They had aired it out and rubbed it with beeswax and lemon oil and hired six strong men to haul it upstairs. It was extremely heavy and very old—here and there the intricate carvings had been worn smooth, and the wood was black with age.

As she reached out to touch it, the knocking suddenly ceased. Ulfra stood staring at the heavy doors of the wardrobe, a prickling at the back of her neck keeping her from flinging them wide.

"Open, please," said a voice, muffled by wool and silk and damask. Fear gave way to indignation. Ulfra threw open the doors with a bang.

Inside, standing among her clothes, was the odd customer from the shop. His mousy suit had been replaced by a magnificent costume of white silk. He bowed low, the sleeves of his blue and silver overrobe sweeping the ground.

"I am sent at the queen's bidding to bring you back to the court Below," said he. "Will you come of your own free will?"

Ulfra laughed. "I should be very surprised if the back of my wardrobe was the way to the court of the elves. Tell me, when did you manage to hide in there? And why did you steal the suit?"

He smiled. "The suit will be returned. It is because it so pleased the queen that your services have been engaged. Will you come of your own free will?"

The tone of his voice and the cool gleam of his quicksilver

eyes were together so compelling that Ulfra found herself nodding. In a wink he had seized her hand and was drawing her into the wardrobe. What had always been a solid panel at the back of the wardrobe had become a brick wall set with a small door. The messenger in blue and silver opened it and helped Ulfra down a narrow staircase. They passed into a clean and spacious tunnel lit with ether. The silver gaslight showed walls covered with rich tapestries, surpassing in skill any Ulfra had seen, even at court.

The messenger led Ulfra to a room where elvish handmaidens gave her a silk coat with trailing sleeves to slip over her muslin nightdress. Returned to the custody of the messenger, she was led finally into a chamber that held a strange group of personages.

In the center, seated in a chair that was very grand yet not quite a throne, was an elf woman of extraordinary beauty. Her opal eyes betrayed both boredom with the situation and the hope that it might yet prove in some small part diverting. She held in her lap a small, furry creature, which Ulfra at first took for a rabbit, then saw was a mole.

To the queen's right stood an elvish woman whose bearing and clothing bespoke a position more of merit than birth. A close handmaiden or, more likely, a governess. Ulfra thought she was anxious, hiding something. Guilt, or fear.

At the queen's other hand stood a lean, elvish man with a face so expressionless it seemed a mask. Even his eyes were unreal, and they kept a sort of loathsome watchfulness, as a carrion crow keeps on a flock. Nastily keen for opportunity—that was it. Ulfra disliked him.

By far the most compelling person in the room was the boy seated at the feet of the queen. He sat on a small miniature of the queen's chair, and the queen's hand rested on his shoulder with the same lazy air of possession with which she petted the mole.

To judge by his face, he was no more than six, dressed after the elvish custom in many underrobes of sheer silk and an overrobe of heavy damask. This outermost robe was deep blue, embroidered in silver thread with a pattern of fireflies and lamps. For want of sun, his skin had grown almost as translucent as that of the queen. His legs seemed too long for the rest of him, as though enforced inactivity had thwarted a natural sturdiness of limb. He stared at Ulfra, trying his best to pass it off as mere gazing and not succeeding. The stare from his odd, amber-colored eyes was the only warm thing in the room.

The lean man took a step forward and read rapidly from a parchment. Then a set of papers was passed to the queen, who added her signature and seal. Once the wax was cool, the man nodded to the governess, who relieved the boy of his layered ceremonial robes. He stood before them in his smallclothes, unembarrassed. Ulfra assumed he was used to being dressed and undressed at the whim of his elders. A measuring tape was presented to her on a small cushion. Ulfra took it and began to measure the boy, stretching the tape taut along his shoulder and then down his back from the end of his neck to the bottom of his spine. He laughed when she measured his inseam, and his laugh, at least, was not pale and thin from lack of use. Like the look in his eyes, it spread through the room like the warmth of a fire.

"Does it tickle?" she wanted to ask, but in this dream she apparently had no power of speech. Still, the boy seemed to understand her, for he nodded and smiled.

The measurements taken, contracts were produced and she was made to sign the papers in several places. The queen extended her hand, and Ulfra knelt to kiss the signet ring, startled at the sting of the cold elvish silver. Then the original messenger appeared and led her away. Over her shoulder she caught sight of the boy as he lifted his chin so that the governess could button him all the way up. Ulfra thought he winked.

The messenger walked so quickly down the corridor that

Ulfra could barely keep up. They passed the changing room without a pause, and she was about to ask if she should return her borrowed robe when she suddenly woke up.

Sunlight was slanting through the dormer window; from the foot of the bed the wolf watched her. For a moment she forgot where she was. Tansy came in with a cup of tea, and Ulfra laughed and related her dream.

"Isn't it funny? When I woke up I was so confused that I thought it was yesterday and that Opaline had been changed into a wolf!"

Tansy did not laugh, but went and examined the wardrobe.

An odd feeling came over Ulfra as she watched the leopard-woman push aside the hanging clothes and rap the back of the wardrobe with her knuckles.

"Tansy!"

The leopard-woman came and sat on the bed. "I'm sorry; I don't mean to frighten you. It's just that you're not the first person to have an odd dream after spending a night in the same room with that wardrobe. It came down in my mother's family, from a relative said to be one of the Banished. It was careless of me to give it to you."

"But it was a dream!"

Tansy shook her head. "I'm afraid not." She drew from her pocket a small folded paper. "This was tacked to the door when I came back from the baker's."

It was parchment, folded into a tight square and sealed with wax. Ulfra stared at the sign embossed in the wax and felt her lip; where she had kissed the signet ring, there was a small spot blistered from cold. She broke the seal and unfolded the parchment.

The sheet was large and closely written in a runish hand. At the bottom someone had signed a large letter Y with a flourish. Beside it, in her own hand, was written her name.

Tansy shook her head. "This is no rune hand I've ever seen.

31

Look at the tails on the runes. Perhaps Lady Twixtwain will know someone who can translate it. In the meantime, we'll have that damn thing"—she nodded at the wardrobe—"hauled back downstairs!"

"No." Ulfra half shrugged, half shuddered, as if shaking off a chill. "I remember what it says. It's a contract for a court suit for a small boy, to be made in black velvet, with silver buttons. I must complete it before the new moon, but I may only work by moonlight, and in silence. I remember how the last part goes: 'And lest my task should come to grief, No man so much as touch a sleeve.' "

Tansy stared. "Well," she said when she found her voice again, "in that case, you had best go back to bed and get some sleep. You have your work cut out for you."

3.

The Goblin Pretender

◆

"Tomus. Tomus!"

Tomus's dim form stirred at the foot of the bed.

"What?" he answered, his voice thick with sleep.

"What's a consort?"

Tomus yawned. It was the deepest part of the night and they both should have been fast asleep.

"Dunno. Nothing good."

"What happened to the last one?"

"The R.H.A. declared him an Official Disgrace—you can't speak his name anymore and it was erased from all the royal books. You know, the heavy ones."

"The Chronicles."

"Yeah, those. In the hall, where there should be a picture of the last Consort, there's a tapestry of some old battle."

"Was he banished Above?"

Tomus yawned. "I can't remember. I think he became one of the weavers."

🌿 🌿 🌿 He had no better luck with Morag the following morning.

"What's a consort?"

Morag smiled her half smile, the way she did just before she was about to tell him something that was half true.

"Well . . . I suppose it's a little like Vervain's elixir: a necessary unpleasantness." The Universal Mineral Elixir for Complaints Royal, Goblin, and Mortal was a thick, bitter syrup compounded of rootwine, honey, and herbs.

"Who are the weavers?"

This time Morag's hands paused in their gathering-up of a blue stocking. She cast a brief glance at the boy, then swiftly pulled the gathered stocking over his toes and heel, past his ankle, and up to his knee. "Why ever should you want to know about weavers, Pending?"

"I've never heard anyone mention them before. I wondered where they were."

Morag smoothed the stocking up to his knee. "They're off in one end of the palace, Pending. No one goes there. There's not much to see but some dusty old tapestries."

"What do the weavers do, then?"

"Mostly they repair the seats of chairs and things." She sat back on her heels and smiled, staring off into the air behind Pending's head. "By all Below, I haven't thought of them in years. My family lived in quarters quite near the workrooms. When I was a girl, I used to fall asleep to the noise of the looms."

"Are they really all mad?"

"Gracious, Pending! Where do you get all these questions? Has Tomus been filling your head with nonsense?"

"Morag," he said sternly, "this is *very* important. Are they all mad?"

34

She looked at him, then at the door. Something in her face relaxed slightly and something else in it tensed.

"Some. Not all."

"Were they mad when they became weavers, or did the weaving make them mad?"

"I can't say. And now," she added in a tone that marked the matter closed, "you know as much as I do about weavers."

He didn't believe her.

❦ ❦ ❦ It is a lesser-known trait of the elvish race that it harbors a superstitious dread of throwing anything away. The lower levels of Ylfcwen's palace were honeycombed with storerooms dating to the Early Epochs. Ethold and Pending had brought a picnic by dumbwaiter to one of them, spreading their feast on the floor among broken tag ends of furniture and dusty, rolled-up carpets.

They came upon an entire royal barge wrapped in muslin like a gigantic moth in its cocoon. Ethold discovered a child-sized copy of the barge, complete with movable oars. There was even a wooden elf queen with rooted silk hair and real dragonfly's wings. Ethold gently worked the wings back and forth. The fifth time Pending said his name, he looked up.

"I'm sorry, Pending. What did you say?"

"I asked if you knew anything about the weavers."

Ethold nodded. He fitted the elf queen into the throne of her barge and, rewrapping the whole, placed it carefully back on the pile of forgotten playthings.

"That's a funny coincidence, Pending. I was just going to take you to see them."

They passed through what seemed like miles of corridors, through heavy curtains that hid much older passageways.

"Tomus and I play hide-and-go-seek everywhere. We've never gone anywhere near *these* tunnels."

"Well, I'm sure Tomus has his orders," said Ethold.

35

They came to a small door set in the tunnel wall. It was barred and locked. Ethold took out a set of keys, identical to the set Vervain wore on a ribbon at her waist.

Pending stared. "Those are keys from the Royal Household Agency!" It was a high crime to steal or duplicate keys to the palace.

"Very observant, Pending. Could you speak more softly? It wouldn't go well with me if we were to be discovered."

Ethold turned one of the keys in the first lock and carefully drew back the bolts. He laid an ear to the remaining lock.

"Charmed. They must know I have keys and are hoping I will trip an alarm." Ethold drew from his pocket a pouch of silvery-grey dust and blew a pinch of it into the final lock.

The door opened soundlessly, at least to the boy's human ears. Ethold paused, listening for something Pending couldn't hear.

"Forward, quietly. No whispering; it carries. Just keep your voice low, the way I do."

The door opened into a large workroom, empty but obviously still used; it smelled of lamps lately extinguished. Taking up one end of the room was a huge loom upon which a carpet was taking shape. It was unlike any of the tapestries that hung in the halls of the palace. Those weavings showed royal processions or represented the feasts of the elvish calendar: the dedication of the gifts, the blessing of the mines, the festival of the fireflies. This tapestry was something else altogether.

Cords of silk, knotted one strand at a time, formed an intricate pattern of twined leaves and flowers. The blossoms shown were unlike any Pending had seen or sketched in the extensive palace hothouses and nurseries.

Ethold fingered a small, white, heart-shaped flower. "They only bloom Above."

Stepping closer to see the weave, Pending saw brilliant flies and glossy beetles, perfect to the smallest detail, as though nature and not the weaver's skill had made them. The carpet was cool to his touch and gave off a smell of crushed flowers and something he could not name.

"Sunshine," Ethold said, as though reading his thoughts. "Sunshine burning the dew off a meadow."

Pending looked at him blankly.

"Ah. Dew—how do I explain? It's a kind of rain that springs from the ground. Here, there is something else I have to show you."

At the other end of the workroom a low door opened on a bunk room, narrow and poorly lit, the air blue with the smoke of dreamlily. In the middle of the floor a few weavers shared a common water pipe. Others lay stretched on low cots around the room, dozing until it was time to return to the looms.

"Can they hear us?"

"Yes, but only as you hear your own breathing without paying it any mind. They don't know peace or pain—just oblivion. Their wages are paid in dreamlily, which dulls their wants and obliterates their cares. Even when they earn their freedom and can return Above, they seldom go. This is the only life they remember."

Only one of the weavers took any notice of them. Seated apart from the others at a small table, he was thumbing through a thick sheaf of papers. He glanced at them and went back to his papers.

"That's the timekeeper," Ethold's voice said in the boy's ear. "He assigns the work and doles out the dreamlily."

🐾🐾🐾 Ethold and Pending returned to the storeroom, but the picnic had lost its savor. Pending climbed into the royal barge and sat banging his heels against the base of the gilded throne.

Ethold climbed in and sat at the boy's feet. He picked up the toy barge and worked one of its oars. "There is something I must tell you, Pending."

"About the weavers?"

"Yes. But not just about them." He paused, as if searching for the right words for what he had to say. "The first weavers were human, like you. They came Below by accident and were given a place at the looms. Some married elves of the lower ranks, and their goblin children were sent to work in the gemfields. The gems they harvested made the elvish queens wealthy.

"One year a fever came. Many weavers and miners died. Suddenly there were fewer of them to work the looms and the mines. The elves could make do without tapestries, but gems were the lifeblood of the realm.

"So the queen of that time sent a servant Above to take a human child and leave a goblin infant in its place. This was the first changeling. More followed. Some became weavers, gem cutters. One changeling, a tavern keeper's son, became the queen's cellar master. One became the first human Consort. They had a son, and for the first time, there was a goblin of royal blood. When that son grew up, he began to wonder why it was that the weavers lived as they did and why goblins worked the mines to make elves rich.

"That was the beginning of the Goblin Wars."

Ethold came out of his tale as if out of a fog, startled to find himself seated in a decrepit old barge with faded cushions and cracked gilt. He looked at Pending and shook his head.

"They'll have raised the alarm for you hours ago. I had better get you back."

They gathered up the scattered plates and knives. Rather than wrap up the rest of the cake, Ethold broke it in two and crammed half into Pending's mouth.

"Eefold," said the boy, muffled by cake.

"Whmmf?"

Pending swallowed. "There was something else you were going to tell me. Not about the weavers."

Ethold shook his head. "Another time."

*   *   *

38

"We have it on the most reliable confidence that the Pretender has planted a spy in our midst."

Ylfcwen was trying to teach her pet mole to open pistachio nuts for her. She paused and looked up. "Why must I be concerned with it? That's what the Agency is for."

The director's face was smooth and professionally expressionless. "In another situation, we would not have had to involve madam. But, regrettably in this case, the infiltrator is one of madam's own personal attendants. The Consort Pending himself has unwittingly carried messages."

The queen held up a hand. "You know I'd rather have a tooth pulled than speak of such things. Just take care of it in the usual manner. I wish to hear no more about it."

The director bent low in a deep obeisance and noiselessly removed himself from the royal chamber.

The queen looked down. Her pet mole had eaten all the pistachio nuts. She had picked up the creature and was cradling it beneath her chin when it came to her, what the director reminded her of: a statue before the sculptor had gotten around to the features.

A chill crept over her, and she called for hot rootwine.

🌿🌿🌿 Ethold waited an hour, and still she did not come. He had given up hope of her when a hooded figure approached. At the last moment his hand went up to make sure his mask covered his eyes. She made the secret sign, and he returned it.

"Well met," he said.

"Well met. Why the mask?"

"A sensible precaution." He laughed, shaking his head. "Tonight I had the strangest fancy that you had been found out and replaced by an agent of the R.H.A."

She laughed and pulled her hood a little closer around her face. "A strange fancy indeed."

"You do not sound like yourself. Have you caught a cold? Here, let me feel if you have a fever."

As he reached out a hand she drew back, then lunged forward in an attempt to snatch off the mask. He seized her wrist in a tight grip. The imposter twisted but could not break free. The hood fell back to reveal the queen's Mistress of the Stones—an agent of the R.H.A.

"Don't feel bad—it very nearly worked. You were the right height and size. Even the voice wasn't too bad. You couldn't help it if your feet gave you away." His voice grew cold and quiet. "Now, listen and listen well: Tell your director to inform the queen that we will not be turned back by so shabby a ruse."

He released her, and she fled on the feet that had betrayed her. Like all agents of the R.H.A., she had a completely silent footfall, but her feet were too big to be those of the woman she was impersonating.

If they knew the secret sign, then they might know the rest. He thought of his love. She had been found out; it would not go well with her. She had, as they all did, a poison pellet. By now she had surely taken it. Ethold pulled the mask from his face and stared at the strip of black bandage, fighting back a choking terror that rose in his throat. He sank to the floor of the tunnel in a crouch, clutching his head in his hands.

Surely, she had taken it.

🌿🌿🌿 The suit was done.

Almost all of the silver had gone to purchase the pearls and the silver thread. Tansy had let her have the velvet and lace as an advance on her allowance.

The workmanship was particularly fine. Tansy counted twenty stitches to the inch on the seams and gave up counting on the buttonholes.

The leopard-woman glanced at her apprentice. Ulfra was

somewhat thinner and her hair wanted washing, but her face brimmed with an exhausted elation usually seen in women who have just given birth.

"And six hours to spare!" Ulfra said through a great yawn.

Tansy folded the suit and laid it in the box. "I have to admit, I had my doubts you could finish it in such a short space of time. You certainly deserve a rest. Why don't you have a bath," she said, "and I'll fry you a chop."

But Ulfra was fast asleep, her head on the worktable. Tansy tucked her in on the workroom sofa with a hot brick at her feet, then gave the suit a final pressing before wrapping it. She wondered where to leave the parcel—the messenger hadn't said—before deciding the wardrobe was the most logical place. Tansy wrote out the bill and slid it beneath the cord that bound the box, then placed it on a high shelf and closed the wardrobe doors.

In the morning, the box was gone, but the bill remained, beneath a large sum in new-minted silver. At the bottom someone had added in pencil, "Many thanks. It suits perfectly."

🌿🌿🌿 Things, animate and inanimate, that make the passage from the one world to the Otherworld often undergo a transformation. The arrival of the examination suit was anxiously awaited, and when it arrived it was unwrapped with no little trepidation. Ylfcwen was quite pleased; at a Royal Examination long ago, a suit of ermine had fared badly, arriving as no more than a moth-eaten muff.

The examinee was forbidden to wear the suit before the appointed day, so the goblin whipping boy was fetched to model the suit before the queen.

Ylfcwen lay on her lounge and gazed at the suit; Tomus squirmed and was pinched by the queen's dresser.

"One sleeve is a little longer than the other," observed the queen.

The dresser cleared her throat. "Rather, madam, one is a little shorter so the examinee shall not get ink upon his cuff."

"Ah," replied the queen. But she no longer saw the suit, for she was remembering her fourth husband and only beloved as he looked the day he was examined. Above, he had been a soldier turned highwayman, sentenced to hang for his misdeeds. The day before he was to be led to the gallows, he had tunneled from his cell into the Otherworld.

He had an eye for gems, and was being trained for work as a gem cutter when he caught the queen's eye. A tall man of fine form, with red-gold hair like pale flames and eyes so dark a blue that they seemed black ice.

A mortal tailor, long since dust, had fashioned a suit to the style of the day: blue-and-gold brocade touched with snowy ermine and lined with crimson silk. In it, he had seemed all fire and air and light, a fearsome angel summoned from the blue void at the edge of the world. She had stitched the examination answers into his cuff herself. There was no sense taking chances when you were up against the R. H. A. When it was over and the crown was on his brow, she had held to his lips the silver cup of forgetfulness. Then she had inscribed his name in the registry beside her own, the fourth Consort Royal, and, she devoutly wished, the last.

But mortal love is a fickle thing. Deprived of light and air and freedom, the new Consort did not thrive. Perhaps he took no joy in riches freely given, only in those stolen in the night. Perhaps he had drunk too deeply from the cup—her hand *had* been unsteady. From the occasional medicinal tipple, he took to soaking up cordials of rootwine and stronger stuff. He grew suspicious and fearful and, in the end, quite mad, a ravaged figure roaming the corridors in tattered raiments. At some point, he had become a ghost. The actual point at which he ceased to number among the living was difficult to determine. By then he had become a weaver.

42

*   *   *

❧❧❧ The director of the R.H.A. had just asked a question. Ylfcwen shut her eyes and snored a subtle snore. After much whispered discussion, they left the room. When the sound of their withdrawing subsided, she opened one eye. The whipping boy was sitting there, like a forgotten comb or shoehorn: something not thought of until it was required.

"Come," she said. "Sit here."

Tomus clambered up into her lap.

Ylfcwen trained her opalescent eyes on him. "You thought I would be bony."

He returned her gaze unblinkingly.

"I am very light, you see. Without weights or rootwine I lack the gravity to touch the floor. As I grow older it will get worse. I will grow less and less substantial, until I am overwhelmed by a compulsion to fly. At that time my reign will come to an end, and a new queen will be crowned in my place."

Not sure what to say, Tomus said nothing at all.

Ylfcwen's arms crept around the goblin boy. Late one night her son had slipped from his handlers and she had left the Consort Royal to his rootwine to meet the boy in a forgotten storeroom. For an hour mother and child had huddled in a silent embrace, each lulled by the heartbeat of the other, until the handlers found them and pried them apart. After that, she saw her son very little. There had been a sudden increase in documents requiring her urgent attention; the documents had been very long.

The director of the R.H.A. reappeared. He stood and stared at the sight of the queen holding the palace whipping boy upon her knee.

"Madam."

Ylfcwen opened one eye. "Surely it has occurred to you that I do not wish to be disturbed."

"This is most unseemly—"

43

"I shall do what pleases me. And it pleases me that this child should sit on my knee as my own son could never do."

A rare expression crossed the director's face. It had something in it of glee and something else of malice. Then it was gone.

"It is about your son, madam, that I must speak with you."

❦❦❦ Vervain was late for the Consort Pending's appointed geometry lesson. To pass the time, Pending dragged the heavy Chronicles from their high shelf, nearly toppling down the library steps in the process. To his disappointment, there was nothing about weavers, but there was an interesting entry under *Consort.*

> In the twelfth year of the Fifth Cycle of the Tenth Epoch of the Dynasty of the Lily, her supreme and divine majesty Ylfcwen, daughter of Yvaine, granddaughter of Ylyssia, great-granddaughter of Ygwynyd, took to her a mortal wanderer who, beseeching her with a comely face and plaintive way with a harp, had escaped indenture at the looms. Crowning him Consort, she bore of him a son, named ▄▄▄ [here something had been blotted out by the censors of the Royal Household Agency] who was raised to take his place as the first king in three Epochs. In his sixteenth year, however, ▄▄▄ spurned his place at his mother's side and entered a self-imposed exile Above, where he lives to this day as a mortal man. The queen's Consort was so grieved at his son's behavior that he drowned himself in the sacred lake. Since that day, there has been no other Consort Royal.

Try as he might, Pending could not lift the censor's blot. He even tried a little of Vervain's Universal Mineral Elixir on the end of his pencil eraser, to no avail. No doubt the ink had been charmed. Pending was peacefully engaged in mixing hot candle wax and spit into ink lifter when he heard a disembodied voice call his name.

"Ethold? Where are you?"

"Over by the bookshelves. There's an old spy hole. Put your ear to it."

Pending obeyed.

"Listen carefully, Pending. There isn't time for long explanations. Vervain has been arrested by the R.H.A."

"Arrested!"

"They have charged her with being a spy for the goblins. She had been an agent of the R.H.A., but she was swayed to our cause by you, Pending. She couldn't bear to see you become the next Consort."

Pending's eyes filled with hot tears. "Can't we save her?"

"No, Pending. But you must listen carefully and do exactly as I say. Go back to your room as if nothing has happened. Tomus will be waiting for you. Change clothes with him; he will take you to the tunnel that leads to the underground lake. I'll meet you there."

"But—Morag—"

"I'm sorry, Pending. It would be too dangerous. You can send word to her after. Now you must hurry."

🌿🌿🌿 In Pending's clothes, Tomus looked remarkably like a Consort Pending.

"Do I look like a whipping boy?" asked Pending.

Tomus squinted at him. "You'll do. Here—Ethold said to give you this." He handed him a bundle. "Now we've got to be quick. Follow me."

They left the main corridors for the less-used passageways.

"Tomus. When he showed me the weaving rooms, Ethold said you never took me there because you had your orders. Whose orders?"

"The R.H.A. Don't give me that look—I wasn't *with* them; I just pretended to be. Vervain used you to send messages, but she was afraid that if she did it too often she would be found out. So sometimes she used me, in the dumbwaiter. If I was caught, I was to say I was playing hide-and-go-seek with you."

They had come to a branching of tunnels.

"Here's where I leave you. Ethold will meet you here." The whipping boy put out his hand. Pending grasped it and shook it.

"Maybe they won't find you out and you'll have to sit for that examination. And that's another thing—you knew what a consort was all the time!"

Tomus shrugged. "Maybe I did. Now I have to get back, before you're missed. Good luck."

And he was gone back down the tunnel, the way they had come.

Pending was shifting from foot to foot, thinking that whipping boys' clothes weren't quite as warm as those for consorts pending, when Ethold appeared, carrying a bundle like his own. He was changed. It was not just the light and echo of the tunnel; something about his face and voice was not the same.

But he came up smiling and rubbed Pending's hands in his own great ones to warm them.

"Have you grown cold waiting? I'm sorry—I had some loose ends to tie up. Now tell me, can you swim?"

"Only a little."

"No matter. I can swim for us both, as long as you can hold your breath. Can you do that?"

"Yes, but where are we going?"

"Above, through the underground lake."

🌿🌿🌿 Morag discovered the substitution at once, but was too frightened to say anything. She gave Tomus a bath and put him to bed early and told the director of the R.H.A. that the Consort

46

Pending was upset about Vervain, having been close to his governess. Morag could not tell whether he believed her.

She stood in the doorway and watched the goblin boy sleep. He was some relation of hers, distantly descended from the same human ancestor, a renowned goldsmith who had had quite a way with the ladies of the elvish court. The human features were uppermost in him. Could it work, could he possibly pass for the human boy? But even if he did, how was she to explain the absence of the goblin whipping boy?

There came a soft knock at the door, and she found herself staring down at a goblin boy just Tomus's height. Armon's boy, Fegyn, if her memory served her right.

"Let me guess: You are the new whipping boy."

He smiled shyly and nodded.

Morag opened the door wider. "You'd best get to bed, then. I am sure the Consort Pending will explain your duties in the morning."

🌿🌿🌿 Ylfcwen retired to her chamber to find a parcel on the foot of her bed. It was about the size of a shoe and was wound tightly with fine muslin. The object was familiar but unexpected, as though it were something she had seen in a dream and had not expected to encounter while waking.

She sat cross-legged on the bed and unwrapped it. It was a perfect model of the royal barge, beautifully carved and gilded. On the throne sat a tiny elf queen with rooted silk hair and real dragonfly's wings.

There was a slip of paper rolled tight and tucked into one of the oar locks.

Mother,
I know when I have been bested and so I will for a little time

withdraw. I have wounds to lick. Perhaps the rarer air Above will restore me. It is said to have such powers.

You will forgive me, I think, for taking the boy. Perhaps you will eventually thank me. For a while I have suspected it was not a consort you saw in him but a less rebellious son. But he has a mother and he shall be returned to her. You will find another left in his place—a sort of changeling. You may think it a poor joke, and perhaps it is. Yet with the advantages you can give him, he might prove devoted enough.

When the R.H.A. came to you, did you know it was Vervain? I like to think they kept it from you. You didn't love her as I did, but I don't believe Vervain ever disappointed you. You must admit, the absence of disappointment has a faint whiff of love about it.

Until we meet again, I am your well-meaning son,
Ethold-that-was-Aethyr

Ylfewen furled the note and hid it in the hollow handle of her ivory wing burnisher. She was feeling light-bodied and poured herself a glass of rootwine but did not drink it. She lay back on the bed and gazed at the walls of her bedchamber, covered with a tapestry of living violets. She did feel very peculiar, as though the air disagreed with her. Perhaps she needed to fly a little. She slipped off the ankle weights and drifted to the vaulted ceiling.

I must tell the dresser to have it dusted up here, she thought dreamily. There were fewer fireflies than she remembered from her last flight, and more cobwebs and moths, but it was pleasant all the same.

It seemed a shame about the suit. By the time they had coached the new Consort for the examination, a new suit would be required. But perhaps there would be no Consort at all. If it weren't for the fact that goblins were sterile, she would almost have suspected Tomus the whipping boy of being Vervain and

Ethold's son. She was sometimes struck by the fact that she had so far escaped having a grandchild, despite her rapidly advancing years. Five marriages and only one child to show for it, and him the Goblin Pretender. It was too much.

🌿🌿🌿 The sacred lake glittered cold and smooth as a facet of onyx. Its shores were littered with drifts of dried jasmine flowers from the most recent dedication of the gifts. Far off at the lake's center, Pending could make out the cold gleam of the shrine's silver spires.

"There's a long dive to a tunnel, and at the end of that a shorter dive that will bring us Above." Ethold was tying their bundles tightly to his back. "The other routes will be watched, but they don't remember this one. If we're traced, they will assume we drowned."

Pending shivered. They had stripped to their smallclothes for the dive, and this place was still and cold. "Then we're not coming back? Not ever?"

It was then that Ethold sat him on one of the carved stone seats and told him of his real name and his mortal mother. He pictured a house with spires at the edge of the blue void, surrounded by all the flowers from the weavers' carpet. His mother was at the door. Her face was a little like Vervain's and a little like Morag's, and her hair was rooted silk.

Ethold had led him to the point along the shore where the water was deepest. They were standing on the brink. Ethold's voice was telling him to fill his lungs, to hold on tight and jump at the count of three.

There was no splash. The cold waters of the lake closed around them.

4.

The House
in the Wood

✦

As it happened, Pending's mortal mother lived not on the edge of a blue void but in the heart of a great and ancient forest that divided the three realms of Twinmoon to the north, Thirdmoon to the east, and Fourthmoon to the west. This was the Weird-wood, its green twilight ruled by the Direwolves and watched over by the silent flights of owls. At its center stood a massive oak, set with a red door, that had once been home to a witch. These days there were different tenants, the Binders and their boy.

It was early morning on a cold spring day. A man and boy emerged from the thick growth of hemlocks into the small clearing surrounding the oak. Binder's hair glinted gold in the weak sunshine; his darker beard was well trimmed and he wore round spectacles. The boy was about seven. His face peeked out from a blue hood, apples in his cheeks from the cold, his eyes an odd, pale brown.

The man had a basket strapped to his back; the boy carried five trout on a string. They paused by the door to use the boot scraper (added since the witch's time) and let themselves in.

The boy took off his coat. Beneath the hood, his hair was the deep russet of a fox's tail and stood up in unruly peaks. His eyes were not pale brown after all, but yellow as a cat's. His ears were small and flat to his head and slightly pointed. He was, in other words, a goblin child. He went and stirred up the fire.

Binder shrugged the basket off onto the table and began to remove its contents: a honeycomb wrapped in leaves, some speckled eggs packed in spongy moss to keep them from breaking, and a number of more ordinary parcels: butter, cheese, candles, a piece of soap.

"When you've put the kettle on, why don't you clean those fish?" said Binder over his shoulder. "Out by the stump would be a good place."

The boy fetched the scaling knife and took up the string of trout. He turned back at the door. "After, can I go see Sleeker?"

"Yes, but don't be long. We'll have breakfast soon. If I know your mother, she hasn't taken so much as a cup of tea."

The boy nodded and went out.

Binder put away the provisions and went down the twisty, narrow stairs. The tiny room had once been a root cellar; now it held a finishing stove, sewing frame, and lying press. Beneath his short beard and behind his wire spectacles, Binder had the look of the perpetual wanderer come to rest. He once had been a knight of Chameol; now he was a binder and mender of books.

He lit the finishing stove and set the glue pot on it to warm, then went upstairs, where the water had come to a boil. He brewed a pot of woodmint tea and took it up the ladder to the room nestled among the oak's uppermost branches.

From the look of the workroom, it seemed as though the

old witch was still in residence. Among the pots of shade-loving herbs that lined the windowsill were lizards in bottles, moths on velvet, eggshells speckled like stones, and the eerie, white masks, no bigger than acorns, that were the skulls of shrews and mice.

At a worktable piled with books and papers, Caitlin sat bent over a sheet covered with runes. Seer's eyes, one blue, one green, gazed out from a face pale by nature and made more so by overwork. She had wound a length of her blue-black hair around one hand and was tugging at it absently as she worked. Binder noticed a pair of hair combs—his present to her on their last anniversary—lying on the worktable and smiled. She was always complaining of her hair and threatening to cut it. He told her that if she did, she would never get anything done; she could only think, he chided her, while tugging at her hair.

Binder handed her a cup of tea. She shook her head, as if coming out of a spell, muttered thanks, and took a scalding swallow.

He watched as some color returned to her cheeks. "How goes it?" he asked, nodding toward the book.

Caitlin grimaced. "Not so well. As soon as I think I've got the hang of it, the text shifts and changes. I suppose it's just eyestrain, but I'd swear the damn runes are doing it on purpose."

Behind the spectacles his eyes gleamed dangerously. "Well, if you *will* stay up all night and not come to bed—"

"If I recall correctly, you were the one who fell asleep taking his boots off. I came to bed to find you snoring away, one boot on and one boot off."

"No changing the subject," he said, taking the tea from her hand and holding it out of her reach. "You have been sadly derelict in your wifely duties."

Caitlin smiled and reached for her tea. "You know very well that I wouldn't know a wifely duty if it bit me on the nose. Let me have my tea and I promise to be more tractable. Ow!"

A wifely duty had bitten her on the nose. A skirmish broke

out, and they fell to the floor with a bump. The tea spilled and went unnoticed.

She laid a finger on his lips. "Before this goes any further—where's Grimald?"

He kissed her finger. "Looking for his otter. Damn!" He sat up, raking a hand through his hair so that it stood on end. "I told him not to be long."

Before she could answer, there arrived at the window a pigeon with a green band on one leg. Caitlin went to the window. As she was unfastening the capsule on the bird's leg, she caught her husband's eye.

"I'm sorry—it's from Iiliana."

He gave the bird a dark look and smiled wryly. "It's all right. I have fish to fry." He swung down the ladder and out of sight.

She placed the pigeon in a cage and gave it seed and water, then sat down to read the message from Chameol's former queen, now its High Counsel and Ambassador to the Thirteen Kingdoms.

> My dear,
> I am in Twelvemoon, heaven help me, trying to sort out which of the late monarch's offspring has a legitimate claim to the throne. There a great many contenders from both sides of the blanket, as they say, and I will be detained here until the turning of the year. I am very sorry, and not just for the dreariness of life here. It's past time you visited me and Chameol. The sun and sea would do you good and, besides, we could put our heads together about the Books.
> —Iiliana
> P.S. The library here yielded nothing about the runes you sent. The best I can do is confirm your suspicion that they are not a living rune tongue. They are most likely Iulian.

When she left the isle of Chameol, where she had been apprenticed as a seer, Caitlin brought with her the ancient book of incantations that had belonged to old Abagtha, her late guardian and the original tenant of the oak with the red door. The book held the secrets of the long-lost kingdom of Iule, long buried beneath the waves by the necromancer Myrrhlock. Now that the wizard had been defeated, the secrets of Iule remained to be uncovered. Chameol had been the kingdom's seat of learning, with a library of fabulous books, the jewels of which were four powerful books of magic: the Books of Naming, Healing, Summoning, and Changing. When Iule sank beneath the sea, the Keepers of the Books had smuggled them from Chameol. It was said that in the centuries since, they had been broken up and sold for relics; the pages that survived had been stitched together by some long-dead owner into Abagtha's book of incantations.

Tackling the runes had been a penance of a kind, a compensation to Iiliana for abandoning Chameol and life as a seer. Raising Grimald in the harsh Weirdwood, there had not been much time for runes at first. Now they were a welcome obsession. In the hours she sat occupied with them, Caitlin did not dwell on the fact that her seer's gift had abandoned her. Since her marriage her visions had grown less and less frequent. Two years ago, they had stopped altogether after the death from fever of her only daughter, Rowan. The runes had that power, at least: They kept her private ghosts and demons at bay.

Caitlin sighed and glanced at the piles on the worktable, pages from Abagtha's book, which had been pulled to pieces. The leaves were sorted by kind into four piles. Some were richly illuminated in brilliant reds and blues and burnished gold leaf. Some were closely written in crabbed, dark runes. Others flowed with an elegant cursive hand, with cryptic diagrams and marginal notes in red. The last pile held leaves from an herbal, so lifelike that it seemed the plants were not painted but pressed between the pages.

As she looked at them, Caitlin felt compelled to resume her work; the impenetrable runes seemed to exert a strange pull on her mind, and in the green light from the window, the pages seemed to cast a faint, irresistible glow.

But as the smell of frying trout reached her from below, a pang hit her in the pit of the stomach, equal parts guilt and hunger. Caitlin went down the ladder.

Grimald was laying the table. Besides the smoking hot trout, there was sour rye bread, a cheese, and applesauce. Caitlin bent to kiss the boy's forehead.

"Did you find Sleeker?"

Grimald shook his head. "It's days since I saw him. I'm thinking—I'm thinking maybe a wolf got him." He said it matter-of-factly, but she knew how he really felt. The otter had been hand-raised since before his eyes were open. He was not truly wild and not as wary of the wood as he should be. A Direwolf would make short work of him.

"Oh, I don't know about that," she said. "After all, he's grown now. Maybe it was time for him to find his ladylove and settle down."

Binder set the platter of fish on the table. "Just think: If he's being shy with *you*, he'll be that much safer around wolves and such."

This seemed to cheer the boy, and he held out his plate.

🦡 🦡 🦡 Grimald had cleared the table and gone back out into the wood. He had his lessons at night by the fire; as long as it was light, the Weirdwood was his teacher. Now that it was beginning to thaw, there were shrew skulls to be dug up and nets to check for bats.

And otters to look for, Binder and Caitlin thought as they watched him go. Binder divided the last of the tea between their cups.

"Do you think a wolf really got Sleeker?" he asked at last.

She shrugged. "By now Grimald knows the wood almost as

well as I do. But I don't think even he knows. You always hope they will get to be a little older before they first lose something they love."

They both fell silent, thinking of Rowan. If she had lived, she would now be five. Caitlin had stayed by the child's sickbed until she, too, fell ill. To keep the boy from the infection, Binder had walked him to the nearest farm. When he returned at last with help, Caitlin was delirious and the fever had settled in little Rowan's lungs. She was buried in a quiet, mossy spot marked with a white stone and grown over with lilies-of-the-wood.

They had each blamed themselves and, in the worst moments of their grief, each other. They thought of leaving the wood. Binder had been unable to set himself up as a printer, and to keep body and soul together, Caitlin had had to bottle herb remedies to sell in the nearest market town. Her researches into the runes had been abandoned. Grimald had developed night terrors and could only sleep if one of them spent the night beside him.

Then Grimald had ruined one of her books, a volume borrowed from Iiliana's library at Chameol. In mending the broken spine and torn pages, Binder found a craft that could support them. Once a month he collected mending from an old bookbinder whose fingers were grown too stiff to keep up with all the work. Caitlin still bottled enough simples to pay for the little books of gold leaf for the binding and new shoes for Grimald.

Binder laced his fingers with hers and gave her hand a squeeze.

"Back to work, I'm afraid. I promised Femius I'd have the next lot for him a little early. One's a real bear—thirteen fold-out charts in need of patching."

"So much for my wifely duties. Well, I have a letter to answer and runes to crack."

He shook his head at her. "For heaven's sake, try to get some sleep first."

When he had gone down to the bindery, Caitlin went back

up to the workroom, pausing at the basin to bathe her eyes. Her reflection in the glass was a reproach. Though Binder would never say it, she looked more than tired. Her face was lined with weariness. She cursed the runes under her breath. For their sake she was ruining her health, straining her husband's affection, neglecting her child, and wearing away her sanity—yet their meaning remained just beyond her reach.

He's right, she thought, I *do* need a nap. She kicked off her shoes and stretched out on the cot. The runes still danced before her eyes, but she made herself draw even breaths, imagining a vine of ornament growing over the runes, shutting them out. Between the leaves of the vine she imagined a door. She opened it and saw the gardens of Chameol, Iiliana seated on a stone bench reading a book. Seeing Caitlin, the High Counsel of Chameol smiled and held out the book so that Caitlin could read the cover: *Ancient Rune Tongues Explained.*

Caitlin walked toward her.

🌿🌿🌿 There never was a colder place or one more lonely than the half-frozen spring hidden by a deep thicket in the heart of the wood. In its black surface, last fall's leaves were frozen in a thin glaze of ice. Grimald knelt on the bank, a dark, wet bundle in his arms.

He had found Sleeker. One of the otter's hind legs had been crushed by the jaws of a trap. He had bound the leg as best he could, but Sleeker had stopped moving. Grimald was sure Sleeker was dead; as soon as he was done with his good-byes, he would bury him. His thick tears fell onto the otter's glossy pelt.

"Hello. What have you got there?" said a voice softly.

Grimald had not heard the man approach. He was young and clean-shaven, his hair pulled back in a lock beneath a wide-brimmed hat. He wore a heavy traveling cloak and carried a pack.

Without ceremony he crouched beside Grimald and examined Sleeker with hands that were as kind and gentle as his voice.

"I think he's dead," Grimald said, shuddering with cold.

"No—not quite. It's good you tied up his leg the way you did. Here, we'll bathe him in the spring and then take him back. He's your pet? You live in the Weirdwood, then?"

Grimald nodded. He watched the man pick up the wounded otter and break the thin ice to bathe the injured leg. The boy turned his face from the sight of the otter's teeth bared in a grimace of pain. When he looked back, the man had wrapped the otter in the folds of his cloak.

"What's your name?"

"Grimald."

"Well, Grimald, I'm Fell. It's a lucky thing I found you, for I'm lost. I'd be grateful for a chance to warm myself before I make my way out of the wood."

🐾 🐾 🐾 Binder met them at the door, his heart in his throat. He had not seen Grimald, only a man bearing down on the house, a bundle wrapped in his cloak.

"Sweet heaven, you scared me witless. Get inside before you freeze solid."

Caitlin appeared at the top of the stair, barefoot, clutching her box of remedies.

As his father helped him out of his wet clothes, Grimald shook his head, his teeth chattering. "No—Sleeker first—"

Fell gave a loud yell. He had just received an otter bite on the hand. He handed Sleeker over to the boy, who had struggled from Binder's grasp. Speechless, the boy nuzzled his face in the creature's fur. Sleeker gave a weak *prrt-prrt* of contentment.

Caitlin examined the young man's hand. Luckily the otter was tame to start with and weak from his own wound; an otter bite can break bones. She did not tell the young man this. When the bite was dressed she turned her attention to the otter.

"It's a simple fracture. If we can keep him still and warm, it should mend. Grimald, go cut me some green wood for a splint."

Grimald let his father bundle him in dry clothes. Dwarfed in one of Binder's wool shirts and clumsy in his mother's boots, the boy stomped out, glad of something to do.

As Binder pressed a cup of hot rum into his hands, Fell turned to Caitlin with a stunned look. "But the trap . . . that leg was badly crushed. I saw it. And when we came up to the house, he had stopped moving. I was sure the creature was dead."

Caitlin shook her head. "It was hard even for me to tell, with the blood and the fur around the wound. It must have looked a lot worse to you. But tell me, how did *you* happen into the middle of all this?"

The young man blushed. "I set off to seek my fortune. I'm afraid I got lost." He lifted his chin. "My late father was a gold-smith; I am the youngest of his sons. Between them, my brothers have spent what fortune there was. I am hoping to find a trade. I came to the Weirdwood looking for a binder I was told lived here."

"My husband is the bookbinder, if it's that kind of binding you want."

"It is. So I am not lost, after all."

Binder shook his head. "Even if we could offer room and board, I couldn't take on an apprentice. I'm not a master yet myself; I rely on the binder in town to give me what work I have. Besides, to become apprenticed you need to be sixteen."

Fell drew himself up. "I'm nineteen! Nearly twenty." Without the wide-brimmed hat and cloak, he was revealed as the youth he was—tall for his age but slight of frame.

Binder smiled and tried to repair the slight. "Then you are more skilled with a razor than I was at your age. No offense."

"None taken."

Caitlin looked at Fell closely. He was telling the truth, as far as it went. But his clothes, though simple, were very well made, not those of a youngest son without prospects. Some impediment other than lack of fortune stood in his way.

Fell seemed uneasy beneath her gaze. He turned down their invitation to stay to supper, reaching for his hat.

"I have no wish to outstay my welcome."

"Nonsense; your cloak is not yet dry. If you can't stay to supper, at least let me show you the workshop. You'll still have time to reach the edge of wood before dark."

Once in the workroom, Fell's shyness fell away, and his features grew almost animated as he asked questions about the tools and materials. Binder watched him thoughtfully. At last Fell's departure could be put off no longer, and they ascended to the kitchen to retrieve the cloak, now dry.

"Bookbinding's hardly the only trade you could learn," said Binder. "I hear there is a good living to be made as an engraver." He gave Fell the name of an artisan in the town.

"Thank you. I am sorry you cannot take an apprentice, sir, for I feel we should have got on well. Good day to you."

"Best of luck to you."

He bowed his way out. Through the window they could see him saying his farewell to Grimald where the boy was cutting splints of green ash.

"It's a shame, in a way," said Binder. "He would have been a friend to Grimald."

"Yes," was all Caitlin said. She did not like to tell her husband so, but she thought the young man more secretive than shy and, no matter what his story, he was no poor youngest son.

🍂🍂🍂 That night, Caitlin came late to bed, hours after her husband had carried Grimald up to the workroom to kiss her good night. She crept down the ladder to the room they shared, a tiny chamber taken up almost entirely by the bed and the heavy chest at its foot. Binder had made shelves for the curved wall at the head of the bed, the brackets carved in a pattern of ivy and fitted to hold candles. She placed her candle in the headboard.

He had fallen asleep half dressed, without climbing all the way beneath the covers. One hand still clutched his spectacles. Caitlin eased them from his grasp and laid them on one of the shelves. Hurrying in the chill of the room, she changed into her nightclothes and climbed into bed. At this slight movement he turned toward her, still deep in sleep, burrowing his face into the warmth between her neck and shoulder.

She lifted her head and gazed at him for a time before she blew out the candle, thinking, searching his face for traces of her lost Rowan and of another child, the son whose place Grimald had taken, whose place he could never take. Binder had changed—in name, for one: Only she called him Badger now. To Grimald he was Baba. To others he gave a new name, Matthew Binder. In appearance, too, he was altered. The close work of the bindery and the scant light of the Weirdwood had taken their toll on his eyes—thus the fine lines in their outer corners and the wire-rimmed spectacles. He had grown the beard during the dark days surrounding Rowan's illness and death. He wore it now, years later, less a badge of grief, more a kind of remembrance.

Binder had never believed that Grimald was a changeling. As the child grew and began more and more to resemble a goblin, he remained convinced that Grimald was his child. And in many ways human love *had* made the boy human. The boy was too young to know he was different from them. Caitlin was resolved to tell him—and loathe to.

So she alone knew, knew and remembered. Dark-haired Bram, her firstborn, her first-lost. Rowan had been flaxen-haired, a rebuke to her hope that Bram somehow might be reborn in their second child. No sooner had she begun to love her daughter for the gift she was than she was taken, too.

That was why she came late to bed, well after Binder was asleep: to deny herself the comfort and solace of her husband's arms, to atone for trying to remake Bram, to make certain there would be no more grieving for another lost child.

She blew out the candle and lay back in bed, turning her back to him, hugging her knees. With effort she emptied her mind of all thoughts, slowing her breaths until at last she drifted off. In sleep, he drew nearer again, matching his posture to hers limb for limb, twining his fingers in her loose hair.

🌿🌿🌿 Pending was cold, so cold he burned with it. He did not remember surfacing; he did not remember setting foot Above. Cold made all his senses shrink until they were a shuddering core in his numb body. A voice came to him faintly. Hot liquid passed between his lips, like rootwine, but not so bitter.

He came to briefly and struggled to sit up but could not. This frightened him, until he saw that he was only weighed down by heavy furs. He was in a small space with irregular walls and a roof only a few feet above his head. There was a strange, thick smell made up of many other smells; it was not unpleasant. He was aware of being warm. Eyes glinted at him in the darkness. Goblin eyes.

"Here. Take this," said Ethold's voice. The boy heard the light scrape of a spoon against the side of a bowl.

He had never tasted anything like it, but it was hot and sweet and thick and delicious. He ate every spoonful and fell back upon his bed into a deep sleep.

🌿🌿🌿 Binder stood and scowled at the open cupboards.

"Did you give Fell any food?"

Caitlin looked up from the floor, where she and Grimald were sprawled over a game of his invention called liar's checkers. "No, why? Is anything missing?"

Binder shook his head. "Yes. Odd things. At first it was a

crock of honey here, a loaf of bread there. I figured you'd gone on one of your midnight cupboard raids."

She smiled. "I see. Go on."

"Then some cider went missing—and the bottles turned up, empty. We're low on candles, and I know I bought enough to last another three weeks. And just yesterday I set some applesauce on the table by the window to cool, and a little while later it was gone, bowl and all."

Grimald captured the last of her dried lizards, winning the game, but Caitlin didn't seem to notice.

"Come to think of it," she said, sitting up, "someone's been at my herb garden, too. I thought it was rabbits, but it was too regular for that. And they were peculiar herbs—things a rabbit wouldn't eat."

"But medicinal?" said Binder.

"Not in themselves. They'd have to be boiled with—"

"Cider, perhaps, and honey?"

"Yes. What will you do?"

"Hang some sausages up in the shed. A neighbor's a neighbor, invisible or not." He put on his coat and went out.

"Who's invisible?" Grimald asked.

"No one. Your father only means that we've never seen the person who's been taking the food. Now, are you going to give *me* a chance to win a game and redeem myself?"

"All right."

"Well, I get the lucky piece this time. Fair's fair."

❦❦❦ Pending opened his eyes, and for the first time in days he could really see and hear and smell and think. He lay on a bed of furs in a small room with earthern walls and a low earthern ceiling from which tree roots protruded like crooked beams. Through the low, arched entrance he could see Ethold outside, crouched by a smoky fire.

He struggled out from under the heavy covers and found his clothes. When he got to the door the light of the clearing struck his eyes and made him dizzy.

Ethold looked up from the cider he was warming. "Well, Bram, how are you feeling?"

The boy remembered what Ethold had told him at the edge of the underground lake. This was his new name, his real name. It sounded strange.

"Achy. The light hurts my eyes. Did I almost drown?"

"No, you made the dive beautifully. But coming Above affects people differently. You got a bad case of light sickness, on top of a nasty cold. Here. Drink this." Ethold handed him a cup of cider with honey and herbs.

"Is it a wolves' den?" he asked, after he had swallowed. There had been pictures of wolves in the Fabulous Beastiary Vervain had given him for his fifth birthday.

"No, a poacher's den, I think."

"Is this where we are going to live?"

Ethold's eyes were unreadable. "No. The poacher will want it back. You're going to live with your mother."

Then Bram remembered. The light sickness had driven it from his mind. Anticipation and a sick dread gave him a queasy feeling in the pit of his stomach. He spoke around the knot that had formed in his throat. "Where will *you* go?"

"Away, to a new life." The goblin stared into the coals, then looked up at the boy, his amethyst eyes bright. "I will have a new name, like you."

Bram opened his mouth to ask another question, but Ethold gave the smallest shake of his head. Then the goblin opened wide his arms and the boy stepped into them. The hot knot in his throat untied itself, unraveling in hoarse sobs that echoed in the little clearing. Even muffled by the goblin's coat, it was a dismal sound.

*   *   *

❦ ❦ ❦ It was early and grey. Though she had been up for hours, Caitlin had not been able to get anything done. Binder and Grimald had gone off before dawn to walk to the nearest farm; the Harriers' mare had had twin foals.

The house, indeed the whole wood, seemed to ache with stillness; Caitlin fought a temptation to leap and stamp and shout to dispel it. There was something uncanny, almost otherworldly about the heavy quiet. It was as if, once alone with her, the runes were trying to speak. The air hummed with the silence that was almost itself a sound.

She got up from her worktable and went to the basin to wash her face, glad of the noise the water made pouring from the bright blue pitcher. As she bent to cup the cold water in her hands, there rose in her mind a fragment of a remembered dream: a woman seated in a garden, holding out a book. It was the garden on Chameol, the woman was Iiliana (no mistaking those coppery tresses), and the cover of the book read *Ancient Rune Tongues Explained*.

Caitlin sank to a crouch on the floor, the basin, the room, everything else forgotten. Could she remember the rest of the dream? She had been awakened abruptly, when Fell and Grimald had brought the wounded otter into the house, and had not thought of it since. As a seer on Chameol, she had been trained to remember and interpret her dreams, even to summon them. Since Rowan's death she had all but abandoned the practice, but it was as much a part of her as memory and needed only to be called on. She called on it now.

She was back in the palace garden at Chameol. Iiliana was sitting on a stone bench, reading. She walked toward her. Iiliana held out the book. She took it. It was heavy, much too heavy for its size. She opened it, but it was unreadable. The runes upon the page shifted and buzzed before her eyes, then slowly resolved into the shapes of bees, circling on a blank page.

She turned to Iiliana to complain that the book was full of

bees, but Iiliana was gone. In her place on the stone seat sat a boy of seven or so, with black hair and eyes as amber as honey. He gazed at her solemnly and held out his hands, which were full of jasmine petals.

No sooner had she taken the flowers from his outstretched hands than the bees began to desert *Ancient Rune Tongues Explained* for the sweet, papery petals. When the last bee had left the page, ghostly shapes could be seen to form there, the shadows of the shadows of runes.

And there the dream ended. Caitlin let loose a shout of frustration.

"It can't end there! It simply can't!"

She went downstairs and put the empty kettle on the fire. When it squealed immediately in protest she took if off the fire, filled it, and stood a minute staring at it. Then she emptied the kettle and put it away. She took up her cloak and a basket and left the house.

It was really still too early to gather mushrooms. As she walked through the wood she listened intently for a twig snap, a sleepy birdcall, any sound breaking through the oppressive stillness, the great held breath of the Weirdwood.

The place where she usually found the best mushrooms was not far from the mossy bank where Rowan was buried, but Caitlin did not stop to visit the grave. Her errand, begun out of exasperation, somehow had become too important to be put off. When at last she reached the spot, she understood why. There were no mushrooms after all, only a small boy, curled up asleep at the base of a tree, his grimy face streaked with tears.

Caitlin stood a long time, wondering at him: at his hair, sooty as a raven's wing; at the strange silver ring upon his finger. She stood clutching her empty basket, afraid to wake him lest he should prove a trick of her dreams, another taunt of the runes.

At last she did reach forward and gently shook him by the shoulder. They looked at one another, each a little afraid, and then the boy held out his hand and she took it and led him through the wood all the long way home.

🍂🍂🍂 Binder looked from one boy to the other and saw the truth of it, the truth she had tried to make him see from the beginning. Despite his amber eyes, there could be little doubt that this boy, with his pallid skin and blue-black hair, was Caitlin's child. And the more he looked, the more Binder believed it must be his son. That hair was hers, but the cowlick and forehead, nose and chin were his own.

As Grimald had grown, Binder had stubbornly ignored the boy's peaked ears, his yellow eyes, his fox-red hair. He could not believe the boy a goblin or suspect he was some other man's child. It was less confusing, less painful, to continue to accept him as his own. Besides, he loved the boy.

Now the changelings (for his eyes told him they were) stood before him, of an age, of a height, one unmistakably goblin, the other so clearly human. The boys looked at him, the dark one waiting for him to speak, the ruddy one waiting for him to make everything right.

He could not make everything right (which for Grimald meant returning things to the way they had been a half hour ago, before Caitlin came in the door with Bram). But he could still speak.

"Welcome—Bram." He cleared his throat and began again. "Welcome home. All right—fish traps. First we'll go check the fish traps, and then I suppose we had better get started building you a bed."

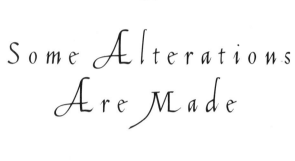

5.

Some Alterations Are Made

◆

Ulfra had been mistaken about the injured wolf. Several weeks passed, and the other wolves did not come for it. As the wolf regained its strength it became harder and harder to conceal it from customers. Still worse, Lady Twixtwain refused to cross the threshold while the wolf was in residence; so she wrote from the sanctuary of her well-appointed house in Goldenmouth Street.

> I know Ulfra would not let the creature harm me, but I can't make my poor Opaline understand that it will not harm her. And I cannot think of leaving her behind. It seems the only solution is for you to come to my house for our next game of cards.

"Dinner at Lady Twixtwain's!" Ulfra's eyes shone. She had been in bed with the measles the last time an invitation had been

68

extended. The tales Tansy had brought back of painted ceilings and a glassed-in fish pond had only sharpened her disappointment.

Now Tansy shook her head. "The wolf can't be left alone. You'll have to stay home and look after him. A half-grown wolf can get into too much mischief in the workshop."

There had already been an unfortunate incident involving a ball gown decorated with plumes. The feathers gave the dress the appearance of a startled bird rising up in flight. How else, Ulfra argued, could a wolf have been expected to act?

She had not won the argument then and she did not win it now.

So this evening found her home alone. The wolf had denned himself in underneath the workshop sofa; there came to Ulfra, as she sat at the drawing table with her sketches, the crunching of his teeth on a bone.

Since the episode of the examination suit, not a day had passed in which Ulfra had not revisited Ylfcwen's court. These were not mere daydreams—they struck her imagination with a force daydreams do not have, and they stayed with her, begging to be put down in pencil, chalk, whatever was at hand. Later, she put them down in watercolors, filling sketchbook after sketchbook with vivid renderings of fabrics so delicate of pattern that they seemed to shift and shimmer beneath the eye.

Page after page blossomed with gossamer silks of peacock and canary, rich brocades of ruby and emerald and silver-shot azure. Her pencil struggled to capture the intricate shape of a silver buckle before the vision fled from her mind. Then there were ear bobs, carved buttons, elaborate clasps, and a strange article of which she could make no sense—something of starched linen, laced like a corset but shaped like an archer's quiver.

Sighing, Ulfra erased, redrew a line, and began a sketch in the pattern of a gold brocade. She hoped it was not an article of underclothing. Something told her that gold brocade was just the thing, and more and more lately, Ulfra found herself paying attention to that something. She set the sheet aside to dry, feeling a bit guilty that she had spent the whole evening doodling, neglecting the rack of dresses that needed finishing. She cast a final glance at the sketch, wondering what the strange corset-quiver could be.

The something that guided her hand chose not to inform her that it was an elvish wing case.

She was about to start sewing tiny jet beads onto the bodice of a gown when the wolf growled. It was an alarm growl, and Ulfra turned to look.

The wolf was at the window, intent on something in the street outside. His ears were laid flat along his head.

Sewing on the tiny jet beads, each no bigger than a grain of rice, promised to be tedious indeed, so Ulfra was glad enough of a reason to set them aside. She went to the window and drew back the curtain just a little so that no one in the street would notice.

It had rained a little while ago. The cobblestones glistened under the light of the lamps, and the gutters of the house opposite still dripped. A few passersby, huddled against the damp, hurried on their way to late dinners. After a moment it became clear that one figure was not hurrying to dinner or anything else. He was loitering in a doorway across the street and a few doors down from the Cat's Face. His cloak was pulled close around him against the creeping damp.

The wolf had known him at once by his smell, a curious blend of boar grease and oil of bitter-orange. Unlike the wolf, Ulfra could not catch a scent through a closed window and across a rainy street. She recognized the man by his shape: a great bear balanced on its hind legs. It was the king's huntsman.

The wolf's growl changed to a wheedling sort of whimper. Let me out, he was plainly saying. Oh, just let me out.

"It would only be trouble if I did." She forgot to speak in

Wolf, but by her tone of voice she made herself understood. The wolf reluctantly rested its muzzle on the sill.

She wondered what the huntsman was doing here. He wasn't looking in her direction; she didn't think he knew the Cat's Face from any other shop. If he did, he wouldn't be standing in the light where she could see him.

Just then the door of the house opposite opened and a young man stepped out. The lamplight picked out the gleam of a silver button, a lace cuff. Though he was the shorter and slighter, this other man managed to be commanding, even next to the bearish figure of the huntsman. In the tailoring trade, one learned to notice how people carried themselves. This man carried himself like a nobleman. (Though sometimes one couldn't tell: There was a wellborn customer of theirs who bore himself as though bound for the gallows and another, a reformed highwayman, who carried himself as though he were destined to wear the crown.)

A sudden gust of wind worried and tugged at the young man's cloak, and Ulfra saw a flash of purple silk. The sumptuary laws decreed that only those of royal blood could wear purple. So he carries himself like a prince for good reason, she thought.

Lady Twixtwain had told them tales of the crown prince, how he had made a double-faced cloak that he could turn inside out and so go unnoticed when visiting his mistress, "an—*unpedigreed* woman, shall we say?" The prince had recently become betrothed to a suitable princess, well dowered, sufficiently pretty, and moderately clever. The commission of his wedding clothes was hotly sought after by the Cat's Face and its competitors.

"And there are some," Lady Twixtwain had said, "who would gladly sew *themselves* into the linings of his clothes, if they could manage it."

At that point, Tansy had abruptly sent Ulfra to buy thread, so she had been unable to satisfy her curiosity on the matter of the prince's clothes and their interesting linings.

Prince and huntsman moved off down the street. Ulfra let

the curtain fall back into place, but did not return to the tiresome little jet beads. She stood there, absently stroking the wolf and thinking.

🌿🌿🌿 The farmyard was strewn with the litter from a wedding. Flowers had been trampled into the sawdust, and one of the garlands to which guests had tied money and good wishes had come untied and trailed in the dirt. In one corner of the yard, the dogs fought over the tag end of a ham. Farmer Goody had said farewell to the last straggler and fled to the barn to smoke a pipe, digest his ale, and ponder in solitude the solemn sums lavished on the nuptials of his youngest daughter.

Hazel had some months before grown past the pencil mark on the pantry door, the acknowledged signal that it was time for her to leave the household and make a home of her own. Happily, a love match had been arranged with the neighbors' second son, and an hour ago the new bride, not yet sixteen, had driven off in a cart to her new life.

Nix sulked. Though Hazel had been his favorite, he had not gone outside to see her off, and as she waved from the wagon, the new Mistress Brown had cried as though her heart would break. Now Nix sat alone with Mistress Goody in the kitchen, helping her clean up the remains of the wedding feast. Neither said a word, but their thoughts ran along the same lines: Nix would never grow past the notch.

Mistress Goody could not be displeased at this prospect. For all his small size, Nix was sturdy and clever, unquarrelsome, and a wizard with money. Mistress Goody's income had increased twelvefold since she had put Nix in charge of the eggs and butter, and as for the jam and pickles, well, they had taken off like a house afire.

Nix had appeared on their doorstep out of the dusk seven years before, a strange note and a purseful of money pinned to his shirt. The note had been written on the back of a bill for a troupe of acrobats. "Take good and amazing care of Nix, the albino deaf-mute," it had said. He had been six, perhaps seven years old, with odd hair as white as an old man's and so soft-spoken that at first they had thought he really was mute.

Farm life had made him sturdier and browner, so his milk-weed-pale hair stood out with striking whiteness. Like any boy his age, he was all elbows and knees, but for months now he had not grown any taller. It was a mystery, but then everything about Nix was a mystery. He never spoke of the days before his arrival on their doorstep. When pressed, he retreated to a dumb stare. So they had not pressed him, grateful for the money that arrived at regular intervals, enough to keep him in shoes and to pay for the bonesetter when he fell from the apple tree retrieving Hazel's cat.

🌿🌿🌿 Dusk had fallen when Farmer Goody strode in, grim-faced. The chairs were still against the wall and the floor was invitingly bare. Wordlessly he seized his startled wife and spun her across the farmhouse floor in a country dance.

"Tom!" she protested. "Did the ale bring this on?"

"Can't a man—a newly impoverished man—dance with his own wife?"

"But the floor still has to be scrubbed. I can't leave it for Nell. She won't do it properly. It has to be *scoured*—people have been treading ham rind and beer into it all afternoon."

"Hush, woman."

"But I'm out of breath."

He laughed. "But never out of words, damn you. Hush, I tell you, and dance."

Nix picked himself up from his chair by the fire and went out into the farmyard. The youngest Goodys, seven-year-old Pippin and nine-year-old Jack, were upstairs sleeping the uneasy sleep of boys who had discovered that it was possible to consume too many sweets at one sitting.

The dusky sky was already thick with stars, large and low to the earth. In the western half of the sky the world curved away to a thin crescent of purple and gold. The air was chilly and Nix wished for his woolen shirt.

It had been an evening like this one, the day Ulfra had left him here. When she had picked out the Goody farm, he had thought at first that she meant to steal a pig, but a cuff on the ear had taught him otherwise.

The Goodys had taken him in and raised him as one of their own. But it had not been the same. He missed life on the road with Folderol's band, picking pockets, performing with the wolves. For the first year after he came to them, Mistress Goody would come downstairs in the morning to find Nix curled on the floor with the dogs. When he had been Nix, the Albino Deaf-Mute, his bed had not been a pallet of straw but a drowsing heap of wolves.

Nix looked up at the sky and found the group of stars called the Greater Wolf. Ulfra had been named for its brightest star; Nix was in the habit of wishing on it.

"Please, I want to grow," he said. "Not just past the mark on the pantry door. I want to be *tall*."

The wolf star shone no brighter or dimmer and stayed exactly (as far as Nix could tell) in the part of the sky where it had always been.

It had granted a wish of his once before. He had wished to see Ulfra, and promptly the wolf star had produced her, grandly dressed, turning over crocks of jam at the Goodys' stall in the marketplace. She had recognized him but had not spoken to him except to buy three crocks of jam. There had been nothing of wolf left about her. Worst of all, she had overpaid for her purchase, so he thought she had lost all her sense, along with her good wolf smell.

74

Still, it had shown that the wolf star granted wishes. Nix turned and started back toward the house.

🐾🐾🐾 The lamplighter had just started his rounds, putting out the lamps. The night owls of the town had barely gone to their beds, passing in the lane the early birds, laborers and tradesmen whose day began before dawn.

In the bleary half light, the baker's boy hurried past shuttered inns and the grey, sleepy fronts of houses. His mistress would have set the loaves for a last rising before she went to bed. It was his job to put those in the oven and form the loaves for the next baking. Today was to be a busier day than usual. It was the eve of a feast; there were seedy loaves to make, and sweet braids, and a special holiday loaf in the shape of a crown. He rounded the corner to the street where the bakery stood and stopped short at the sight before him.

Eight wolves trotted swiftly at the heels of a ninth, a great she-wolf, grizzled black and silver. They made a perfect triangle but for the back row, where there were three wolves instead of four.

The baker's boy shrank back against the wall, but the wolves took no notice of him, loping past in silence.

After they had gone, the boy let himself into the bakery and set about his tasks. He was a little rattled; though he did not burn the bread, he shaped the seedy bread into braids and the sweet bread into round loafs, instead of the other way around.

🐾🐾🐾 The wolves reached the Sign of the Cat's Face and sat down on the cobblestones, still in formation. The she-wolf went to the front door and scratched on it with her claws—too lightly to wake Tansy, or even Ulfra, but just loudly enough to wake the wolf inside. In a trice he was at the front door. There he sat back on his haunches and gave a whimper, for the door was latched and bolted. He communicated this fact through the key-hole to the she-wolf.

The other wolves, overhearing, lay down to wait. One of them yawned, and was bitten on the ear by his neighbor for bad manners.

The she-wolf tasted the air. By the smell of him, the lamp-lighter was still several blocks away. There was time. *Draw the bolt with your teeth,* she explained in Wolf, *then press the latch with your paws.*

The younger wolf saw how this was possible and, after several tries, got it right. He took his spot in the fourth row, and swiftly the pack moved out of town. No human had seen them except the baker's boy. The baker would shake her head at the seeded braid and the sweet round loaf and sell them anyway. And, from one end of town to the other, householders would wonder why their cats perched on the highest beams, fur on end, impervious to coaxing or saucers of milk.

Tansy, when she came downstairs, assumed that she herself had left the door unbolted. Only after they realized that the wolf was missing did Ulfra find the scratches on the front door.

❦ ❦ ❦ Lady Twixtwain paid a visit that very afternoon. Opaline stood in the doorway uncertainly. Though the house had been well aired and the rugs beaten, there was still a faint whiff about the place that made the dog tremble. But on seeing Ulfra she overcame her fear and came inside, beating her tail against the carpet apologetically.

"No, no tea, thank you," said Lady Twixtwain. "Now the only thing I take is this water." She held up a small, stoppered flask. "If you have a little wine . . ."

Tansy rose to fetch some.

"The man I see about my foot recommended it most highly,"

76

said Lady Twixtwain, pouring a fingerful of the water into the glass provided. "It purifies the blood, sweetens the breath, promotes concentration, *and*"—she filled the glass the rest of the way with wine—"improves the complexion."

"I can see it does," said Tansy. "Your complexion is *very* much improved."

"But does it help your foot, Lady Twixtwain?" asked Ulfra. Lady Twixtwain had handed the flask to her. Its label, covered with crabbed writing in brown ink, did not mention afflictions of the hands and feet.

"Alas, no. I must sleep with them above my head, he says, and bathe the left in milk and the right in vinegar."

"But your right foot is not afflicted," said Tansy.

"I thought the same thing, but he set me straight. The humors in my feet have become imbalanced, you see. It is all very complicated."

"And expensive?"

"Oh, not half so expensive as I feared. And I do not mind the taste at all. Now, Ulfra my dear. You were going to show me the sketches you made for my dress for the masked ball."

"I have them here." Ulfra took out her watercolor board, to which several drawings were pinned.

"*Ah.* A charmer of snakes. Oh, how well you have drawn me! And Opaline peeking out from under my skirts.

"And here I am as Night, I presume? A celestial look. See, Tansy, she has made my skirt out of a comet's tail. Alas, I fear it would not be proper to wear in front of royalty."

Lady Twixtwain admired in turn sketches of herself as a black swan on a lily pond (complete with embroidered frogs, dragonflies, and carp), an aviary (a cage of gold wire worn over a skirt embroidered with birds), and the personification of a rose—a gown of the palest ivory silk over green hose, embroidered with crystal beads of dew.

"And what is this?"

It was one of Ulfra's doodles, a gown of layered silk in blue-violet and cloth of gold, with a strange corset-quiver affair on the back, and a strange staff topped with a jeweled orb.

"Ylfcwen—the queen of the elves," Ulfra said, the something of her daydreams speaking for her.

"It will answer handsomely, though we will have to change the colors. I wouldn't want to be fined for breaking the sumptuary laws. But tell me, what is the strange apparatus on the back?"

And at once Ulfra knew. "It's a wing case." In her mind she was already envisioning how it might work, how a small cord, when pulled, would release the wings of stiffened gauze.

🌿🌿🌿 "Grimald!"

Grimald drew further into the shadows of the shed and held his breath. The door hinge squealed and a patch of dim light slid across the earthen floor in front of his hiding place. His father's boots strode into view.

"You'll have to come out sooner or later. It might as well be now."

Grimald made a face. He was sorry now that he'd chosen this hiding place. The hollow oak down by the stream would have been better. He knew how to live in the wood. A bundle was ready under his bed. He knew how to light a fire and keep it alive. He knew where all the fish traps were, and the beehives, and the places the wood-hens laid their eggs. He and Sleeker would live by the stream.

"Come on," said his father, drawing him by one arm from his hiding place. "That's enough of this."

Bram was at the table with Caitlin, helping with the week's bread, when the door opened and Binder entered, steering Grimald before him.

"Tell your brother you're sorry."

78

Grimald glowered. He was not sorry and he certainly had meant it. Then he caught his mother's eye. He mumbled something in the direction of the new boy.

Binder shook him gently by the shoulder. "Again, with feeling, and look at him this time."

"I'm sorry I locked you in the cellar."

"And?"

"And I'm sorry I put a walkingstick in your bed."

Caitlin made a face. "Oh, Grimald."

"It gets worse," Binder said. "Go on."

"And I'm sorry I put grubs in your porridge."

"That's better. Now, you, say you forgive him."

Bram raised sullen eyes to Binder's. "But I don't, and I won't lie and say I do."

Grimald wriggled from his father's grasp. "I take it back! I'm not sorry at all and I'll do it again!"

The taunt was on the tip of Bram's tongue—the elvish slur for goblins—when Bram caught a fierce glance from Caitlin. Then he thought of Ethold, and shame soured the word in his mouth.

"All right, that's enough. Grimald, no more trips to see the Harriers' foals. As for you, Bram, you're as much in the wrong as he. Lights out for you early the rest of the week."

The boy's sullen look was gone. His face wore a look of blank misery. His only pleasure was reading.

"Now I want the two of you to go together and get the water and wood for tomorrow. No, Grimald, not another word. Go on."

In silence they went, Grimald abristle with suppressed fury, Bram unreadable. When they had gone, Caitlin shook her head. "I can't really blame either of them. Think how they must feel. All of the sudden I bring home this strange boy and expect them to behave like brothers."

"That's just the problem. They *are* behaving like brothers."

"But grubs in the porridge. It has to stop." Caitlin slashed the tops of the shaped loaves and slid them onto the floured shingle, ready for the outdoor oven.

"What about these?" Binder said, pointing to two smaller loaves.

"Bram made them. They need a second rising."

Binder looked at one of the loaves and then picked it up to examine it closely. Carefully, he pulled the dough apart.

"Oh, Badger, you'll ruin it. He spent a lot of time getting it right."

"In a way." He held out the halves of the unbaked loaf for her to see. Embedded in the dough were some dozen fat, white grubs.

That night Grimald lay in bed and plotted his escape and fell asleep to pleasant dreams of living by the stream with Sleeker.

In the other bed, across the chalk line that divided the small room in two, Bram lay awake trying to remember faces. Ethold's was still clear in his mind, but Tomus's and Vervain's and even Morag's were not so easy.

He stared at the ceiling and willed himself to remember.

Hours later Caitlin paused in the doorway to look in on them where they slept. Grimald slept on his stomach, his breathing slow and heavy. Bram's face was turned to the wall. She thought he was awake but let him feign sleep, going up to her own bed.

Binder opened his eyes when she came in.

"Go back to sleep."

"I wasn't really asleep. What time is it?"

"Late." She undid her braid swiftly and, too tired to be bothered with brushing it, got into bed with her hair loose around her shoulders.

Binder reached out and looped a few strands behind her ear.

"A silver one . . ."

"More than one, thanks to the boys."

"And other things." The litany went unuttered but understood: the isolation, the death of Rowan, their marriage.

80

She smiled, working a dab of greenish paste into her roughened hands. "Ah—this is a well-worn theme. My life of ease as a seer on Chameol, revered, serene, and *chaste*."

"Something like that." The warmed beeswax released its scent and he breathed in the green perfume of balm and woodmint. At least the scars on her hands could be seen.

"If you think my hands wouldn't have been callused on Chameol, then you don't know liliana." She blew out the candle.

She never feigned sleep to deceive her husband. It was to lull herself into sleep, to turn her mind from incessant worries, that she turned her back, slowed her breathing.

Since the day she had found him in the woods, Caitlin had spent sleepless nights thinking of all the ways Bram might come to harm. In secret, because she was ashamed, she had schooled herself in all the old lore of mortals released from the Otherworld. She read up on the shaking fever called elf's dance and the ailments known together as elf's kiss, manifested as fainting spells and fits of paralysis that came on and passed with the new moon.

Those were no more than superstitious tales. What she could not shrug off were the recurring references to changeling sight, Otherworld visions manifested in childhood that led to blindness, madness, and death before the age of twelve.

Binder was not asleep either. He knew she was only pretending to be, for reasons he did not like to think about. But, asleep or not, she was beside him. In seven years, they had not driven each other to madness or violence or flight.

And that was balm, of a kind.

🌱🌱🌱 Lady Twixtwain's costume was a great success. The final color scheme was silver-and-blue brocade reversing to magenta. Ulfra had sacrificed the spring mechanisms from several mousetraps before perfecting wings that would unfurl when a hidden string was pulled.

Lady Twixtwain had created a sensation. The crown prince

himself had come over to compliment her (*"much* to the chagrin of his bride-to-be"), and within the week a woman of any social standing could not be seen at court without a wing case. Mechanical wings were not a part of the new fad; the cases were used instead to hide everything from illicit love letters and unfinished needlework to the emergency pair of silk hose or the secret flask of gin.

Ulfra's designs were much copied by other tailors around town, but the Cat's Face got the lion's share of the business in wingcases. Tansy was perplexed but uncomplaining, and gamely produced a new design on a weekly basis.

They had to hire three women to handle all the work. When the house next door was vacated, they expanded into it. Amid the workmen and plasterers they stood and toasted their new good fortune with expensive wine, casting their glasses into the unfinished fireplace.

"We're rich," Tansy said, wonderingly.

"No," said Ulfra, with an uncharacteristic giggle. "We're *extremely* rich."

A workman came up to them, hair and face whitened by plaster to the aspect of an unkempt ghost. He spoke in a thick Se'enmoon accent. "Summun left this inna dur."

Tansy took the proffered letter, a heavy vellum packet sealed with red wax. She broke the seal and scanned the letter's contents, then sank down on the plaster-strewn floor in shock. Ulfra picked up the letter where Tansy had let it fall.

Let it be known that, by royal appointment, the tailoring establishment known as the Cat's Face, with premises in Everlasting Lane, has been awarded the commission to make the wedding clothes for His Most Serene Highness, Prince Berthold of Twinmoon. (Details of said commission will be forthcoming from the Valet Royal.)

6.

Barter and Trade

◆

The fad for wingcases had played itself out, but over the course of the next nine months, the name of the Cat's Face became so imprinted on the fashionable mind that anything produced by their shop became a mania in its own right.

First came black velvet mitts called cat's-paws; then sheer, stiff embroidered sleeves called dragonflies' wings; and then a fad for women to go about in blue tunics—the Elf-Prince look, they had called it.

Meanwhile, Tansy and Ulfra worked on the prince's wedding clothes. This included the actual suit of clothes he was to be married in and a cloak with a long train, as well as his traveling clothes for the year-long pilgrimage he and his bride would undertake while the new summer palace was being constructed.

At the start, nine months had seemed more than ample for the work to be completed. That was before they made the acquaintance of the Valet Royal. A strict procedure had to be adhered to; sketches and patterns and embroidery designs examined, approved, and notarized; dyes formulated and fabrics certified; workers bonded and sworn to secrecy.

There were to be two formal winter suits (best and second-best), two formal summer suits (ditto), five costumes for attending the theater, six different dancing costumes, and various outfits suited for sleigh riding, falconing, hunting, fencing, and sampling the hot springs at Se'enmoon.

Bolts were only rolled out to impress clients; to choose fabrics, Tansy and Ulfra referred to large ledgers. Pinned to the felt pages were swatches of fabric, with notations of the shelves in the workroom where the bolts could be found, as well as which customers had garments made up in them already. This was to reduce the chance of embarrassment at balls, where a guest might find, to her chagrin, that her next-door neighbor had a dress made out of the same fabric.

Ulfra let her fingers skim the surface of the fabrics, mulling over nap and color and weft and weight. There were light cambrics, soft challis, and chambray for shirts and blouses and underskirts; an ivy-green damask worked in a pattern of vines and leaves, another in pale grey with a pattern of doves and roses; fine dimity for starched collars and sleeves; rubbed silks tender as doeskin; rich silk luster and delicate messaline; precious sarcenet and shot silk.

At last she found what she was looking for: wool combed from black mountain sheep, woven with silk into a light, flexible fabric of lustrous silver-black. This Ulfra chose to make the prince's hunting coat.

She sat down with her watercolors to sketch out the embroidery that would band the hem and sleeves: hunters on horseback and their hounds, twined with branches and leaves. The buttons would be horn in silver mounts: one a fox, one a boar, one a stag.

Ulfra worked, unaware of Tansy's scrutiny from across the workroom. The leopard-woman studied her former apprentice; her apprenticeship had ended on her twenty-first birthday. She was now a master tailor, entitled to all the rights of the guild. As a birthday present, Tansy had made her a full partner in the business.

"You realize," she had told her, "that you are a very wealthy young woman. You need not remain with me to make your way in the world."

"But what else would I do?"

"Your painting, for one thing. Explore life outside this damned workroom, for another. You could be presented at court."

Ulfra had shook her head stubbornly. She had known the wild Weirdwood in winter, when it was left to the wolves; she had known life at the court of mad King Milo and life on the road with Folderol's band. And she wanted none of it. She wanted only to be left alone with her sketches.

Tansy looked at her now and turned things over in her head. A farce was being staged in the town, playing to packed houses. It featured a girl tailor at an establishment called the Dog's Muzzle. The prince was lampooned, too; he wore a cloak of mourning that reversed to a wedding suit. Tansy badly wanted to see it, but could not bring herself to. Lady Twixtwain urged her to go (she herself had been three times), but to Tansy it seemed somehow disloyal.

Ulfra sat and sketched. In a portfolio case under her mattress she kept sketches she did not show Tansy, scenes of the Weirdwood and life with Folderol's troupe, and sketches of a boy with strange, pale eyes and a shock of unkempt hair, milkweed white.

One such sketch, of this odd child with his arms around the shaggy neck of an old she-wolf, was tacked to the back panel of the cedar clothespress in Ulfra's bedchamber. There she retreated to sleep and think, the din of hawkers' cries and the rattle of cart wheels on cobblestones muffled by the thick woolen folds. Breathing in the mingled lavender and cedar, Ulfra would sleep, dreaming, as she had not done for years, of wolves.

The clothespress featured a false bottom. Tansy might have known of its existence, but it would never occur to her to look for anything there. In the hidden cavity, Ulfra kept the relics of her past life. A small strongbox held a strange inventory: strung on a leather lace, two teeth, one from a human child and one from a wolf cub; a small velvet pouch full of large, fine pearls; a handbill, luridly illustrated, advertising "The Wolf-Girl, her Ferocious Direwolves, and the Albino Deaf-Mute"; several large, colored spangles and dyed plumes, as from a gaudy costume; the coiled, translucent skin shed by a snake, and, the most recent addition, a carefully folded handbill advertising *The Dog's Muzzle*.

🐾 🐾 🐾 Neither Caitlin nor Binder could recall exactly when the chalk line had disappeared. Apparently, a truce had been in effect for some time when, stooping to pick up a vole's skull that had rolled under Grimald's bed, Caitlin noticed the line had been rubbed out. It seemed not to be the act of a deliberate hand, but of feet scuffing back and forth over the disputed border.

By the end of the first three months, the boys had advanced from tolerance to cautious overtures of friendship. By the end of six months, they had begun a commerce in mantis egg cases, moths, and owl pellets; and soon after that, they developed a private language, in which they traded secrets. Now they went together to visit Sleeker at the creek.

As the months passed the boys grew ever more different in both looks and temperament. Grimald was more foxlike than ever, ruddy and mischievous, nearly impossible to catch red-handed at anything. His temper was hot, his fancy impulsive. He could climb any tree in the Weirdwood and had once crept the length of a rotten branch to rescue a nest of owlets. His greatest joy was helping Binder tool a leather binding in gold leaf. It was marvelous how such a chatterbox and creature of impulse could sit still for hours on end in perfect silence. He was just learning how to stitch gathered pages together in the sewing frame.

Bram was the cool one, quieter, more likely to bide his time than to act in the heat of the moment. If Grimald was the fox, them Bram was the owl: watchful, silent. Many nights he would seem to be dozing by the fire but afterward could repeat to Caitlin every word that had been spoken. When he did lose his temper, Bram was capable of a cold rage, and when he laughed (which he did even more rarely), it was a sweet sound, a sound Caitlin liked to hear above every other. His keenest enjoyment came from the hours he spent sitting motionless in Caitlin's workroom, watching her restore the vivid, gilded pictures in the margins of books.

🌿 🌿 🌿 There came one day to the oak with the red door a strange figure, frail more from illness than age, his reddish hair thinning and the soles of his shoes almost worn away. His shabby coat of red and gold brocade was cinched by a stout leather belt with a heavy silver clasp. Beneath the coat his shirt was riddled with moth holes, the collar and cuffs foxed with brown stains. One ear was ragged, as if the moths had moved on to it after finishing the shirt.

"Is the binder about?" he asked. His voice was surprisingly sure and sound, as if it had been spared the forces that had ravaged the rest of him. His eyes, too, were clear and bright.

"If it's books you want bound, then I can help you," answered Binder. Occasionally a determined customer would track him down in the Weirdwood. The present visitor, however, did not seem to be a man of great means.

"I have some scraps to sell, bits and pieces of old books, good enough for patching things up."

He opened a satchel that stank of must. Inside were sorry

remnants that had once been books, a sad catalogue of fates: books worried by dogs or gnawed by mice, books with the boards and spines charred away to the bare cords, books swollen and splayed from lying in the rain, their pages obliterated by mildew. Oddly, none had been damaged by bookworms.

Binder selected two or three books whose leaves could be used to mend other books. He also took a crudely sewn volume of scraps, thinking to make it into a practice rune book for the boys.

As payment, he offered the bookman six coppers and the hospitality of their pantry. Grimald hurried down to the cellar for a pitcher of cold cider.

The ragged bookman sat and ate steadily without uttering more than a sigh or grunt as Binder refilled his plate. At last he pushed the plate away and wiped his mouth carefully with his napkin; one could guess from the state of his sleeve that this was not his usual habit.

"Tell your wife she makes a good crab-apple pickle."

"Actually, I do. Thank you all the same." Binder nodded at the stranger's satchel. "Business any good?"

"Middling, alas, middling." The man drained his cider mug and smiled at Grimald when the boy refilled it. "Mind you, middling is a damn sight better than business has been for years. Some of those, the burned ones, were pulled from bonfires back when a man could be flayed for reading in the wrong rune tongue. When I think what was lost . . ."

"Do you know rune tongues? You must stay and meet Cait. She's been studying runes these last seven years. She'll be glad of the company of someone who can speak the language, if you know what I mean. She's in town at the moment."

A spark of interest flickered in the visitor's eyes, but he shook his head. "I can't wait. I must see a man today on urgent business. Payment on a debt, alas. But if she will visit me in town, we might talk of runish things. Have you a pencil?"

Binder found paper and pencil, and the bookman labored some time with these. When he at last sat back, the paper and the man's hands were both much begrimed with pencil lead. Beneath the smudges the sheet was covered with odd markings.

The bookman rubbed his hands together. "She will understand that. I need not trouble you longer, I think." But his eye strayed toward the pitcher of cider.

"Well, if you can't stay for another cup, will you take a jug with you?"

The bookman protested, but the short of it was that Grimald was sent down again, returning this time with a corked jug, and the visitor went on his way.

❦ ❦ ❦ Caitlin and Bram returned at dusk, laden with supplies. Caitlin set out on the table several bundles of smooth calfskin in blue and red and green, tiny pots of pigment from the apothecary, a new bloodstone burnisher, spools of stout thread. Binder's eyes scanned the goods as if looking for some object he did not see; he opened his mouth and closed it again without saying anything.

"What," said Caitlin sharply, "not satisfied with all that? Everything *there* is for you except the little pots of color for *my* work. Isn't that so, Bram?"

"Well," said the boy, "there *is* this." He drew out a small bundle, no bigger than a pencil.

Binder seized it and happily undid the cloth tapes of a doeskin pouch. Inside were six new finishing tools, made to his own design by a metalworker in the town.

Grimald hung back until Caitlin gave him a smile and said, "Right coat pocket." He dug a hand in and drew it out, clutching a tiny book of gold leaf.

Caitlin picked up the bookman's note, then sat down to work her way through the runes.

"Who—" She looked up, but Binder and Grimald were gone,

down to the binding room to try out the new tools on some scrap leather.

Bram rubbed his eyes. "Pickles and cider."

"What did you say?"

"A funny man—all red and gold—with a ragged ear." Bram pointed to the chair Caitlin was sitting in. "He sat there. I can see where he was. Da gave him pickles, and Grimald brought him cider."

Caitlin spoke calmly, though her heart was beating fast. "Come here a moment. You can tell me about the man later. Right now I want to see those poor eyes you keep rubbing."

🌿 🌿 🌿 Getting ready for bed, she told Binder about it.

"Now I can see them, all the signs he showed before that I didn't *want* to see. But at this distance—"

Binder removed his glasses and polished them before setting them out of the way on the carved headboard. "Are you so sure it's such a bad thing? Couldn't Iiliana teach him, the way she taught you?"

She shook her head. "It isn't the same kind of sight. He wasn't just seeing what could happen or what would happen. He spoke as though the bookman were still in the room—as if he saw him in the chair where I was sitting." She paused, gathering words. "Some people who have been Below can see—auras, *presences*—the way a wild animal can 'see' a scent. These people can see traces of the Otherworld."

Binder looked at her closely, narrowing his nearsighted eyes. "You're not telling me everything."

"I don't know everything."

"May I have that in writing, please?"

Her reply was wordless. He was taken aback (though not unpleasantly), and replied in kind, feelingly.

So she banished from that room for a little while the cold shadow that was her dread.

90

❦ ❦ ❦ The Binders had another visitor before the week was out. A prosperous guild master arrived on a cold autumn morning.

He was a well-fed man who had once made his living with his hands and now made it with his wits; a man who had married late or perhaps for a second time, to judge from the ring upon his finger: A young man might buy such a thing for his bride, but not for himself, and it was not old enough to be an heirloom. All in all, thought Binder, a man much risen up in the world. He grew hopeful in the anticipation of well-paying work.

But his hopes were dashed as soon as the guild master spoke.

"I have a daughter of marriageable age who is, shall we say, recalcitrant. In all other matters, she is sweet-tempered, but the merest mention of matrimony turns her into a shrew." The guild master smiled bitterly and turned his own wedding band upon its finger. "I had been told that you sold potions, and I hoped . . ." He let his words trail off, embarrassed to be be dealing for such goods at a hermit's hut in the middle of the Weirdwood.

"I don't handle that kind of binding," said Binder. "But you're in luck. The spellbinder of the house is at home."

❦ ❦ ❦ Caitlin listened to the man without sympathy. She did not go in for love potions. Compared to real feeling, they were an unsatisfactory substitute, a cheat. She only prepared them for couples who had fallen out of love with one another, and then only half-strength. When it came to love, she found the mortal mind capable of sufficient magic of its own.

"Why do you think your daughter needs such a potion?"

"She will not marry." The guild master paced the workroom, taking up a shrew's skull and putting it down again with distaste.

"She will not marry the man of your choosing?"

"A man of mine or her or the man in the moon's choosing. She does not wish to marry. She is the elder of my two daughters. There is a legal difficulty. If she marries, she will inherit a small

91

fortune from my father's estate. She was his favorite grandchild. If she does not marry, the fortune will enrich a charity house for orphans. In either case, my younger daughter, the child of my second marriage, is dowerless, dependent on the generosity of her sister."

"You appear prosperous. I should think a dowry for your younger daughter within your means."

"Money does not make itself. I have a workshop to run, two sons to educate and set up in life. I must maintain a house in town."

"And no doubt your wife is expensive to maintain."

The guild master blustered and changed colors. "You do not see how it is."

"No, I see precisely how it is. There is nothing wrong with your elder daughter that I have a cure for. Good day. And watch your step going down."

🐾 🐾 🐾 The king's huntsman glanced around the darkened gallery of the theater and felt beneath his coat for his dagger. The prince insisted on attending performances in disguise, even though he could command a performance at the palace when the fancy struck him. It was foolhardy, but Galt understood the impulse. After the finery of court—men and woman starched and laced, wigged and perfumed within an inch of their lives—it was something of a relief to come to this place, to feast the eyes on women whose figures had never seen a stay, their complexions florid, not from the rouge pot, but from hard work and a little too much gin. From the cheap seats there rose a ripe smell mingled with the bitter steam of the roasted chestnuts being hawked up and down the aisle. It was a barn smell, a clean stink. Galt liked it.

The crown prince sat back in his box, his cloak turned purple side in, brooding into a cup of ale. To say that he was unhappy at the prospect of his approaching marriage did not do justice to the prince's mood. He was in a sour, princely sulk. His affianced bride was undeniably beautiful, of the best bloodlines, and had been schooled in all the arts deemed appropriate for a marriageable princess. She could make small talk in six languages, sing and play the harp, and draw in perspective. In short, her manners had been developed at the expense of her mind. "She is," the prince complained in private, "incapable of *having* an opinion, much less expressing it."

His father-in-law had, however, formed an opinion about his daughter's married life and had expressed it to the prince in no uncertain terms through the dowry negotiators. When their life together commenced, he expected the prince to give up many things, the chief among these being the theater "and all that attends it." "All that attends it," of course, meant his mistress, Lucivia, a woman of irregular reputation, who lived in Everlasting Lane.

Now the players strolled onstage, and the prince was able for the space of a few hours to forget his marital worries.

The Dog's Muzzle; or, The Tailor's Business was a fine bit of farce, with barbs aimed to skewer lords and ladies of fashion and the tailors who lived off them. At one point the heroine, Modesty, and her sister, Pulchritude, entered with velvet cats' tails peeking beneath their skirts. While the audience roared, the hero, Prince Lovelorn, entered with his friend, a huntsman named Gout.

The prince swore in Galt's ear. "By all the honey in heaven above, if it isn't you, my old friend!"

Galt watched as Gout tried unsuccessfully to plead his case to Pulchritude. He grinned back at the prince uncomfortably. Beneath his leather vest Galt began to sweat. But worse was to come.

The girl tailor entered, wearing wolf's ears and carrying enormous tin shears that were half her height. She began to give Gout advice on how to win Pulchritude's heart, and convinced him to strip to his smallclothes in order to be measured. While his back was turned she produced, with much winking at the stands, a "measuring tape," and when Gout turned around again she thrashed him about the head and ears with a stout leather strap, singing,

> Beat a wolf, sir, wolf, sir, wolf, sir,
> (Beat a wolf, sir, wolf, sir, wolf!)
> Come a day, sir, day, sir (yes, sir!),
> The wolf will come and beat—on—you."

The audience roared its approval. The crown prince glanced at his friend. The huntsman was tight-lipped. The incident of Ulfra and the injured wolf had, over the months, taken on a life of its own. No one seemed to remember that it had not been the huntsman himself who had baited the wolf. Poor Galt would never live it down.

But it so happened that the playwright had been magnanimous. In the end, the thing had a happy ending, and the huntsman Gout was married off to Pulchritude. It was the girl tailor, though, who wed the prince. Modesty, wearing her cat's-tail finery, was pursued and eaten by wolves.

It was, after all, a farce.

When the crowd had thinned somewhat, the prince and Galt left the theater by a back door. The prince cast sidelong glances at his friend as they wound their way to the guild district and Everlasting Lane.

"A nice bit of work. My sides quite ache. I had not realized my little tailor had achieved this degree of fame."

"I did not know the Dog's Muzzle was your tailor. Anyway, whatever fame your tailor has achieved has come from her dealings with you."

"You sell yourself short, my friend. Surely her fame comes from that incident with the wolf. Ah—now I have offended you. But you *will* allow me to lose to you at dice, and make up for it.

"Now let us quicken our steps; 'All That Attends' is keeping supper hot for us."

❦ ❦ ❦ The cast of *The Dog's Muzzle* trooped into a tavern, where their supper had been laid by the innkeeper. There were jugs of cream-and-black ale, smoking-hot meat pies, cheese-and-leek tart, and a boiled pudding called drunken lords. It was midnight, and the actors were in high spirits. They would sit, eating and drinking and otherwise making merry, till dawn.

The part of the girl tailor was actually played by a sly-faced boy of fourteen who used the name Trammel. He strode to the head of the long table and handed to its sole occupant a purse.

"Your fee, sir!" he said, with a smart bow. It was a little too smart; something about Lord Gobeleyn made Trammel uneasy. He did not smirk or joke with him, as he did with the others. Lord Gobeleyn was the author of *The Dog's Muzzle*, and in a way held the fate of all the actors in one hand.

Lord Gobeleyn smiled the smallest wisp of a smile and waved a negligent hand at the repast. The company sat and fell to.

Their author and benefactor did not eat, but filled and refilled his cup from the jugs of ale. Lord Gobeleyn had an otherworldly capacity for drink, known colloquially as "a goblin's leg." In truth, Lord Gobeleyn had not one goblin leg but two, neither of them hollow.

7.

Some Suitors, Keen and Reluctant

✦

Royalty cannot be stuck with a pin. A prince who must be fitted with enough traveling clothes for a year-long pilgrimage must have a manikin to take his place at those fittings where the garments are stuck through with pins like some vestment from a torture chamber. A prince, of course, must have a living manikin.

The prince's present manikin had grown up in the palace kitchen, turning the spit, until one day all the young men of likely height and breadth had been summoned into the courtyard to be measured.

It was not bad work. He must eat what the prince ate and exert himself as the prince exerted himself—at riding, falconry, dance, everything—on the theory that by living like the prince, he would keep the prince's figure.

This evening the prince was dining with his lady in Everlasting Lane. The prince's manikin, by name of Tod, was finishing his supper by the kitchen fire, in the company of the maid.

From the other room there came a loud crash and clatter of glass and metal and crockery, as though a supper tray had toppled to the floor. Gales of laughter reached the two by the kitchen fire. Lily got up, but Lucivia's voice from the other side of the door stopped the maid with her hand on the knob.

"Never mind, Lily—I've got it."

The maid retook her seat. "Now, you don't suppose the prince was exerting himself, do you?" Lily said, all innocence. She and the prince's manikin had an understanding of their own. He removed her hand from his knee.

"Hold a moment; let me finish this pie. I get measured tomorrow."

🌿🌿🌿 It was not Lily but the pie that undid him. That one slice, eaten by the fire, was not the culprit; it was all the slices of pie that had come before. For, exert himself as he would, Tod could not eat pie as the prince ate it and keep the prince's figure. The next day the Valet Royal weighed him, and he was found wanting—or, rather, found not wanting enough.

"It's back to turning the spit, I guess," he told Lily. "I don't suppose I'll be back." There would be another manikin; wasn't their understanding at an end?

Lily burst into angry tears. "You have another thing coming, Tod William, if you think I'll let you exert yourself with anyone but me!"

And, in the end, it was all right. He and Lily kept their understanding and, when it suddenly became necessary that they tie the marriage knot, Lily's mistress made her a nice settlement. Tod was pleased with the way things turned out. The falconing thing had been all right, but he had never been keen on the dancing.

*　　　*　　　*

97

❦ ❦ ❦ After he had wished on the wolf star, Nix had started to grow. Within two months Nix had shot up four inches and added half again to his weight. Within six months, he had not only grown past the mark on the pantry door but past the door frame itself. He had to duck his head when Mistress Goody asked him to hand something down from the top pantry shelf. Silently he cut and hauled wood, lugged pails of water for the wash, and scoured the stables. Watching him, Mistress Goody shook her head and marveled.

"Late grower," said her husband. "Some start out runty and catch up later. Think how much of your good soup has gone down that gullet!"

She thought it was something other than her soup: magic or sheer will, maybe some of each. With a heavy heart she knelt by her blanket chest and took out a parcel of plain brown paper. Inside was a boy's coat and a shirt of fine linen. They had arrived six months earlier, with a modest sum in silver and a dress for Mistress Goody. The coat and shirt were hopelessly small.

"But yours, all the same," she said, laying them before him. "There was always a little money, too, which we used for your care. But I saved whatever was left. It's a nice sum and will get you settled somewhere."

Nix nodded. He raised the coat to his nose and breathed in. It smelled faintly of dust and lavender and the old cat that liked to nap in the blanket chest if it was left open. Beneath those smells rode another—old, familiar, but faint. Too faint.

Nix let out his breath with a sigh and opened his eyes to see Mistress Goody looking at him strangely.

"Thanks, Mummer."

Her eyes smarted; he hardly called her by that name anymore.

"I packed you a meal for the road," she said, handing him a tin box.

He nodded and added it to his pack with the clothes. The

silver he added to his purse, which he wore around his neck beneath his shirt. Then he kissed her good-bye and left. Through the window she saw him cross the turnip patch to the field where her husband was mending the fence.

"And not even one of mine!" she said, weeping, watching them embrace, Nix now a few inches taller than her husband.

So he left them not quite eight years after he came.

🌿 🌿 🌿 In the most prosperous (and therefore respectable) quarter of the town, a house presented a demure aspect to the street. In the smaller of its two dining rooms Niccolaus, engraver and guild master, sat at the head of his breakfast table and surveyed the scene before him. It was prosperous and respectable. His two young sons, Albert and Bastian, were attacking the sausages with vigor. Columba, his daughter from his second marriage, was breakfasting on cream puffs, careful not to spoil either her gown or her artfully applied complexion. His wife Ermingrude's delicate disposition forbade breaking her fast before suppertime. She sat at the foot of the table, sipping limeflower tea while she read a letter from her sister.

The merchant frowned. "Where is Iona?"

His family looked up from their respective preoccupations and stared. Columba laughed shortly.

"Where is she ever, father?"

Niccolaus waved away the servant who had stepped forward to distract him with smoked trout. "Call her again."

His wife set down her tea. "She has been summoned three times already, my lord."

Niccolaus pushed back his heavy chair, startling the small dog curled asleep beneath it. "Then I shall go myself a fourth time!" He strode from the room.

Ermingrude sighed and nibbled a dry rusk. The boys went back to sawing sausage into the lengths that could be crammed into their mouths most efficiently. Columba admired her reflection in the back of her spoon, licked some stray sugar from her little finger, and smiled.

Iona was in her attic bedroom, bent over a block of boxwood, the handle of a burin cradled in one hand. She wore fingerless gloves over hands ingrained with ink and covered with innumerable nicks and tiny scars in various stages of healing. Her hair was pulled indifferently back with a plain black ribbon, and the only pigment on her face was a smudge of ink where she had wiped her brow. Her lips were chapped; she bit the lower one as she worked. From time to time, she blew wood chips from her work and held the block up to the light from the window.

It was a sunny room, and pleasant, but one would not have called it clean. One wall had been covered with cork, and to this were pinned prints in various stages of completion. Efforts that had pleased their maker less lay wadded in drifts under the workbench. A neglected tray held an all-but-uneaten meal—last night's perhaps; perhaps the night before's. Under the workbench a tabby cat was picking clean the bones of a chicken wing. On the worktable beside Iona lay an apple core, so browned it might have been carved of wood. If it were, thought Niccolaus, studying the scene from the topmost stair, his elder daughter might pay some attention to it.

"Iona."

She blew a final shower of wood curls from the block before looking up. "Hello, father." She reached for her spectacles and wiped them on her smock. A look of dismay came over her features. "Oh, dear—have I missed dinner?"

"Not dinner. Breakfast. Tell me, what is it that so absorbs you this morning?"

Iona held up the block. Half of it, still uncarved, bore a charcoal transfer pattern; the other half had been transformed into a scene of an underwater palace, with a queen upon an underwater throne surrounded by sea serpents and a garden of watery ferns.

Iona happily pushed back a lock of hair. Her sleeves were rolled up and both elbows were black where she had leaned on the inking table. "It's one of a series of blocks on tales from the Elder Age. When Columba and mother and I went to the sea, I visited the new water gardens to make sketches and called on an elderly gentleman in the old quarter who keeps specimens from the deep. It was the first holiday I ever really enjoyed, Papa."

"Yes." Niccolaus sighed. "Your sister told me about it." They had been unable to get Iona to dress respectably for meals at the inn, and so had had to hire a small villa to keep her scandalous behavior from public view. He took the block from his daughter's hand.

"The work is quite good. But tell me, what use do you think it will be to you? The trade will pass to Bastian, as my eldest son."

"I know, Father—that is both customary and right. I only ask to keep my small room and to be allowed to do my part to pay my keep."

"Until you marry, you mean."

Iona laughed and shook her head. "Oh, Papa! Me, marry? Who would have such an oddball as I am? What man would take a wife who burns the roast because she is bent over a block of wood all the day long? I would rock the dog in the cradle and throw my child a bone."

"Silence!" Niccolaus brought his fist down on the table, making the tools rattle and the curls of wood jump. Iona flinched.

"What—what have I said?"

"I will hear no more shocking nonsense! I will not have you making a laughingstock of the family, and I will not have Columba's position imperiled by your willful disobedience!"

"Willful disobedience! Papa, that is not just! I have missed a meal or two, but that is hardly disobedience!"

Niccolaus held up a hand. "The fault is entirely my own. You are my firstborn child, and for many years, for lack of a son, I taught you my craft, proud to have such an apt pupil in my daughter. But it was one thing when you were eight or ten or even twelve. When you were fourteen I hoped you would turn your energies to more seemly pursuits, such as Columba has always preferred. Nothing, it seems, can make you take an interest in the impression you make on others or how you present the family face to society."

Iona flushed scarlet. "The family face! What in hell is the family face, may I ask?"

"Here it is, profane willfulness! Can you deny it?"

"Not willfulness, Father. Indignation! Would you have me give up all you taught me and devote all my time to adjusting the lace of my cuffs and painting moles on my cheek?"

"No! I would have you marry!"

"And perhaps I *will* someday, when the time and the man are right. But what and who am I harming up here? I hurt no one."

"And how is Columba supposed to marry? She is the younger; no respectable young woman marries before her elder sister. And what man of good name would marry into a family with such an infamous eccentric?"

Iona studied her father's face as though something had become clear to her. "Obviously, some man of good name *has* asked her. Which is it, the paper merchant's prodigal son or the not-so-young duke? Let me see—which would most benefit the family? A prosperous match ensuring a supply of fine paper at a substantial discount, or marriage to a generous patron under whose protection the house is sure to prosper?" She sat down at her workbench and took up her block. "I see from your face that I am right in part, if not all. Willful, disobedient Iona must marry so that Columba can make an advantageous match. Now I understand."

102

Niccolaus raised a hand to strike her and for a moment froze with his hand in midair. Then he took the half-carved block from her hands and cast it into the grate.

Iona did not stir. "The fire went out long ago. And if it had burned, I would simply begin again. Not out of willfulness—but because I can't *not* do this work you taught me to love."

🕊 🕊 🕊 "It was *so* mortifying, Mother!"

Columba leaned toward the mirror to examine her beauty spot. Her father often marveled that the spot appeared and disappeared and was never to be seen before noon.

"There she was in the high street at two o'clock in the afternoon with her hair loose, hanging on the arm of some old bearded fool. I was with friends, so of course I had to pretend I didn't know her. She didn't see me, but I was mortified just the same. She was wearing an enormous black smock that flapped behind her, like some great black goose. And spectacles! I swear I would rather be struck stone blind than be seen in the street wearing spectacles. *Can't* you say something to her?"

Ermingrude lay back upon her cushions. "Oh, she never listens to me. Only her father can get anything out of her."

Columba darted a glance at her mother in the mirror, then began to apply a rosy stain to her lips from a small gilded pot.

"I only hope that Mathias does not lose all hope of me and find himself an heiress. He might marry that merchant's daughter, the one with vulgar dimples whose father sells those gorgeous silks we saw in that shop in Thistledown Street."

"That reminds me," said Ermingrude. "Aren't you due for a fitting today for your new gown? We will go directly. Smuggs is done with your hair. Iona will come, too. Your father has declared she is to have a new gown from the Cat's Face."

Columba was not pleased and had to redraw her mouth.

*   *   *

✿ ✿ ✿ While his wife and daughters were occupied on the premises of the Cat's Face, Niccolaus was engrossed across the street in a business transaction of great importance.

"Where did you find him?"

"It does not matter where," said the marriage broker. "He finds your terms acceptable."

"I must at least know the name of his family."

The marriage broker laughed, a low, throaty chuckle. She refilled their glasses with plum brandy, colorless, tart, and strong. As she poured, a few dark gems winked on her fingers. "Do you want a young man of spotless reputation or a young man with a fine family name? If you must have both, it will cost you."

"So long as he is not a thief or a scoundrel."

Lucivia gazed at her customer dispassionately. "I will vouch that he is not."

"Well, then." Niccolaus picked up the sheaf of papers and signed them where Lucivia indicated.

"It's all set, then—he will come for his interview tomorrow at four o'clock."

"How will I know him?"

"He will know you."

✿ ✿ ✿ "It is really going to happen," said the prince.

"What?" Lucivia looked up from her accounts. She was seated at the window, and the morning light played on her face and hair. It was not a young face, but it was, in the prince's experience, surpassingly beautiful.

"My marriage." The prince spoke from the bed on the other side of the room. The clothes he had worn to the theater the night before had been cleaned and pressed and lay awaiting him when he should emerge from his bath, which steamed behind a screen in front of the fire.

"Well then." Lucivia dipped her pen into the inkwell and

bent her head over the account book. "I don't see what is so startling about that. Several hundred people have it as their full-time occupation. It would be a wonder if it did not come about."

The prince sighed. "I know. It was seeing the sketches for my wedding clothes nearly complete. I wish I was at least indifferent to her. It would be preferable to finding her unbearable."

"You have had my professional opinion on this subject before. Didn't we agree not to speak of it between ourselves?"

"We did indeed." Rather than getting up and having his bath, the prince poured himself another cup of tea. He always postponed his bath at Lucivia's. Bathing meant getting dressed, and getting dressed meant leaving. "I wish I could marry you—"

Lucivia threw down her pen with a laugh.

"No, don't laugh. I wish I could marry you instead—"

"As if I would have you," she chided.

"And I most heartily wish you would make my wretched wife-to-be a brilliant match with someone else."

She came over and took the teacup from his hand.

"Stop talking such nonsense. You are a prince and she is a princess. What could be more eminently suitable? I am a marriage broker. With what I know, I would not be any man's wife. Our present arrangement suits me as it is; if you must give me up, so be it. Now, are you going to get into that bath or not? If Rose has to lug any more water upstairs, you'll have her to answer to."

🌾🌾🌾 Niccolaus watched the tall young man circle the room, scrutinizing every tapestry and silver ornament. He had not removed his hat upon entering and did not surrender his cloak. A servant, hovering expectantly, cleared his throat. The young man spoke over his shoulder.

"Your servant seems to have a cough," he remarked thoughtfully.

Niccolaus waved the servant away.

The young man stopped by the window. In the courtyard below, two women could be seen making a circuit of the garden. The younger wore a grey smock and her hair hung loose, the color called gilt-and-ashes. At one point the older woman took the younger's elbow and spoke earnestly in her ear. The young woman pulled away, casting her eyes up to the very window where the young man stood watching. Startled, he withdrew from the window. The young woman strode from the courtyard, her arms held stiffly at her sides, fists clenched. The older woman trotted after.

The young man let the curtain fall into place. "At what price?"

Niccolaus cleared his throat. "My advisers in such matters have drawn up an inventory of the proposed dowry." He placed the document on the table between them. The young man reached over and picked it up.

" 'One linen press . . . one bed with tapestry curtains . . . one ebony-and-silver clothes chest . . . one dozen silver plates and goblets . . . one small coffer of assorted books . . . silver-and-ivory dressing-table set . . .' " He looked up. "This is over-generous. The sum you mentioned would be more than sufficient."

"Nay, sir," said a woman's voice, "it is not compensation enough."

In the doorway stood the young woman from the courtyard; her hair had been tied back and her grey smock removed to show a dress of blue silk damask. Though the blue became her, someone had pinned to the neck a bit of lace frippery. With the distaste of a cat ridding itself of a bow, Iona snatched off the collar and cast it onto a chair.

"No, not half compensation enough to make up for the sacrifice of saddling oneself with such a virago!" She seized the dowry list and laughed out loud. "Oh, Father! A cradle! You *do* have great plans for this match!"

The young man looked at her with renewed interest. Niccolaus hastened to repair the damage.

"Master Fell, allow me to present my daughter Iona and my wife, Ermingrude."

Iona nodded. Ermingrude held her hand out to be kissed. When Fell instead seized it and gave it a vigorous shake, she colored deeply but recovered herself. "Master Fell of . . .?"

"Just Fell. Of no fixed abode." He turned back to the window. The sky had opened up, and the orange trees and fountain of the courtyard were obscured by grey curtains of rain. A servant ran out into the downpour to fetch something that had been left on a stone seat. Gloves, perhaps.

Niccolaus cleared his throat. "Master Fell."

The young man once again dragged his gaze from the window and gave his attention to his proposed father-in-law. Iona studied him with interest. As it was, she found him repellent only on principle; he was tall enough and broad enough in the shoulders. His nose was just shy of straight and his chin not quite square, but these flaws made him more attractive rather than less. He was clean-shaven, his light brown hair pulled back in a lock. His grey eyes were serious without being sober, perhaps because he always appeared on the verge of a smile without seeming to smirk. He gave the impression of one perpetually alert and pleasantly surprised by everything around him.

"I hope I satisfy."

"Whether I am satisfied hardly enters into the matter, I think. It is my father you must please. I am sorry if you find me ill-mannered; I was only curious to see the sort of man I am to be appended to."

There it was: a fleeting smile. "We shall get stares in the street, going about joined at the hip."

❦ ❦ ❦ Nix walked into the town as the inns were putting up their shutters. He followed his nose until he found a place that reminded him of the Goody farm: sweet straw and clean horse dung. He slept that night where cart horses were stabled and drank from the animals' trough.

As he lay in the straw, Nix let the smells of the town waft over him, sorting them over in his memory, looking for one small scent, a certain faint note. But among all the smells of the town, hot coals and cold embers, sour beer and overcooked cabbage, soot and dishwater, fresh pig's blood and new sawdust, horse sweat and human piss, he did not smell the one smell he was searching for. He did not smell so much as a whisker of wolf.

Nix rose at dawn to look for work as a laborer. The streets were just coming to life as he walked past the taverns and inns, oblivious to the many bills and notices that plastered their sides, many overlapping and obscured by mud and whitewash.

One such bill extolled the virtues of a new play, *The Dog's Muzzle*. Another called all young men "of sound limb and good character," urging them to report to the Valet Royal in order to be weighed and measured for possible work in the king's palace.

Nix saw neither.

"Know anyone needs a laborer?" he asked of a man loading barrels into a cart.

"Try the Tart's Nose," said the man, and guffawed at some private joke.

"He means the Turtle and Rose," said another. "It's a tavern across from the theater in the Compass. The owner wants someone to help him hoist the wine casks and such. From the size of you, you'll do."

Following their directions, Nix made his way to the circle known as Compass Street. The Turtle and Rose was not in the best part of town, and Nix's purse with its silver coins was not as well hidden beneath his shirt as it ought to have been. All along the street, people apparently engaged in their own business traded winks and nods.

The tavern was not yet open. Even as Nix raised his hand to knock on the shutter of the tavern, someone kicked his feet out from under him and threw a sack over his head. Then he saw stars, and not the kind for wishing on.

He came to in an alley alongside the Turtle and Rose, just as someone in an upper story tipped a pan of wash water out the window. Nix sat and dripped, knowing without looking that the silver was gone.

"It might have been worse," said a voice. "It might have been the chamber pot."

A well-groomed man stood over him, remarkable for his violet eyes, which sparkled in the dim alleyway. His clothes showed him to be a man of no small means: His coat was as black and glossy as a horse's hide, and his immaculate cuffs gleamed in the dimness.

Nix could not place the man's accent, but he trusted him on instinct. When a gloved hand was extended, Nix took it and was hauled to his feet.

"That's a nasty gash. It should be looked to. And here is Winsom with the carriage. Will you accept the hospitality of my house? It is some distance, but you can be better looked after there. Heaven knows, Winsom can look after a gash."

So Nix began his singular education under the roof of Lord Gobeleyn.

8.

Tea and Tales

◆

The twenty-third Lord Gobeleyn lived behind a high wall in a district of town where guildhalls and artisans' workshops outnumbered houses. Here twenty-two previous Goblin Pretenders had retired in defeat, each assuming the wealth, title, and house of his predecessor. The wall presented to the street a face of bare grey stone festooned with iron spikes. This appearance led passersby to speculate about the mysterious house and its even more mysterious occupant. Such a wall bespoke vast wealth, cold splendor, vicious hounds; gargoyles on either side of the gate suggested that something worse than mastiffs awaited the unlucky trespasser. The truth was rather different.

The garden side of the wall was inlaid with an intricate mosaic, nearly covered over by ivy. The mansion itself, of pale russet stone, rambled in porches and terraces down to the hot-

110

houses of tousled roses and sleepy peonies. An unseen fountain burbled; from a hidden dovecote came a low cooing and the soft flutter of wings.

Lord Gobeleyn sat on one of the terraces, bundled like an invalid in several dressing gowns, his feet clad not in slippers but in boots, in case he should be overtaken by an urge to walk in the garden before first being overtaken by an urge to get dressed. His pale, red-gold hair stood up on his head like flames; his eyes, a violet of startling intensity, were set deep in a face that had lost some of its high color to fatigue or illness. His face was a poor-fitting mask of languor; through the gaps one could occasionally glimpse the features beneath. His eyes especially gave him away, for they brimmed with remembered loss and ever-present pain, a keen violet sorrow.

Beside him a sideboard on wheels held a silver urn the size of a small child. This contained a quantity of tea strong enough to tan a mule skin. Close at hand sat a cut-glass dish of jam. No one of his acquaintance had ever observed Lord Gobeleyn to take any more nourishment than tea. This was, of course, romantic exaggeration on the part of both admirers and detractors, for he did take the occasional sardine on toast or egg beaten with brandy.

A smock-clad someone appeared, short of person, round of shoulder, bland of face. Nothing of this someone's appearance or manner, neither hair nor voice nor bearing, revealed whether this was Lord Gobeleyn's footman, valet, or housekeeper.

"Lord."

"Yes, Winsom."

"The young man is now presentable. Shall I present him?"

"Has he been fed?"

"Yes, my lord. I also took the liberty, while his clothes were drying, to avail him of some of your own, as well as a glass of the brandy."

"Then bring him to me."

111

Nix was brought before him, his recently washed hair drying in white peaks around the expertly bandaged gash. He wore some of his benefactor's old fencing clothes: a full white shirt gathered loosely at the wrists and neck and straight black trousers tucked into high, glossy boots. As he walked out onto the terrace, Nix caught his reflection in a looking glass and stared.

"It is a difference, is it not? Please sit by me. Will you have tea or more brandy?"

"Tea," said Nix.

"Just the thing for an insult to the skull. Winsom will attest that tea has done wonders for me. Was I a shadow of my present self when you met me, Winsom?"

"You were, sir."

"Did tea do wonders for me?"

"It did, sir."

"Most people," said Lord Gobeleyn, filling a bowl with tea and spooning jam into it, "make the mistake of not brewing it long enough. It should steep overnight at the very least. You want it full strength. Here—have a swig of this and tell me what you think."

Nix took a sip and felt, in the words of Mistress Goody, his eyelashes straighten and his spine curl.

"It is strong."

"Long brewing makes all the difference. Now tell me how you came to be lying in the alley of the Turtle and Rose."

Nix began his story, from the time he left the Goodys.

Lord Gobeleyn raised a hand. "Begin," he said, "at the beginning."

So Nix began again, this time with his earliest memory: a beggar and guttersnipe eating stolen bread. Through chance he had met Ulfra, who was then living at the court of mad King Milo.

"When Milo went mad for good, we joined Folderol's troupe with the wolves. And this was all right for a while, for we had all the geese we wanted and we were setting some gold aside. Then the contract with the wolves ran out, and we had to return them to the Weirdwood, and on the way back she left me with the Goodys." The tea (or those violet eyes) had loosened Nix's tongue; he had never spoken so much at one stretch in his life.

Lord Gobeleyn seemed to follow this disjointed narrative perfectly. He made no connection, however, between the wolf trainer of Nix's tale and the heroine of *The Dog's Muzzle*.

"And now you have come in search of her."

Nix nodded.

"So you know where she is living?"

Nix shook his head.

"Well, then. I would suggest to you the following plan. The lady you describe has some means, for she has sent you money and fine presents. In order to circulate—to go around in such company as she keeps—you must learn some things you may not have needed to know on the Goody farm, things with which I am intimately acquainted. I would be happy to teach them to you and to take you to such places as she is likely to be."

This was a kingdom unknown to Nix. "Where is that?"

Lord Gobeleyn shrugged expressively. "The court, the theater, the baths, the falcon grounds, the tailor."

"Will it take a long time to reach it? I would like to begin at once."

Nix's benefactor shook his head. "It is not far, but there is much we must do to prepare. You must first learn the language."

Nix felt his heart sink. He was clever enough to realize he was not clever enough. "What language is that?"

"Conversation."

🌿🌿🌿 Iona could not make Fell out, not at all.

His manners were curious, to say the least. He was taciturn to the point of rudeness, and when he did speak he was so blunt

113

that she wondered whether some mockery underlay his seemingly simple words. Iona suspected Fell kept his hat and gloves on when they met only to irk her and spent all their conversations gazing out the window only to test her patience.

While he was not unhandsome, there was in Fell's look nothing that strived to please. There was a subtle anticipation in his every word and gesture, as though he were prepared to fight or fly or, at any moment, turn into something else entirely, as though released from a spell.

Iona laughed at herself. And what would Fell turn into? A prince, or a tusked beast in ermine and velvet? Had she to choose, Iona thought she would much prefer a beast for a husband. Humming, she sketched a well-dressed beast on the back of a proof.

She was so engaged when there came a knock. Iona turned from her work to see Fell ducking his head to clear the low doorway. As she followed his gaze around the room, Iona blushed, seeing as through his eyes the clothes draped over the furniture, the unemptied basin from her sponge bath, yesterday's stockings discarded in a snarl in the middle of the floor.

"I'm sorry," said Fell. "You are at work."

She wiped her inky hands on her smock. "That's all right. I was going to stop in a bit anyway. I keep a little stove hidden up here so that I don't have to bother anyone when I only want some tea. Father would never allow it—certain I'd burn the house down while they all slept."

Fell smiled. "No, if *you* were ever to burn anything to the ground, it would not be accidentally. Well, if you're quite sure I won't bother you. . . ." He lifted the cat from the chair and sat down.

She brought out the small, tabletop brazier and lit it. All the cups that did not leak had been used for mixing ink. While she was wiping out the two least objectionable, Fell picked up the heavy folder of finished prints.

"May I see?"

Fell had already untied the cloth tapes that held the folder shut, and Iona could only murmur her assent.

He leafed through the folder, examining each print carefully, hardly noticing when she pressed the cup into his hand. He did not look up except to hold a print to the light, nor speak except to ask how a certain effect had been achieved. When he had gone through the entire folder once, he turned the pile over and gave his attention to certain prints again, admiring a print of a warrior woman, helm on one hip, sword aloft. Iona sat in agony and watched him.

At length he set the folder aside.

"I asked your father's permission to speak with you alone, but he does not know what I plan to say to you. I know you do not wish this marriage. You see me as a fortune hunter, and I cannot deny it. All I can do is offer you compelling reasons why this match is in your own best interest, as well as mine.

"I offer you this: marriage in name only. You will keep your own workroom and, if you so desire, a separate bedchamber. You may come and go as you wish, travel abroad as you wish. I only ask that you spend part of the year under the same roof with me. I should add that, legally, I may not share in your marriage portion unless we reside together at least six months and one day of each year."

Iona could not at first reply. "Forgive me if I seem ungrateful. This does not strike me as a happy prospect."

He bowed. "I misunderstood you. When we met, I received the strongest impression that the idea of marriage to anyone was repellant to you."

"It is," she said uncertainly.

"Then the plan I have outlined must be the least objectionable form of matrimony imaginable. You could do exactly as you pleased."

She looked at him, her eyes narrowed more out of suspicion than nearsightedness. "There are plenty of marriageable maidens with larger dowries and better manners than mine. Why me? What do you get out of the bargain?"

Fell shifted his grey gaze out the window, where pigeons were fluttering and cooing among the decorative chimney pots. The noise they made, rising and falling among the red-tiled roofs, was at once soothing and mournful, a sad cradle song. "When we met, you seemed so determined against the match that I thought there was nothing for it but to withdraw. But it seemed to me, Iona, that your father would eventually attach you against your will to someone without my views on marriage. I suggest that you stand a better chance of happiness under the arrangement I describe."

"How gallant of you!"

He raised an eyebrow. "Is it? When I first came up these stairs today, it was to tell you I was abandoning my suit. You seemed to have so much spirit that I doubted the arrangement would work at all."

She laughed bitterly. "Then you admit I *am* a shrew."

Fell shook his head. "No. You need the only thing I cannot bring to the match."

"And what, may I ask, is that?"

"Love."

She had no answer. He set his cup on the dresser and rose to leave. When he was halfway to the first landing, Fell turned and called back up to her where she stood at the top of the stairs.

"By the way—your warrior woman. You have given her left hand a right-handed thumb."

"What?"

"The hand that is holding the sword—the thumb is the wrong way around." He turned and went down the rest of the stairs.

When her mortification had passed, Iona gave rein to her temper. "I wouldn't marry you if you were the very *last* man Above or Below or in All-in-Between!"

116

This did not seem to surprise her cat, who reclosed one eye and returned to a dream of plump, flightless sparrows.

Iona turned and took up her own, untouched, tea. It was stone cold and tasted emphatically of ink. Fell had drunk two cups of it without complaint.

🐝🐝🐝 "Let's see, now," said the old apothecary, rummaging in a wooden box full of bits of glass and wire. "I seem to remember I got some small ones in."

Caitlin did not like to think about how the apothecary came by the secondhand spectacles: At best, she got them from starving widows parting with a last momento; at worst, from unscrupulous grave diggers. Or perhaps the old woman procured them herself, through the occasional embalming she did on the side. Easy enough to substitute plain glass for the valuable lenses—the embalmed tell no tales.

Bram's eyes were much worse. As the episodes of changeling sight had become more frequent, his eyesight had dimmed. He suffered from frequent headaches and had to lie down for part of each day.

At last the old woman pulled a pair of spectacles from the box, spat delicately on each lens, and polished them with a filthy cloth.

"You, boy—leave that be and come here."

Bram left the stuffed owl with its single dusty glass eye and went to Caitlin's side. The apothecary set the spectacles on the bridge of the boy's nose and hooked the wires over his ears. The old woman was as grimy as her tiny shop, the whorls of her fingertips ingrained with dirt, but she had a clean smell, sharp with juniper and fir smoke, sweet with beeswax and mint.

Bram was fascinated by her large ears. The pendulous lobe of the left was hung with a lizard's foot, the right with a glass owl's eye. As her ears came into focus, he saw inside them tufts of grey hair. Startled, he stepped back. The apothecary cackled.

"Ah, he sees—sees how ugly I am!"

Bram grinned uncertainly back at her, glad of Caitlin's hand on his shoulder.

"What do we owe you, besides our thanks?"

The old woman waved her hand, dismissing the notion. "Just bring me some of those wood herbs you dry, next time you come. I am getting too creaky in the knees to bother with them myself."

"Done. Say thank you, Bram."

They had barely reached the corner when he burst out, "Did you see the hair in her ears?" Caitlin smiled. "Yes, I did. It was good of you not to ask her about it."

"I don't think she would have minded."

"Probably not, but it'll do you good to practice your manners. Heaven knows you don't practice them at home. Now, I have one more call to make before we go. You can come with me or meet me back here in an hour. You have so much to see with your brand-new specs."

Bram weighed his options. He could go to the canal and watch the floating market, the brightly painted boats stacked with tubs of live turtles and wicker baskets of crabs and eels. Or he could go to the square, where the old men who idled in the tavern doorways would buy him lime punch if he beat them at checkers. Lime punch was a delicacy unknown to the Binder table. Bram was very fond of it and very good at checkers.

"Where are *you* going? he asked, nibbling his thumbnail.

"To see a book peddler."

"Then I'll come with you."

❧ ❧ ❧ The bookman's directions led them to an unlikely street. Caitlin was beginning to think she had mistranslated the runes when Bram spotted a shingle hanging from the uppermost story of a tall, narrow house.

☞

BOOKS
BOUGHT
&
SOLD

They climbed the narrow staircase until they reached a door. A small shutter set in this at eye level was closed. Tacked below the shutter was a notice, written out in an elegant hand.

BEMBO GILL, BOOKSELLER

Books may be left on consignment,

but the Owner reserves the right to

examine them for bookworms, &c.,

before they are brought onto the

premises. Sweetmeats out of wrapper,

uncorked bottles (esp. ink), &c.,

must be surrendered to the Owner

upon entry. Live animals are to be

left in the yard.

☞ALL PIPES Must Be PUT OUT

While they were reading this notice, Caitlin became aware that they were being observed through the small shutter. At once the shutter slid closed and the door was opened. The bookman peered out at them.

"Master Gill?" said Caitlin.

"Yes, yes, but please call me Bembo. No one calls me Gill, let alone Master."

"It's Caitlin Binder. You left a note with my husband."

"Ah, yes. Come in—I have been expecting you—your husband gave me to understand you have an interest in runes." He turned a sharp eye on Bram. "You—little man. Have you got any candy in your pockets, hmm? Peppermint whistles? Treacle mousetraps? Larks' tongues?"

"I haven't even got *pockets*," Bram protested.

"Well, that's all right, then. Come in, come in. And watch your step!"

They entered a maze, a room filled halfway to the rafters with books. The floor was covered in piles waist deep, through which the bookman threaded his way. Caitlin caught glimpses of heavy oaken boards set with iron bosses, slim volumes bound in creamy vellum. There were atlases that were taller than Bram, and a book small enough to fit entirely into the palm of his hand. Bembo fetched it from the glass case where it lay with other tiny volumes, none quite as small.

"It's a treatise on bees, written by a monk. This is not his smallest book; he wrote subsequent volumes on ants, fleas, and mites. Eventually he went stone blind."

Bram turned the tiny pages, each no bigger than his thumbprint. The bees were shown life-size and, at the end of the book, there was a fold-out cutaway diagram of a hive.

"A lovely thing, a lovely thing," muttered Bembo, returning it to its glass case. "Now, will you take a little tea? Never mind that smell—it's only camphor, to keep the bookworms away. The tea is verbena, very nice verbena, at that." He looked from Caitlin to Bram anxiously and was relieved when the offer was accepted.

They emerged from the maze to find a worktable. At least, a worktable could be deduced from the four legs that supported the heaps of parcels and papers awaiting the bookman's attention. Mismatched and mended chairs were ranged around the fire that burned in the grate.

Bembo put the kettle on and began to scrounge around for three uncracked cups with handles.

"Little man," he said over his shoulder, as he searched for spoons, "will you fill the dish with milk and put it on the floor? I've not been around to the fishmonger today, and the mice have been scarce of late."

A pie tin and a covered crock of milk sat on the dresser. Bram filled the dish and set it on the floor. He was immediately up to his ankles in cats: big, middling, and tiny; tortoiseshell, smoke, marmalade, and harlequin; a few missing bits of ears or tails; several with extra toes. There had been no sign of the cats among the stacks of books, though Caitlin now recognized the shop's faint oily smell to be the odor of sardines long since eaten.

"Keep the mice down, you know. A mouse would rather eat the glue out of a bookbinding, I think, than a whole Six'moon cheddar. Have a seat—tea's ready. That's the secret to good tea, you know. Mustn't let it steep too long."

The tea was scalding, fragrant, and pale green; Caitlin sipped hers cautiously and studied their host. He did not square exactly with Binder's description of an impoverished man selling ruined books. The bee treatise alone might have made him a rich man, but he fed his cats better than he fed himself.

As if reading her thoughts, Bembo spoke.

"The problem, you see, is that no one reads. In these sorry times, the purpose of a book is to show everyone else that you are rich or learned or devout or well connected. See that pile over there?" Bembo indicated a pile of books tied in bundles; they were all of a size, all bound in vellum. "Those don't open. They are wood blocks covered with sheepskin and gilded along the edges. And others are just old bindings. Back when the rune tongues were banned, you could have your eyes put out for reading the wrong book. So they tore out the offending pages and sewed new ones in. That atlas? It was used by a horse breeder to record the bloodlines of his stallions. And this, this was once a bestiary. Now it is the account ledger from a pawnbroker."

121

It seemed to Caitlin that the time had come to broach the real purpose of her visit.

"What do you know of the Books of the Keepers?"

"Well, that depends," Bembo said, without a hint of craftiness. "What do *you* know of them?"

Caitlin was caught up short by this but soon recovered herself. "Not counting the Book of Seeing, there are four of them: the Book of Naming, the Book of Healing, the Book of Summoning, and the Book of Changing. They were written during the Elder Age, before Chameol was an island, when it was a cloister on a hill above the lost kingdom of Iule."

"Go on."

Bram settled back, tucking his feet up under him and blowing on his tea contentedly. His mother told good stories, and the best ones began "Long ago, in the Elder Age . . ."

Caitlin suspected she couldn't tell the bookseller anything new, but resolved to leave nothing out all the same.

"In the Elder Age, when this world and the Otherworld were one, Chameol was a cloister, a walled city within the royal seat of Iule. The women of the cloister were dedicated to knowledge and the Elder Arts, what we call magic. The Keepers' task was to study the Books and guard them, for the magic they contained could be dangerous in the hands of the unwitting. Each book was protected by a powerful spell.

"The Book of Naming set forth the art of calling things— stones, beasts, herbs, winds, beings mortal and immortal—by their true names. It was bound in ivory that had been carved in the shapes of fabulous beasts. It was protected by wailing runes that would bray and howl and shriek when the book was opened without permission. Its Keeper was Gudule, who is shown in later books holding a pen and inkhorn.

"The Book of Healing was the grandmother of all herbals, for all those that survive today descend from it, sickly children though they are. The pattern of its binding was a knot garden, planted with precious stones and set around a silver fountain. It was protected by its pictures. The hemlock on the page was deadly and the thorns and nettles could catch and sting. Edda kept it; she is always shown holding a branch of the elder tree.

"The Book of Summoning taught how to use a true name to summon forth winds and water, men and beasts. In some fables from the Elder Age, the Book of Summoning is used to return wayward husbands to their wives and children. Chroniclers say it was bound in gold set with six cameos of the four winds and the sun and moon. Its protective magic was the loss, bit by bit, of the power of speech: The reader first began to stutter, became tongue-tied, lost his voice, and eventually turned mute. Its Keeper was Orisyn, who is shown with, or as, a wood thrush.

"The last book is the Book of Changing, the art of exchanging one shape for another. Fables have survived with nonsense morals: 'It is easier to change an ass into an angel than a priest into a pin.' It seems that changes from animate to inanimate were more difficult to pull off than wordly to otherwordly. Since the book itself could shift its shape, nothing is known of its appearance. It was said to be protected by shifting runes that could not be read or copied. Its Keeper, Thyllyln, is usually shown as a chameleon, the lizard that changes its color. The least of the arts of changing, those of stealth and disguise, were kept alive by the brotherhood known as the Knights of Chameol."

Caitlin, feeling a little parched from so much talking, drained her cup. Bembo looked at her expectantly.

"Oh, do go on, please," he said.

"I'm afraid that's all I really know about them. I seem to have found out more what they aren't than what they are."

Bembo looked embarrassed. "I'm sorry, I have misunderstood. Your husband told me you had been studying runes these seven years."

"So I have, with precious little to show for it. I have been working from an old book of incantations, pages from each of the Books bound together. But whether because the Books are not complete or because I am not initiated, the runes will not speak to me."

Bembo's distress became acute. He bit his thumbnail and shifted in his chair as if it were acrawl with ants.

"But you know—you *must* know . . ."

Caitlin felt an odd sensation of extreme impatience mingled with dread. "What? Tell me!"

"The Books as you described them to me are quite right. Nothing wrong there. But you do understand—you must know—the rune books you have been working from are only copies."

Caitlin shook her head. She could not have understood him. "What?"

"They are copies. They are from the Elder Age, all right, and the Keepers charmed them, but they are copies." Seeing her face still incomprehending, Bembo bit his lip and searched the ceiling for words. He found the word he wanted and looked back at her, beaming triumphantly.

"They are decoys. Fakes."

9.

Misapprehensions

✦

Bram looked anxiously from Bembo to his mother. Bembo looked at Caitlin. Caitlin's gaze seemed transfixed by an invisible object suspended some six inches from her face. Over her features there played a range of emotions, all strong and none simple.

"Fakes," she repeated at last, trying the word gingerly on her tongue, as though the power of speech were new and strange.

"Yes," said Bembo doubtfully. "I am very much afraid so, yes."

"Ah. *Ah.*" Caitlin collapsed in laughter. Bram joined in, and then Bembo, and the three laughed for several minutes on end.

Caitlin wiped mirth from her eyes. "You have just told me I have wasted seven years' study on fakes, and yet, I feel like a new woman. How do you explain that?"

Bembo shrugged. "Now you know why you weren't getting anywhere with them."

Caitlin shook her head. "But it still doesn't make sense. Scraps from the Books became my old guardian's book of incantations. If they were fakes, how could she use them to perform magic?"

Bembo scratched his head thoughtfully. "The fakes had to fool magicians of no mean talent. Nonsense books, mere puzzles, would have been found out. The fakes had to be convincing. From other books of incantations that have come my way, it seems that portions of the real Books were copied over with mistakes put in and some essentials left out, a powerful cryptic spell cast over it all. Some of the spells would work, others would not. Failures would be put down to copyists' flubs. You and many others have spent lifetimes"—Caitlin smiled ruefully—"trying to decipher them, with nothing to warn you that you did not have a real Book."

"So the real Books were destroyed after all."

Bembo shrugged. "Who can say? Me, I think not. The Keepers were crafty. I think they made up those tales of their own demise and the Books being scattered. Why bother to look for something you think has been digested by bookworms? I think they hid the Books in plain sight so that they would be sure to be found and used again. But the real books were charmed, so they could be found only by one with a pure motive."

Bembo suddenly fixed his gaze on Bram, who had been squirming in his seat for some minutes.

"Speak up, boy! No need to burst your bladder. There is a little closet at the bottom of the stairs."

Bram scampered from the room.

Caitlin saw her chance. "You know so much about old books. Why—"

"So why am I so poor? Ah, that question has been simmering in your eyes since I showed you the bee treatise, I think." The bookseller undid one cuff and rolled up his sleeve. The length of his arm from shoulder to elbow bore an elaborate tattoo.

Caitlin had seen the ancient pattern once before; there was no mistaking the design.

"A shape changer!"

Bembo protested, tugging his sleeve back into place. "Heavens, no. It's nothing so honorable, I'm afraid: a pawn mark, a sort of receipt, if you will, for my true shape." He sighed. "I was once a—well, I came from a very old family, and I was, shall we say, a *wealthy* man. Through an unbridled love of books I became hopelessly indebted to a pawnbroker. He dealt in shapes as well as books, so to settle my debt, I pawned my true form to him."

Caitlin wavered between crediting and disbelieving his story. Shape shifting had fallen from common practice hundreds of years since. "I thought it was a lost art."

Bembo smiled, and his eyes shone as if with a brilliant vision. What does he see? wondered Caitlin, and in his eyes she fancied she saw reflected the spires of his ancient city, its glittering port. "Not in *my* kingdom, it wasn't."

It was time to go; when Bram returned, Caitlin made their apologies. As he saw them out, Bembo said thoughtfully, "Not to say, of course, that the fakes might not have a clue or two in them. Watch your step on the way down—the railing's coming away from the wall."

On the long walk home, Caitlin remembered a story she had heard at Abagtha's knee, of an ancient king who pawned his true shape in order to own the Book of Wisdom. She told it to Bram as they reached the edge of the Weirdwood.

"And so the magician granted his wish, and turned the king into a book. . . ."

🌿🌿🌿 There was nothing quite so tiresome, thought Columba as she sat on the couch of the front room of the Cat's Face, as watching someone else buying clothes. Beside her Ermingrude reclined with her feet propped up, fearfully regarding the proceedings from beneath a damp compress.

"All this white is giving me a miserable headache."

"We must have seen every bolt of white cloth in the thirteen kingdoms," said Columba with a sigh.

"No," said Tansy crisply, unrolling yet another. "Only the best of them."

There were blue-whites like snow under moonlight, green-whites like jasmine in shadow, pink-whites like the wannest rose. There were swan's-breast velvets, moth-wing muslins, and a sheer, stiff silk that crackled with the fire of opals.

Iona agonized. Columba's boredom was palpable. She must pick something. She must decide. Anyway, you may never wear it, she told herself. She could still call the wedding off, so it hardly mattered which.

"This one." She fingered the bolt of jasmine silk.

Tansy held a length of it next to Iona's cheek and nodded.

"Yes—this will be very nice. The color sets off the roses in your cheeks. A simple round neck, I think. And the sleeves should not be too long. Just past the elbow."

Ermingrude protested. "But her hands are so unsightly—cover her wrists, at least."

Her hands *were* unsightly, scarred from the burin and ingrained with ink. Iona scowled and hid them behind her back.

Tansy was firm. "You have very fine hands, long and well shaped. I get a special sort of soap from the dyer. It will get that ink out from under your nails. No, the sleeve must barely cover your elbow." The leopard-woman jotted some measurements on a sketch.

Now that the Cat's Face was well established, Tansy saw customers without a veil. As the leopard-woman calculated the length of silk required for each of several designs, Iona studied her, trying to commit to memory as much as she could. She had that morning prepared a new block of boxwood; as soon as she got back home Iona meant to begin a portrait of the cat-faced tailor.

Tansy caught Iona gazing at her and smiled. "No lace for you, I think. Just some roses worked in silk. And real ones in your hair."

Ermingrude could not decide on a pattern. Certainly the one that used the least silk; but she did not want to be thought cheap. Yet it was important that Iona not outshine Columba. At last a middle-priced design was selected.

Columba had to be shaken out of a reverie of her own wedding clothes: the watery, opal silk, so encrusted with crushed pearl that the dress would stand up on its own. And golden slippers for her feet.

In the street Iona felt a rush of happiness: Her ordeal was over for the moment. Soon she would be home, working on her block.

"I hope that silk will not make you look sallow," said Ermingrude.

"I imagine Master Fell will go through with the ceremony if it makes her look three days dead," murmured Columba.

Iona ignored this remark, but the barb had drawn blood. And at home, in the attic workroom, she stared at the paper pattern for Tansy's portrait, unable to carve the first line in the boxwood block. Lulled by the sound of the pigeons on the roof-tops, she sat and brooded on Fell's strange proposal. Amid these thoughts there cropped up unbidden images of herself at the altar in her wedding finery.

Annoyed, Iona bent over her drawing.

🐛 🐛 🐛 Iona's betrothed was across town, in his lodgings over the Turtle and Rose. He shared a rented room with an actor in the troupe, a lad who was always out drinking his night's pay or sleeping it off. This suited Fell; he liked his privacy. For an extra penny the landlady brought meals up on a tray so that he need not eat in the tavern dining room.

As lodgers went, Fell was unfailingly sober, untroublesome, cool-tempered, and thoroughly odd. His half of the small attic room was strewn with rag pickings, scraps of paper, and boxes of scrap lead. Sweeping the room out, the landlady had discovered drawings of an odd contraption under the mattress.

"A what?" asked her husband, the keeper of the Turtle.

"An odd contraption. Like what you put people on, to stretch the truth out of them."

"A rack!" The landlord laughed until he had to dab his eyes. "Ah, I've married a madwoman. Our tenant, building a rack in the attic. Hee hee!"

His lady pressed her lips together in a thin line. "All right then, Maxwell Hunt. We will just see!"

🦋 🦋 🦋 Nix sat and stared at the objects before him. The mental concentration made the sweat stand out on his lip like nail heads. His glance strayed down to the fresh cherries on his plate, then back to the implements. He pleaded wordlessly with his inquisitors, but Lord Gobeleyn seemed engrossed with his fingernails; Winsom, as usual, was a cipher.

Nix picked up the larger of two spoons, scooped up a cherry, and conveyed it to his mouth without mishap. He managed not to choke on the pit, but then held it on his tongue, aware that something more was wanted. Lord Gobeleyn's glance seemed to lift a fraction of an inch and fasten itself on the spoon in Nix's hand. Nix spat the cherrystone onto the spoon and lowered it to his plate.

Winsom nodded and began to clear away the discarded dishes and linens. Gobeleyn applauded and poured out the brandy, which the boy swallowed entirely. When Wisom had left the room, Lord Gobeleyn leaned over in a conspiratorial whisper.

"I must admit I feared for you, my boy, that fourth course, before the second soup. Stouter men that you have fallen to fish in jelly."

Nix rose from the table on unsteady legs. He collapsed into a chair with a second brandy. At length he opened his eyes and nodded curtly, as though to his executioner.

Lord Gobeleyn hesitated. "We *can* continue tomorrow . . ."

"No! I'm ready."

"All right, then." Lord Gobeleyn poured himself a brandy and studied the ceiling for a moment. "A woman drops her fan. Do you pick it up?"

"Yes, but I don't return it to her hand. That would mean I was consenting to a tryst. I place it where she can see it, say, on a table. Unless her husband is watching, in which case I leave it where it is."

"Good. Now, suppose you do want to accept her offer and her husband is watching?"

"I pick up the fan and return it to her later."

"Any exceptions?"

"The queen or her chief lady-in-waiting. In that case, I leave the fan where it is and show up for the tryst."

"Good."

"But Gobeleyn, what if I don't want to?"

"Have a tryst? Well, in that case there are only two courses of action available to you. Under the influence of wine, you may pretend to fall asleep. Or assume a degree of innocence that suggests you haven't the slightest idea what she expects of you. Neither strategy, I should caution you, is foolproof. If a fan should fall at your feet, don't scruple too much before you pick it up."

Nix yawned widely. "Go on. Duels . . ."

But Lord Gobeleyn had not outlined the first problem when his pupil gave out a faint snore.

Winsom returned for the table linen and paused to remove the glass from Nix's hand and place it out of harm's way.

Lord Gobeleyn studied Nix thoughtfully.

"No luck tracing this mysterious wolf-girl of his?"

"No, my lord."

"It is too bad, you know. I begin to think I was wrong about the source of her money. Perhaps she is dead of consumption or drink or languishing in a brothel."

"It strikes me, my lord, from his description of her, that she is rather resourceful enough to have escaped that fate."

Lord Gobeleyn smiled. "As usual, Winsom, you are full of abundant good sense. Of course she is, and he will find her. Love will have its lovers. And I shall do my part to keep him from the arms of ladies-in-waiting, even if I have to pick up all the dropped fans in the thirteen kingdoms to do it."

"I am sure you are equal to the task, my lord."

"Sometimes, Winsom, I suspect you of making remarks at my expense."

"Never, my lord. Good night, my lord."

"Good night. Leave the brandy."

🌿🌿🌿 "Madam, I told him you were otherwise engaged, but he would not wait!"

Rose—successor to the departed Lily, now Mistress Tod William—looked daggers over one shoulder. A pale young man stood behind her in a state of barely concealed agitation, running his slender fingers ceaselessly around the brim of his hat.

Lucivia pulled her silken wrapper more closely about her and shut the door to her inner bedchamber. "It's all right, Rose; you may go. Bring up some hot wine." She turned to her visitor. "Unless you'd rather have something stronger?"

The young man turned and shook his head. It was Fell.

The door closed after Rose, but Fell waited until he heard her making noise in the scullery below to speak.

"Are we alone?"

132

"If I am alone at this hour I am usually up working. It is all right; he sleeps." She chucked him lightly under the chin. "Now, tell me. What brings you here, with such a look?"

Fell was all smooth composure. "I can't go through with it."

She made a face of sympathy and disappointment. "Is there something about the bride or her situation that does not meet your expectations?"

"No. Everything about her and her situation is as you told me it would be. It's just that—" Here the composure faltered, and Fell drew a ragged breath. "I find myself unequal."

Lucivia smiled. "Nonsense. Never were two more alike, more equal, than you and Iona. These are mere jitters."

Fell shook his head, a little angry. "I see nothing to joke about."

"I was not joking."

"She should not have her affections, her heart, her very life trifled with. It is too much—"

He broke off. Rose had entered with the hot wine. When her mistress had tasted and approved it, the maid withdrew.

Fell opened his mouth to continue, but Lucivia held up a hand. "Drink your wine first. It is late, and I fear you have come through the streets in foul weather. Think carefully, I urge you. Are you really so ready to relinquish your suit?"

"I do not see what choice I have."

"Are you so willing to go back on our contract?"

Fell's spine stiffened and he set his wine down cautiously. He laughed shortly.

"You would not hold me to it! Not with what I know about you."

"Oh, I most certainly would. What you know about me is nothing to who I know. You swore to fulfill a solemn promise. If I release you from our bargain, it will cost you the advance in silver upon the dowry. If I were in your shoes, I should not find it an attractive prospect. Besides, my sweet, where is the hardship in it? So she is not complacent; she *is* very rich." She could not resist a final needling. "All you have to do is be a man."

This final insult was too much. Fell pushed past her out of the room, bowling over Rose, who was engaged in a useless rearrangement of the hall linen chest.

In his haste Fell had knocked the wine cup from Lucivia's hand, and the contents had splashed upon her silk wrapper. She gave a hoarse shout of frustration.

"Love?" called the prince from the inner room.

Instantly she snatched up the paper knife from the writing table by the window and was upon the floor. The shaft of a paper knife protruded between her ribcage and armpit, and a ghastly stain spread pinkly over her heart, smelling faintly of cloves.

Such was the sight that met the prince's eyes as he entered from the bedchamber. With an oath he knelt and slipped an arm beneath her to raise her.

She opened one eye, and with a shout of fright he let her fall back on the floor. The truth dawned across his face like a black eye.

"Damn you, Lucy!"

She clutched herself, shaking with mirth. "Oh, I have banged my elbow, and now I shall break a rib laughing! Darling, you looked so sweet. Really, are you *very* angry with me? How could I resist such an opportunity? My best silk wrapper is ruined. I might at least get a smile out of it."

A frightened Rose peeked in at the door, but an oath from the prince sent her scurrying out again.

Lucivia put off the stained wrapper, and stood by the fire in nothing but a moth-wing muslin gown. "Will you get me my other wrapper?"

"Certainly not."

She made a face and crossed to the inner room. As she passed, he caught her by the arm and pulled her back into a kiss.

"Fiend," she murmured.

His reply was the barest exhalation: "Witch."

🙦🙦🙦 Rose had soon told the tale of the hired bridegroom to her own Matthias, who related it to his cousin Lam at the tavern, who told it to his mistress, who waited upon Lady Littlefoot, who told it to the ostler, who told it to his ladylove, who was Columba's own maid, who told it to the to the housekeeper as they were counting out the linens purchased for the wedding feast.

"Even with the dowry what it is, he won't have her. They say he wanted more money to go through with it."

"Well, it doesn't surprise me. After the first mistress died, the master let her run wild. She was indulged something awful. Once grown, it's hard to bring such a creature to heel. You can comb her hair and put her in a nice gown, but that doesn't give her nice ways."

Unknown to them, Iona had curled up in the window seat of her favorite alcove, the arras pulled across it for privacy. Her book had slipped from her hand, and she sat frozen where she was. When the last napkin had been counted, the two servants moved away.

Iona pulled back the curtain, dizzy and sick to her stomach. She stood, uncertain where to go, wishing she could vanish on the spot and never have to see any inmate of that house again.

Then she began to get very, very angry. A quarter of an hour later, she had put on her black cloak and packed a bag with her tools, any jewelry she could sell, all her money. Once out of sight of the house, she had soot to smear her face, wax to black out one tooth. She would go about as a beggar woman.

She came down from her attic room and met Ermingrude in the hall.

"Why on earth have you got your cloak on indoors?"

135

"I—I'm going out to make sketches."

"Well, you'll have to make them later. Your bethrothed has paid you a visit."

Iona curled her hand confidentially upon her stepmother's arm. "Oh, dearest, will you let us alone a little? The wedding is so soon and we have spent so little time in one another's company, that I fear he will seem a stranger to me on my wedding night. Will you give us half an hour alone?"

This seemed to Ermingrude a very pretty sentiment, and she assented. Fell was shown to the same room overlooking the courtyard where he had first been received.

Iona was seated by the window, looking uncommonly pretty. Her temper had put her in a high color; her ash-gold hair lay in charming disorder about her shoulders, and an unaccustomed brightness lit her eyes.

Fell had brought a posy of geraniums picked from the window boxes of the Turtle and Rose. Iona held them to her nose and inhaled their spicy fragrance and smiled in a way Fell found disquieting.

"Rumors have reached me about a certain business arrangement concerning myself," she said.

Fell swore under his breath. "The damn maid . . ."

"How quickly you defend yourself!" She rose and began to pace the room. Fell picked up the discarded posy and idly plucked the flowers from their stems. Petals began to pattern the carpet.

"You are not in a state of mind to credit what I say."

"I'll thank you not to speculate on my state of mind."

"Your state of mind is closer to my own than you might think."

"Do I really seem such an idiot to you? Did you think I would not learn that you had been bribed to marry me?"

Fell sighed. "My dear, you scruple too much. What else is marriage? What else is a dowry? What else is the entire ridiculous custom but bribery, deceit, and civilized indentureship?"

"Don't make fun of me. I suppose this woman, this marriage broker, is your mistress."

Fell began to laugh in a way that made Iona regret her words. Her composure broke, and in her anger and confusion she began to cry.

Fell sat quietly where he was. When the storm had passed he laid the flower stems upon the table.

"The date is set for two weeks hence. I can't deny anything you have said, except to say that you have put the wrong color on it. I honestly believe this match is the best thing for each of us."

"Then why did you want to be released from it?"

"I feared you might mistake my motives and take it into your head to run away."

"And if I should?"

"For one, I think the scandal would make your father wash his hands of you. There would be no coming home in a fortnight. Shall I tell you how penniless young women make their living in this town?"

Iona did not reply, but picked at her sleeve.

"In any case," Fell continued, "you would have to leave all your prints behind, and Columba would be sure to burn them out of spite."

He got up from the chair and went to the door.

"I know you don't believe me, Iona, but my motives are purer than the driven snow."

"Yes," she said, raising her head. "Why should I believe you?"

"Don't believe me. Just trust me."

He left, and she listened as his footsteps echoed down the hall and ceased. After a time the shadows in the room lengthened, and the light from the windows began to dim.

Ermingrude entered and made a small exclamation. She lit a candelabra and set it on the table next to the piles of flower stems and petals.

137

In the candelight, Iona's face showed traces of her tears. Ermingrude might be languid to a fault, but she was not entirely unobservant.

"Oh, dear, it has not gone well, has it? Did you quarrel?"

Iona laughed. "Yes, you might say that."

"Well, a quarrel is a sight better than indifference, I dare say."

Iona sighed. "I suppose it is."

❦❦❦ When at last the Keepers broke their centuries' silence and spoke to Caitlin across the chasm of ages, it was in the form of a small, crimson scrap of linen.

It was late, the boys long since asleep. She heard Binder go up to bed. She stretched and thought only fleetingly about joining him. She was restoring a page from an herbal, a leaf copied perhaps from the ancient Book of Healing itself. Many of the colors Caitlin used in repairing the illumination came brush-ready in small pots, already mixed with gum. Some colors, however, were left over from the dyers' trade. For these, scraps of linen were soaked in dye again and again until saturated. Caitlin then only had to set a clothlet in a dish and add a little egg white and water to achieve the pigment.

As Caitlin touched her brush to the wet clothlet in the dish and watched the color spread into the surrounding glair, she froze, and began to make a list in her mind. Woad blue, whelk purple, yellow buckthorn and saffron, green woodbine—all came in clothlets. There had been a cloth-making industry on Chameol. What if there had been a connection between the illuminators and the dyers?

She imagined chameol under siege, the Keepers persecuted. Suppose the Keepers had *not* fled after all, but continued to practice their arts in secret, while engaging in other trades. The women who sewed the bindings of the books could have turned

138

their skill with a needle to tailoring easily enough; the illuminators and woodblock carvers might turn their talents to dyeing and printing cloth. The binders, skilled in cutting and paring leather, might have become glovers and cobblers. And the scribes themselves might have turned their pens to pattern making and the design of embroidery.

Caitlin wrote out a short message and fixed it to the capsule of a pigeon's leg. Saying a short charm against owls, she released the bird into the Weirdwood night, and with a few wing beats it was gone, bound for Chameol. She remained at the window a few moments, thinking, before she went up to bed.

Bram was waiting for her. Wordlessly, he crawled into her arms.

"Nightmare?"

He nodded. He didn't want to talk about them, usually. But now for some reason he spoke.

"I dreamed Grimald was beneath the ice. . . . He was all made of glass. I could see his heart inside. And his eyes . . ."

She kissed the top of his head. She wanted to tell him there was no reason to worry, that everything would be all right, that Grimald would be fine, but she could not tell him any of those things.

All she said was, "Do you want to sleep with us tonight?"

He nodded and scrambled into the bed; only when he had been badly frightened did he take her up on this offer. He normally disdained it as babyish. A small creeping fear bit at her heart as she got into bed after him.

He had settled down and was dropping off to sleep again when she realized that Binder was awake, watching them. In the dark his eyes glittered with some wordless mix of emotions that made her heart ache: weariness, love, regret.

She leaned over their sleeping son and kissed her husband's eyes to close them, then his pulse above his ear, and the warm spot just behind it.

"You'll wake him. . . . ," he murmured.

"Oh, he's dead to the world." She yawned into his shoulder. "I had to banish that look in your eyes."

"Is it gone?"

She had to admit that it was.

"Then go to sleep."

10.

The Final Fitting

◆

Winter was beginning to close in on the Weirdwood. The days grew shorter, and with every passing day Bram's sight was growing dimmer. Every afternoon Caitlin made him lie down in the dark with compresses on his eyes. To a boy whose chief pleasure came from reading, this was torture in its cruelest form, and before the first week was out he was wild with boredom. Grimald took pity on him and sat with him during the hours of his enforced blindness, trying to distract him with stories: how many brown bats were in their nets, how their mother had finally outwitted the mice who had been chewing the glue on the new bindings, by reversing a spell that eased toothache.

Bram seemed to be listening, but during Grimald's tale his hand crept up to the blindfold that bound the compresses to his eyes. Caitlin's voice came to them sharply from the kitchen, where she was steeping herbs for compresses.

"Bram—you'll only have to wear them longer tomorrow."

He made a face and let his hand fall down to pick at the embroidery of the coverlet.

"I had a dream," he said. "About the palace."

Grimald knew which palace he meant. He sat and waited for him to go on, if he was going to. Bram hardly ever talked about life before he came to the oak with the red door.

Bram spoke quickly and distinctly, the way people sometimes do in the grip of a fever. "I was in the dumbwaiter, the one they put the food on. It ran between all the levels of the palace. I was in it, and it was falling very fast—my heart felt like it was going to come out of my mouth. Then it stopped, and the doors opened, and I was looking out at the furnace room. There were all these goblins, and the fire made all their faces sooty. Ethold was there, and I called out to him, but he didn't hear me. Then one of the other goblins heard me and turned around. He had your face."

Grimald shifted in his chair. Bram sounded serious—not at all like he was pulling his leg. Like he meant it, like he believed what he was saying.

"Did I say anything?" he asked, laughing uneasily.

"No, I woke up right after that."

In truth, the dream had continued. Grimald the dream miner handed Bram a lump of dull black ore and told him to polish it. He dutifully polished it and polished it, and at last it took on a glossy sheen and passed from gold through several other colors, until at last it became clear, a crystal heart, five-chambered. A goblin heart.

But when he went to show it to Grimald, he saw that his brother's eyes had turned filmy and white, like fish eyes. There was a hole in his chest, and he was dead.

❦ ❦ ❦ Caitlin had carried her tea to her workroom and was halfway through the cup when a pigeon arrived, carrying a letter from Chameol.

When she had unfastened the tube and unrolled the tiny scroll, she saw that the lengthy message had been written in Iiliana's best flea's-eye script. She fetched her hand lens, a birthday present from Binder.

"That's better," she muttered as the words sprang into view.

Cait, my dear,
This will not be as long a letter as I would wish, since I have much to do to prepare for an expedition to the northern isles.

A shipwreck off the Chameol coast was raised six years ago, but the inventory of the artifacts was completed only last year. To judge from the contents of the ship's hold, the crafts of dyer, weaver, embroiderer, cobbler, and tailor were represented upon Iule. That is, if the ship was leaving port with Iulian goods and not arriving with them from somewhere else. (From the surviving documents that we have been able to decipher, it seems likely that this was so.)

One of the objects retrieved from the wreck was a waterproof money box belonging to a cloth merchant from a town in Sixmoon called Madderfields. Madderfields was the country name of a town later known as Isle-of-Praise, a possible corruption of "Iule be raised," the last words of a famous heretic. The box contained some documents wrapped in oilskin, including receipts from dyers, weavers, and tailors. There were notes on the receipts, apparently written by the merchant, that bore a strong resemblance to a script known only from a fragment found at the old library on Chameol. A network of merchants might have avoided the heretics' pyre by conducting meetings under the guise of trade. And, as you guessed, keeping their bookmaking skills alive.

Curiously, one of the receipts was from a tailor's establishment in a town called Moorsedge—perhaps

143

yours? It was marked, "At the sign of the Shears, Lasting Lane."

I hope that gives you something to grab on to. I eagerly await news of further discoveries. Give my best love to Badger and the boys. I am glad the nets I sent met with your bat catchers' approval.

Many blessings,
Iiliana

Caitlin rolled the message and placed it in one of the tiny pigeonholes of the tiny writing desk Binder had made for her when she had despaired of finding a misplaced message from Iiliana. Just the size for a mouse scribe, it had been carved from a single piece of cherry, rubbed with beeswax till it shone like satin. Musing on the mystery of the clothlets, Caitlin pressed a hidden catch. A panel slid back, revealing two glass marbles, blue and green. *Your witch eyes,* his voice said in her brain. The words were spoken with wry affection, vinagered with impatience and something else: the fear that has wonder in it.

Caitlin tried to sort out the facts she was sure of. Before the kingdom of Iule sank beneath the waves, its artisans had carried on trade with a town known as Madderfields. When Iule sank, leaving only Chameol above the waves, all trade had ceased. The town of Madderfields became Isle-of-Praise, a reference not just to Iule but to Chameol itself. Had a secret society of artisans kept the arts of the Keepers alive, or was she letting wishful thinking get the better of her?

But why in Moorsedge, so far from the channel that separated Chameol from the kingdoms of the near Moons?

She closed the hidden compartment and set the mouse-sized desk into a niche in the wall by the window seat. Ink was a disaster around old books; she did most of her letter writing at the window seat, where there were cubbyholes to hold her pen and ink and paper.

144

From the window she could see that Binder had sent the boys out to do their late-day chores. Bram moved through the garden, pulling turnips from the frosty ground for the soup while, further off, Grimald gathered kindling. As she looked at Bram, a wave of cold seemed to grip her limbs and make her heart sink, as though some monstrous shadow had passed over the house, boding ill for all who lived in it.

She had not lately divined with a candle and a basin, afraid of the shape the wax might take in water—the rune for "stone," the rune for "dark."

🐦🐦🐦 Binder looked up from the book he was mending, took off his spectacles, and rubbed the bridge of his nose.

"If you start for town this late, you won't be back tonight."

"No. If I deliver some of the finished books, it should buy me a bed for the night."

She caught his glance; wordlessly it spoke the words his tongue shied from, the irony of her buying a bed in the town with the money he earned mending bindings. Her face burned.

"It's important. I can't explain—"

"No. I know. The books that are done are on the shelf; the addresses are inside. And yes, I'll make sure he wears the compresses." He smiled. "I might try them myself." With the spectacles replaced, his eyes seemed resigned and reproachful.

"I'll be back tomorrow night," she said, frowning unconsciously.

"I didn't think you wouldn't be." He said it a little too quietly.

"I only meant that I'll dose you myself when I get home."

"Is that a promise?"

"A threat . . . as you should know by now."

She kissed him and was gone.

*　　　*　　　*

🌿🌿🌿 The prince soaked in his bath. Not the tub before his mistress's fireplace, but the extravagant gold structure with dolphin-head spouts at the palace.

He soaked and he brooded, and as he soaked, his broodings began to shape themselves into a rough plan. If a manikin could stand in for him at his fittings, why not at the wedding ceremony itself? The reluctant bridegroom sank back into a pleasant reverie of abdication, elopement, and wedded bliss in a shepherd's hut high on some mountain meadow.

Only, he could not put Lucivia's face on the shepherdess. When he conjured the shepherdess in his mind, she had a simple, vacant look, and when he succeeded in calling Lucivia to mind, she was not in the neat little hut but at her table by the window, doing accounts.

The Valet Royal entered carrying a robe. Pages followed, bearing linen, hose, and the royal smallclothes.

"Highness, the tailor awaits."

The prince was most curious to meet his tailor. All the previous transactions had been conducted through the Valet Royal, and all the early fittings on the manikin. She was nothing like the hellion of *The Dog's Muzzle*, this serious young woman, stoic in her deep blue smock. She was accompanied by a veiled woman. He nodded at her, indicating his permission to remove the veil, but the odd figure only nodded back at him in a disconcerting fashion. The Valet Royal stepped forward and whispered in the prince's ear.

"Oh, well, then," said the prince, as he crimsoned to the ears, "in that case, she may remain veiled."

Only the king's wedding suit itself remained to be completed, and this had progressed to the point at which it must be fitted to the prince's own person. In any case, the royal manikin still had not been replaced.

The prince hated finery, or at least the silliness in it. His own clothes were invariably dark and plain. The only concession

146

to sumptuosity that he made was the purple lining of his cloak. So the Valet Royal held his breath as the nuptial suit, basted together, was eased over the royal head. No one noticed the note to the embroiderers pinned to one sleeve.

The heavy blue silk was covered all over with stars in gold thread. The sleeves were not ridiculously large, nor was the skirt of the tunic overpleated.

"Golden hose?" asked the Valet Royal.

"Blue," replied the tailor.

"Ah. Yes. Simplicity itself."

The prince regarded his reflection as the tailor made adjustments to the sleeves. He did not look like himself, but everyone—his father, his friend, his mistress—told him that this was what he must be.

"For the ceremony itself there is a cloak with a train. We brought a sketch and a swatch with the embroidery. Your highness will see it is white velvet embroidered with suns and comets. It reverses to royal blue."

The Valet Royal held his breath and the pages looked at their feet. The prince himself cast a startled look at the tailor. The whole palace knew of the reversible cloak the prince wore when visiting his mistress, but no one spoke of it. The girl did not appear to mean any disrespect. His look seemed to discomfit her.

"The blue side is impervious to rain," she explained.

"Ah," said the prince.

"And at the collar . . . ?" said the Valet Royal.

"Properly, nothing. Perhaps a bit of ermine." Ulfra cast a sidelong glance at the prince to see if she had overstepped.

The prince only nodded absently. "Are you through? Can I—can we—get out of this thing now?"

It was then that the only pin, the one in the note to the embroiderers on the sleeve, scratched the prince's arm.

The pages and Valet Royal and tailor stood in appalled

147

silence. The prince swore mildly and seized the nearest cloth to swab the blood beading the length of the scratch.

"Red after all, like the rest of ours," said a voice in the doorway.

"Ah, Galt. We've managed to cut ourselves on a pin."

It was only then that the king's huntsman saw the tailor. As their eyes met, Ulfra saw the silver wolf pelt fastened around Galt's shoulders.

He waited for a glancing blow from some sharp, wicked shears or at least a tongue lashing. But she said nothing. The dangerous brightness in her eyes suddenly welled up as tears.

"My lord, you must forgive me," she whispered to the prince and, turning, fled from the room.

With a gesture of his hand, the prince dismissed the Valet Royal and the assorted pages. "Stay," he said to the leopard-woman.

"She meant no insult, my lord prince." The slightly lisping voice that issued from behind the veil unnerved the prince. "Your huntsman wears a wolf skin. My young partner has an abiding kinship with that animal. To her, the sight of a wolf skin is abhorrent. Forgive me; I cannot offer you a better explanation without betraying a trust. Now I must go to her."

When they were alone, the prince clutched his arm and stared at his friend in amazement.

"Galt! Either our eyes deceive us, or you're nursing something of a passion for our tailor. Oh, I see I have salted a wound. Come, I'll make it up to you, in pints."

❦ ❦ ❦ Lord Gobeleyn was unwell. Winsom ministered to him, bringing him an egg beaten in brandy and possets of sweet woodruff. When Winsom rubbed a strong-smelling ointment into his chest and Lord Gobeleyn did not protest, Nix knew his benefactor was very ill indeed.

Nix hovered anxiously until Winsom banished him to the other end of the house, where he made faces in the hall of mirrors and practiced his dance steps with the fencing dummy.

At last he carried the dummy back to the fencing salon and hung it on its hook. Giving his dancing partner a parting kiss, he set to with his foil. It was an uneven match; a thrust from his sword gored the headless torso, and Nix stood transfixed, watching the sawdust trickle down onto the highly polished floor.

The sight and smell of the sawdust had recalled to Nix his days among Folderol's troupe and the sawdust put down in the ring, woody, sweet, and sharp. Other memories came flooding back: counting out their stolen gold, Ulfra letting him have the wishbone from the roast goose, sleeping in the crook of her arm upon a bed of wolves, Ulfra singing to him in Wolf under her breath.

Nix licked the sweat from his upper lip and replaced the foil in the rack on the far wall. His hand trembled slightly, and his knees seemed about to go out from under him.

As he passed through the hall he glanced at a clock face and saw that he had spent not one hour in the fencing salon but three. Nix was suddenly aware of a ravening hunger. He called out, but no one appeared. Winsom was still with Lord Gobeleyn. After some hesitation, Nix sought out Winsom's pantry, a plot of holy ground some twelve paces by eight that even Lord Gobeleyn himself dared not violate. The pantry was small and serenely ordered, the crockery and copper and knives cunningly arranged and gleaming. On an upright wooden chair beside the only window lay a long letter in a language Nix did not know.

Nix cut himself some cold meat and ate it where he stood, with the single-mindedness of one who is starving. But as his hunger ebbed, his restlessness returned. He could not stand to remember, or think or feel. And he was afraid—afraid he would never find Ulfra, afraid Lord Gobeleyn would die. So he must not feel, he must not think.

He would go to the Turtle and Rose.

149

🌿🌿🌿 When they reached the Cat's Face, Ulfra, as was her wont, shrugged off all Tansy's attempts to talk about the fitting. She pleaded a headache, took a teaspoonful of poppy syrup, and went to bed.

Tansy turned at last to the wedding clothes for the rich engraver's daughter, a task that could be neglected no longer. She was just turning under the neck facing when a knock came at the door. She gently set the gown aside, careful not to bruise the delicate jasmine silk. She hoped it would not be the little boys who knocked at the Cat's Face hoping the leopard-woman would answer the door. They sometimes pulled the trick five or six times in a single day.

It proved to be something else entirely. Well worth setting the gown aside for, Tansy thought, sizing up her visitor's odd smock and trousers and her seer's eyes.

The visitor was apologetic. "I should come again tomorrow. You have an illness in the house."

Tansy looked at the visitor intently. "So we do—though how it is known to you, I cannot fathom."

Caitlin smiled. "I work with herbs, and my sense of smell is rather acute. I smelled poppy syrup as I came in the door."

"The illness is not serious—indignation and heartache in equal parts."

"May I presume upon you a little while, then? I have come a long way, not to engage your services but to ask some questions I believe you—or this house—may be able to answer."

This struck the leopard-woman as a sound proposition. Besides, she liked the looks of her visitor. Once you have worked in a circus, you give little weight to superstitious nonsense about seer's eyes. Tansy possessed a cat sense, and was able to judge trustworthiness at a glance; the woman on her doorstep could be trusted. Besides, her curiosity had been aroused.

"Will you come in, then, and sit?"

The Cat's Face had been recently refurbished and now boasted an elaborate room for greeting clients. Tansy led her visitor instead to the small sitting room still favored for privacy and comfort. A fire burned in the grate to keep the autumn chill at bay. The leopard-woman waved Caitlin to a deep chair.

Tansy listened intently as Caitlin explained about the Books and the Keepers and the shipwreck off the coast of Chameol, interrupting her only once to get up and nudge the fire when it fell into a slumber.

"You see," Caitlin said, "I believe that these Keepers scattered, but kept their book arts alive by working as tailors. And the papers found in the shipwreck seem to point to Everlasting Lane."

Tansy retook her seat upon the sofa. "Well, there had been a tailor on this spot as long as anyone can remember. This whole district was once called Tailor's Nine. We are the only surviving establishment."

"Have you come across any old documents—letters, ledgers? Anything at all?"

"There are some old pattern books. All patterns and client measurements are written in tailor's code, to keep trade secrets. But these are different. They seem to be written in runes, though I know only a smattering of the under-tongues, as my mother used to call them. They are curiosities, really—we leave them because they give a sense of history to the place, but it would be hard to remove them even if we wanted to—they are chained to the workroom wall."

"May I see them?"

"Of course."

The ground floor of the Cat's Face was deserted. To celebrate the occasion of the all-important royal fitting, Tansy had given all the workers a bonus and the day off. The workroom was a place of cheerful disorder, bright with bolts of fabric, its walls covered with Ulfra's sketches for current commissions, and pop-

151

ulated by headless muslin-and-sawdust torsos in various states of undress. While the room seemed alive with color and industry, it was also unmistakably old—very, very old. Its age radiated from the flagstone tiles beneath Caitlin's feet, from the massive beams of the half-timbered ceiling, from the far wall of dark, smooth stone.

"The latest renovations to the room are at least two hundred years old. I was told by the last owner that the oldest things in it are that low counter over against the wall and this smoothing iron, what we call a goose, after the way the handle curves. The books are over here."

She led Caitlin to the far wall. This was of dark grey stone, worn smooth as glass. Half its length was fitted with wooden drawers and bins that held buttons, ribbon, thread, and such. The rest of the wall was given over to the shelves that held the pattern books.

Six of these were obviously older than the rest, massive volumes bound in oak boards fastened with iron clasps. Each was chained to an iron ring in the original wall. A low trestle lay against the wall to help in consulting the heavy pattern books. Upon this Tansy laid open one of the old books.

"We never have been able to make sense of the runes, though it's become a sort of rite of passage in the trade, when the apprentices become journeymen, for them to try to tell what the runes say."

"How would anyone know the difference?"

"Legend has it that when the runes are translated, a fabulous treasure will appear. The apprentice first makes a wish, then opens the book and points to a passage while blindfolded. Then the blindfold is removed and the apprentice must try to translate the passage she has pointed to." Tansy smiled at her visitor. "Would you like to have a try?"

"I would very much indeed. Do I have to be blindfolded, or can I just close my eyes?"

"You know as much as I do about it—no one has ever succeeded in disclosing a treasure."

Caitlin covered her eyes with one hand and brought the index finger of the other down in a slow spiral onto the open pattern book. She opened her eyes.

The page was crabbed with runes that she recognized as numbers, with occasional words in between.

"They are only measurements, after all," she cried in disappointment. "This is the word for waist, here is shoulder, here is elbow. The spot where my finger came down says 'Waist, eleven; neck, twenty-three; elbow, nineteen; shoulder, six.' "

Tansy laughed and shook her head. "But those are nonsense measurements! A neck twice as much around as a waist."

Caitlin looked at the page more closely. The passage on which her finger had landed was repeated several other places on the same page. She flipped forward and backward in the book and found the passage appeared again. An apprentice picking a passage at random was likelier than not to hit upon the nonsense measurements. But why?

She copied down the passage and closed the book.

"Thank you. I believe I may have found what I have been seeking, if I can only make meaning of it. Now, let us tend to your patient."

Caitlin might have remembered Ulfra as the wild wolf-girl she had encountered many years ago at the court of the boy-king Milo. But the occasion did not arise: Ulfra was not in her bed. The covers had been thrown back violently. Wherever she had gone, she had gone in her nightclothes—her robe still lay upon the end of the bed.

"Does she walk in her sleep?" Caitlin asked.

"No—but in extremes of fatigue or distress she sometimes goes off and hides. I don't look for her. There is something animal in it—she dens herself up to tend to her wounds, and I let her."

*   *   *

153

꒰ ꒰ ꒰ Ulfra was asleep in the cedar clothespress, the contents of the strongbox scattered about. She had been working feverishly on a drawing of Nix, not as the boy she had known and cared for as a wolf might her cub, but Nix as he must be now, at thirteen or fourteen. She could not get the features right, as if her brain refused to frame them, refused to admit the passage of time, of change itself. The drawing lay crumpled beneath her now as she slept.

In her dream she wore the prince's hunting costume and rode a dappled grey through a dense forest. This was the Weirdwood, home to the Direwolves. Galt rode at her side, and when they reined in the mounts on the forest path, the horses put their muzzles together in a companionable nickering. From the underbrush the Direwolves watched and, when they passed, lifted their muzzles in a mournful cry.

They were hunting a white hart. Ahead of them the hounds caught the scent of the quarry and broke into a run. Galt spurred his horse and called to Ulfra. As she urged her horse forward through the trees, branches snatched at the folds of her cloak. Unsnagging it, Ulfra saw that it was lined with wolf's fur. The waving branch spooked her horse, and as it broke into a gallop she struggled to hold the reins in one hand and undo the cloak with the other. Glancing down, she saw that the toggle was made of wolf's teeth.

Ahead, the hounds had cornered their quarry in a glade and were milling in a circle around it, keeping up a high, keening cry. The hart was a magnificent creature, with antlers of burnished gold and a milk-white coat that seemed to gather up all the light of the wood. From the center of the circle where the dogs had hemmed it in, the hart struck out at its tormenters with golden hooves.

Galt drew his horse up beside hers and, drawing an arrow from his own quiver, fitted it in her bow. Leaning from his saddle, he set his grizzled cheek against her fair one and showed her how to set the bowstring in the arrow's notch and, holding his fingers over her own, helped her hold the bow steady while she drew the arrow back.

The arrow sang true to its target and struck the animal in the throat, near its massive shoulders. Blood began to spout like a ruby fountain. Not the way it really would, she thought as she slipped from her horse in the dream, but the way a painter would paint it.

She ran to the animal where it had fallen. Its eyes rolled wildly, then fell on her: blue eyes, uncannily pale. At once the animal grew calm and laid its head meekly in her lap, as though it knew her for a friend.

It was gravely wounded; Ulfra knew it would die unless she could retrieve the arrow and stanch the bleeding. As she seized the shaft of the arrow and tried to wrench it from the wound, it was suddenly not the hart's shoulder but a man's, though still unearthly white. She gazed down into her lap and saw the face she had not been able to draw, the face of her beloved Nix. His strange white hair was streaked with sweat and his face spattered with blood from the wound.

"The spring will heal me," he said, "if you hurry." When he spoke, his tongue was slick with dark blood. Dread brought Ulfra's heart to her throat.

"Where is it? You must tell me where it is!"

Ulfra was suddenly awake, her heart pounding, the very words in her throat. She sat up and leaned her head against the cedar panels of the clothespress until her heart slowed its frantic beat. But though her breaths were less ragged, her mind was still gripped by confusion. What did the dream mean? Was she supposed to find the spring? Was Nix her one true love? Or was she meant to right the wrong she had done by abandoning him at the farmhouse?

Lady Twixtwain would know what to do. Changing by feel in the fragrant clothespress, Ulfra put on thief's black and a black hood to cover her hair. Since the notoriety of *The Dog's Muzzle* and the success of the Cat's Face, she could not walk the streets anymore without attracting a crowd. So the hood and thief's clothes had gotten to be a habit when she wanted to go about her business unmolested. Besides, she knew Tansy would think this a feverish fancy and insist she stay in bed. Ulfra's errand could not wait until morning. It was almost the supper hour, and Tansy would be putting her feet up. It was now or never.

She climbed from the bedroom window to the drainpipe, slid down the drainpipe to the street, glanced up and down the alleyway, and was gone.

11.

Some Suits
Are Pressed

✦

The physician was tall and gaunt; beneath his paper white complexion the blood flowed in his veins as purple as ink. He closed his bag and went to wash his hands at the basin. He enjoyed a thriving practice, for he was both skillful and discreet and did not disclose his patients' identities or the curious natures of their ailments.

Winsom stepped forward to collect the basin of dark blood and the crimsoned toweling.

"When you are done," said the physician, from where he stood at the elegant marble washstand, "I want to speak to you in the hallway."

Winsom gazed down at Lord Gobeleyn. Drained of blood, his naturally ruddy face was as white as the pillowcase beneath it, and his outflung arm black and blue where the physician's

157

sharp lancet had probed for a vein. The faithful servant's eyes filled with tears that could not be shed.

In the hallway, the physician spoke quickly in low tones, so as not to awaken the invalid.

"It is his heart. Some goblins—more often boys born to mortal fathers and elvish mothers—are born with a weakness of the heart. It is not life-threatening so long as they remain in the Otherworld. But should they venture Above, the consequences are grave. In infants and boys, the heart weakens gradually, until death is inevitable, though often masked by some other illness, such as whooping cough. In older boys and men, the course of the ailment can be slowed somewhat, by avoiding exercise and eating a spartan diet. But the onset of the weakening can only be postponed, not prevented. Once it begins, its course is rapid and severe. The only cure lies in returning immediately Below."

"That is quite impossible."

"Then he has a month at the outside, perhaps as little as a week. I can at least make him comfortable. Rouse him every four hours and make him drink a dilute solution of this elixer. I have written out the proportions. Make sure it is well shaken before he drinks it. One of these blue vials broken under his nose will rouse him; do the same with one of the black, and he will sleep. He should sleep comfortably enough. But be careful that he does not harm himself. He will soon cease to think or feel anything real going on about him and will live only in the past. He may have nightmares or rave in his sleep. He may ask to see people who are long dead. Humor him."

Winsom nodded dully. "Is there nothing else I can do to ease him?"

The doctor shot a glance at Winsom. "Unstop the proverbial Spring of the Dead and dip him in it! I must go on now to attend a lying-in."

Winsom nodded and showed the man out, then returned to the sickbed. Lord Gobeleyn opened fevered eyes that looked up vacantly at the ceiling without focusing.

"The boy . . . I must save the boy . . ."

Winsom broke open one of the black vials, and Lord Gobeleyn sank back into unconsciousness.

🌿🌿🌿 The Turtle and Rose was not crowded, in part because the cast of *The Dog's Muzzle* was busy rehearsing a new entertainment, a masque in celebration of the prince's approaching nuptials. In an alcove of the inn that afforded the greatest degree of privacy, Galt and the prince were savoring a jug of cream-and-black. At least, the prince was enjoying it. Galt was in a mood, and the prince knew better than to jolly him out of it, though he could not help making an observation.

"Has it ever occurred to you that the reason you cannot bring yourself to speak to her has nothing to do with wolves or even her wolfish ways?"

"No. But I suspect it has occurred to you. Pray"—Galt cracked a walnut in his fist—"enlighten me."

The prince gazed up at the rafters as if every beam were carved with words of wisdom. The ale had ever so slightly loosened his tongue, else he would have been more heedful of the gleam in Galt's eye.

"It's that you have always surrounded yourself with a certain kind of female company not inclined to the art of conversation, and so have no conversation yourself."

Galt gave the prince a baleful glance, refilled his tankard, and pushed the jug away. "Again," he said softly. At once the landlord was at their table. The empty jug was swiftly removed and a full one set down in its place.

"And how do you know what kind of female company I keep?" he asked when the tavern keeper had moved off to supervise the tapping of a cask of wine.

"I know that you are a not-too-frequent but generous patron of the better sort of courtesan, and that you favor those who, while young and comely, are not given to idle chat."

Galt's mouth twisted into a ghost of a smile. "Unlike a king, a king's huntsman can only choose so far. He must content himself with the selection available to a man of his rank and means."

The prince perceived that the conversation had passed beyond playful bandying to something else. He searched his friend's face for a moment before he spoke, and when he did he chose his words carefully.

"I begin to suspect that you believe yourself incapable of engaging a woman except through a business transaction. Or is it your own affections that fail to be engaged?"

"You mistake me, my friend. I like to leave my heart at the door in such transactions. My affections were engaged once. I did not care for it."

"I see. So the unscrupulous might slit your throat and make off with your purse, but they will never wound you *here*." The prince leaned over and tapped Galt soundly on his leather breastplate.

Galt brushed the hand off with a soft hiss. "Tread softly!"

The prince held up his hands, palms outward. "On cat feet," he murmured.

Galt stared into his black ale. "When I was young—younger than you are now—I married, only to discover my affections had been sadly misplaced. But my wife was so beautiful and her ways so sweet that I could not believe she was capable of deceiving me with another. One day, while hunting boar, my arrow went astray and killed the man rumor called her lover. When she heard the news she took poison." He looked at the prince's face and smiled. "You see, she did not believe I could miss my mark."

❦ ❦ ❦ Three flights above this conversation, Fell was seated at the unsteady table that served alike as washstand, boot stand, and writing desk in the small, ill-furnished room. On this occasion it was a writing desk. He sat with his pen poised over the sheet,

biting his thumb and staring out the window at the distant roof-
tops, imagining the prospect as seen from Iona's attic window,
pigeons rising and falling among the ornate chimney pots.

Before him on the half-filled sheet was a list.

REOPENING THE HOUSE
+ Air out trunk (check for moths)
+ Candles, firewood, cat's meat
+ Wine (Where is key to cellar?)
+ Count linens
+ Have extra set of keys made for I.
+ Pawnbroker for Mother's jewels (Get garnet ring reset for I.?
  Can this be done in three days?)
+ Have press delivered (Do this at night?)

Fell turned his attention from the view to his list and began
to draw on the bottom of the piece of paper. A few minutes'
sketching produced Iona in wedding clothes beside an altar covered with flowers. Then, after a pause during which he stared off
into space, Fell erased the flowers. In their place he drew his own
effigy in armor, stretched out on a low tomb. Then he filled in
Iona's gown with black.

Beneath this he wrote: "Make arrangements for death (Check
on dowry, arrange funeral, decide on day—how soon after
wedding?)"

❦ ❦ ❦ Dusk was beginning to gather. The narrow streets, with
their houses so close that a man could lean out his window and
light the pipe of his neighbor next door, were sinking into an
enveloping darkness, dispelled here and there by the hopeful work
of lamplighters making their rounds. Through these streets Ulfra
made her way, her thief's garb allowing her to pass within feet
of others unnoticed, her face hidden by the close hood.

As it happened, Galt had veered from the route to his lodgings to persuade an apothecary just shuttering his shop to sell him a headache powder. The premises of this obliging merchant were in the same street as the button makers Ulfra had visited the day she had rescued the young wolf, and lay quite close to Lady Twixtwain's house.

Cutting through an alley to shorten his way home (his head was pounding now; damn that last pint) Galt spied a figure in black trying the back door of a house in Goldenmouth Street.

With the ease of one plucking a rabbit from a snare, he stepped forward and seized the housebreaker by the nape of the neck.

"Let's have a look at you," he said. Pulling back the hood, he was astonished to find himself face to face with the prince's female tailor.

"You!" Galt gave a stifled cry, half shout and half laugh, and released her so abruptly that Ulfra fell back on the slick cobblestones. Realizing this was not winning conduct on the part of a suitor, the huntsman hauled her to her feet and suddenly found himself holding her tightly by the wrists, mesmerized by those wolf's eyes.

It is never advisable to kiss a wolf, but that is what Galt did. Taken completely off her guard, Ulfra stood frozen with her fists clenched. When she regained her wits she found she could not shake off his grip. At last Ulfra wrenched her head to one side with a snarl that issued from some place low in her throat. It was a murderous sound—enraged, uncanny, and not quite human.

Galt released her wrists as though they were red-hot pokers. He felt as though he had been pulled from a seething cauldron only to be plunged into an icy deep: His bones sang, his eyes dimmed, and he found himself suddenly drenched with a cold sweat.

She stood before him a girl again, her face damp with tears of outrage, dragging the back of her hand across her mouth. The

162

wolf had receded from her eyes, leaving them indignant and confused.

Her lower lip was bloodied. Galt found a handkerchief and stepped forward to press it to her lip, then placed her fingers over the bandage so that she could hold it herself.

"I'm sorry," he said.

She shook her head and removed the handkerchief to speak, trying the words out gingerly. "It happened when I turned my head."

"I'm sorry," he repeated.

Neither of them had stepped away. It only wanted a glance for an invisible spark to cross the gap between them. Neither knew afterward who had moved first into a kiss that tasted of blood and tears and the Turtle and Rose's best cream-and-black.

Then, with a sudden exclamation, she ducked down and out of his arms, loose-boned as a mink shrugging out of a trap. Before he realized what was happening, she was gone.

What had happened was this: Just as she was about to abandon all caution, Ulfra's hands had closed on the lining of Galt's cloak.

❦ ❦ ❦ The prince left the Turtle and Rose and began to make his way to Everlasting Lane. He had turned from the alley into the wider street when he was nearly bowled over by a strange young man, long-limbed and impeccably dressed, except for the omission of gloves and the less-than-fashionable disarray of his collar and cuffs.

Nix was winded, but between ragged breaths he gasped a hasty apology and made as if to run past.

The prince, staring at him, did not release the boy's shoulders. His mind whirled with new-sprung possibilities.

"You are the very thing! No, never mind, that, I'm fine. Here, hold your arm out."

Nix did so, a little wonderingly, but obeying the easy command in the prince's tone.

They were of a height, their shoulders an equal span, and their arms so alike that if they had been cast in bronze, one could not tell which was the model and which the copy.

"If our faces were anything alike, I should begin to fear for my throne," the prince muttered. "Instead, I begin to hope for my happiness." The prince drew a card from his pocket, scrawled something on it, and handed it to Nix. "Present this at the palace and tell them you are to see the Valet Royal. You will be well paid for your trouble."

❦ ❦ ❦ Lady Twixtwain saw at once how it stood with Ulfra.

She had been quite surprised to discover Ulfra on her doorstep, since Ulfra had both a key to the kitchen door and a standing invitation to let herself in and make herself at home until Lady Twixtwain should emerge from any of a number of baths, naps, changes of wardrobe, and small cosmetic adjustments that made up her daily domestic routine.

Taking the girl firmly in hand, she set her before the fire and gave her a clean compress for her lip, a little of her miracle tonic on a silk handkerchief that smelled faintly of scent. Ulfra haltingly related first her dream and then the encounter with Galt. Lady Twixtwain listened to the girl's expressions of repulsion and loathing for Galt and her bitter self-recriminations with an increasingly unsympathetic ear.

"My dear," she sighed. "I beg you, don't waste perfectly good indignation on the matter! It is quite commonplace to love and loathe the same person by turns, and often both at once. And, if I may further shock your nice sensibilities, you can even be in love with more than one person at the same time."

Ulfra squirmed a little where she sat, looking extremely ill at ease. "I can't believe that."

164

"Well, you ought to. It has been the way of the world since time began. You may very well hate this man with all your reason, nay, even with all your heart, but your blood may sing another tune! Tell me the truth: Did you find his kiss loathsome?"

Ulfra stared down at the handkerchief in her hand. "Yes! No . . . not the second time."

"From what you have just told me, I surmise a few things. You had only just discovered in this dream that you love this lost boy—Nix, is it?—and before you can come to tell me, you find yourself in the arms of the man you most loathe in the world. And now you are feeling guilty and afraid that you have been unfaithful to this Nix of yours. My dear, you are all of twenty-one, and never yet kissed? It is too much for him to expect for you to be untouched by other lips. It would be a crime against nature. It is *beyond the pale.*"

Thinking she had perhaps taken the topic as far as was wise for the time being, Lady Twixtwain took the conversation in a different direction.

"Here—let me have a look at that lip."

Dutifully, Ulfra removed the compress. The bleeding had stopped. Indeed, it was impossible to tell where the cut had been.

"There. Did I not tell you my water works miracles? Now kiss me, my dear, and then up to bed with you. I will send word to Tansy that you are staying with me tonight. Heaven only knows what other adventures you might have on your way home."

🌿🌿🌿 "I tell you, it solves everything!"

The prince spoke these words with great passion and more than a little annoyance that they seemed to carry no great persuasion for his mistress, who sighed and moved to dip her pen into the ornate inkwell.

In a fit of unbidden temper the prince shoved the inkwell

165

away, making a great blot on the page of accounts to which Lucivia had been devoting herself. She looked up at him with an expression of intense exasperation.

"All right, that is it. I have had quite enough, thank you, for this evening. Uninvited, you present yourself during the very hours which we have agreed I am to be left to myself. You then outstay your thin welcome, bend my ear with some harebrained scheme of hiring a manikin to stand in for you at your wedding, and now you have undone an hour's tedious accounting! Really, I have half—no, three-quarters—of a mind to turn you out altogether. No, not a word, I am quite serious. I am tired of your peevish behavior. How can I state it more clearly than I have done? I will not not marry you, under any circumstances!"

His eyes flashed with anger. "Don't scruple about my feelings! Let me have it, madam!"

"All right, then. You do not consider it possible that I should have any business of my own that is more important than your personal and immediate gratification. Simply because you are in a mood you expect that I should cancel all other appointments, set aside important work than must be done, and devote myself to soothing your wounded self-regard."

"What other appointments at this hour, may I be allowed to know!"

Her eyes flashed. "Oh, you are most infuriating! If a woman's attention, let alone her affection, is not engaged entirely, heaven knows she can only be bestowing it upon some other *man!* She cannot possibly be engaged in business, or the running of her household, or her own *thoughts!*"

"That is an unkind cut, Lucy," he said wearily.

"If it is unkind, it is only because it is the truth." She paused to catch her breath and smiled at him wryly. "Believe me, my sweet: We would not suit. We are too different, and ours are not the differences that complement, but those that detract. My ambition, my independence of mind, would only make you unhappy; I am utterly incapable of the sentimentality you so like to credit

166

me with. You would do far better to resign yourself to the bride that I have spent so much time and energy procuring for you."

A stark and dreadful realization was beginning to take form in the prince's fevered brain. "How can I love another, after you?"

This at last made her laugh. "But you do not love me, goose. You are *in love* with me, and only with the part of me that is pliant and pleasing and dresses itself in scent and silk. And that is not who I am the other sixteen hours of the day. If I *were* to marry, it would be to a grey old man who would allow me a good night's sleep."

The prince stood and looked at her, acutely aware that nothing between them could be as it had been before. His eyes had been opened—not to her true nature, which she had never concealed from him, but to his own.

Her anger had passed. She looked at him with affection and reached up to lay her palm upon his heated face.

"Unlace me," she said. "I have something to show you."

When the bodice was unlaced and her back laid bare, Lucivia pulled aside her heavy tresses and revealed the mark, wine-dark and the size of his outstretched palm, that spread between her shoulder blades in the shape of a butterfly.

"What do you see?"

"Your scar," he said dully, "where your brother scalded you in the bath." He thought he heard a note of pity in her voice, and it made him afraid.

"I told you that because it was what you would believe. A discreet surgeon made that scar. Yes, I paid him to do it. Wing removal is a far more common operation that you might think. There," she said gently. "I've told you." She shrugged back into her bodice and turned to face him.

"That is what they removed from me. Now you know what I am. If you will not heed my other reasons, you must heed that one. Go on—leave me. Rose will lace me up again. She is finally getting good at it, the little idiot."

*   *   *

❦ ❦ ❦ The prince dragged his feet up the gilded staircase to his bedroom, where his page kept a sleepy vigil in case his master should make a rare appearance in his own bed before the small hours of the morning.

"Will you bathe, Your Highness?" inquired the Valet Royal.

"No."

"Have you dined?"

"No."

"Have—"

"No! Leave me. I want nothing."

When he was alone, the prince went out onto his balcony to breathe the night air, then came back in and rummaged in the drawer of the massive writing table, never used, that made up part of the princely appointments of the royal bedchamber.

He drew out a packet of documents and took them over to the bed to read: a series of formal letters, from his future father-in-law, and the marriage contract and its many codicils and legal appendages, on thick curling parchment much covered with red wax seals. Among all these papers there was only one short note from his appointed bride, a few lines in a girlish hand. Her accomplishments, the enclosed note told him, included not only the lute and harp, but the mastery of several languages and a decided proficiency at embroidery.

With these documents there was a small ivory box set with diamonds, which, when its catch was sprung, revealed a portrait of his betrothed. She was very young, with quantities of glossy, soft brown hair caught up in a net of pearls. The painter had given her wide-set brown eyes a wet luster; this, with her slightly upturned nose and small chin, gave her the inbred look of a spaniel a little too highly strung.

❦ ❦ ❦ Three days passed, and on the eve of Iona's wedding a package arrived at a house in the most prosperous and respectable quarter of the town. The servant left the enormous parcel in the hallway and went to tell the mistress of the house of its arrival.

Ermingrude set down her letter and her spaniel and her bowl of tea and scurried to the hallway, exclaiming and calling for Columba to come and look, the thing had indeed come in time, and who would have expected it?

Ermingrude and Columba and the housekeeper had spent some minutes exclaiming over the workmanship of the dress and wondering how its folds could be conveyed in a carriage without crushing the delicate embroidery, when they realized the bride herself was not among them.

"How like her," murmured Columba. "If my sister is one thing, it is not *vain*. Shall I find her?"

"Yes, do. You would think she would think of me and be a little bit anxious for my sake. She seems to me such an unnatural child."

"I should hope so, madam, since she is not yours," murmured Columba, gliding out the door.

She found her half sister in her attic room, packing the last of her inks and tools and blocks into a special crate. Iona had removed all her prints from the walls and placed them in the special case that Fell had given her as a token of their engagement. She had thought it a little wrong of her to accept it, but she had not really known what else to do. And it had come in very handy.

"How nice this place looks, now that you've picked it all up," said Columba, leaning in the doorway but disdaining to cross the threshold.

Iona glanced around. "Really? To me it looks rather bare."

Privately Columba thought the room could best be made into quarters for a live-in seamstress. Her own marriage was to follow Iona's at the minimum respectable distance of three months. It would be uncommonly handy to have her own private dressmaker installed at her mother's house, working full time on her own marriage clothes.

"Your dress has come at last. We were all looking at it this past half hour before we noticed you weren't with us."

☙☙☙ Columba had to admit that she had been wrong about the silk. The jasmine white did not make Iona look sallow at all. Rather, it brought the roses out in her cheeks and made her hair glitter like gold leaf glimpsed in a dim chapel.

"My dear, you are quite a vision," said Ermingrude from the couch, where a back spasm had sent her. "Who would have imagined it? Your father was quite right to make you eat a piece of bloody beef once a week. It has done wonders for your complexion."

Iona gazed silently at her reflection in the glass. The dress was marvelous. The cut of the bodice worked wonders, the silk clinging here, skimming there, and finally flaring below her hips into a full skirt. The gown was embroidered all over with intertwined jasmine vines.

The housekeeper appeared in the doorway.

"This was just delivered, madam."

"This" turned out to be another parcel, addressed to Iona, bearing no return address. When the paper was removed it was revealed to be a small box of horn, carved with a motif of doves.

"It looks old," said Ermingrude, wondering if it might be valuable.

"No—he made it himself," Iona said softly. She had recognized the doves for pigeons, and the design on the box as the view from her own window, with its maze of chimney pots.

"Open it, silly," said Columba impatiently. "Of course, it's your ring!"

It was a fine red stone in a setting of reddish gold that curled up around the stone like leaves of ivy.

"It's only a garnet, after all. He might at least have gotten you a ruby," said Columba.

"Be quiet," Iona whispered, turning the ring over in her hand. The inside of the band was engraved. She held it to the light to read the inscription.

It said, "For Iona," and nothing more.

12.

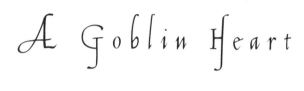

$\blacklozenge$

The vows were sworn, the marriage feast over, the guests dispersed. Good-byes were said, and the small chest containing Iona's clothes was loaded into the carriage.

As part of Iona's dowry, her father had intended to make the couple a present of a modest house close to his own, with a dozen or so rooms. But Fell quietly insisted on a house with only eight rooms, on the fringe of the artists' quarter. No argument move him on this point, and rather than see his daughter settled in a still less respectable part of town, Niccolaus grudgingly conceded. Fell had engaged the servants himself, claiming that he was quite particular about the management of his household.

As they rode in silence through the streets of the city, it occured to Iona that it was no longer her wedding night but early in the morning hours of the first day of her married life.

Fell sat with his face turned to the carriage window. She thought that perhaps he had fallen asleep. Something in the set of his shoulders bespoke a profound weariness, an intense fatigue he hid from the world when awake. Shyly Iona stretched out a hand and touched her husband's shoulder.

The carriage had stopped, and Fell stirred, from sleep or contemplation, and turned to her. His face was unreadable, but in the pale lamplight it seemed young and uncertain. He smiled at her wryly.

"Your new home, madam."

In the hallway the sleepy housekeeper helped them from their cloaks. Iona glimpsed crates and trunks and furniture draped in cloths.

Fell knelt to pick up a large cat that was weaving between his legs. He buried his face in its plush grey fur, and for a moment she did not recognize him, so unaccustomed was she to seeing an expression approaching tenderness on his face.

He set the cat down and cast a quick glance at Iona, seeing the draped forms of the hall through her eyes. "I thought you would want to arrange the furnishings to your own liking." Fell turned to the housekeeper and ordered hot wine. "Bring it to madam's bedroom."

The housekeeper led the way up the staircase. Fell paused at a different door along the passage.

"I'll join you when I've bathed and changed." He dropped a kiss on her cheek.

Iona paused in the hallway, suddenly feeling oddly disembodied and confused. The housekeeper waited, holding the lantern aloft. Iona hurried to catch up, lifting the heavy skirts of her wedding clothes.

The housekeeper showed her into a spacious room furnished with a clothespress, a writing table, and a carved bed hung with silk curtains. In an alcove, a cushioned seat looked out through leaded windows to the park below.

"Shall I help you out of your dress, madam?"

"No—yes. If you would just undo the back, I can manage on my own."

When the woman had gone Iona washed her face at the basin and combed out her hair. When she went to change the heavy wedding dress for her nightclothes, she found that her mother (or possibly Columba, in a fit of spite) had substituted for her maidenly nightdress another of diaphanous muslin that, in the candlelight, was entirely transparent. None of her other clothes had been unpacked, so Iona left her shift on. The housekeeper returned with a tray containing a jug of spiced wine and two goblets. Iona filled a goblet with a fingerful of wine and tossed it down. Her throat was parched. Unconsciously, she wiped her palms on her shift.

She could not bring herself to wait on the bed, so she sat in the window seat and looked out at the park below, angry at herself for being so nervous. She had made her bargain, and now she must live by it. Columba's taunting words about wedding nights rang in her ears and made her cheeks burn. Opening the window a crack, she inhaled the cool night air. Behind her a door opened and softly closed again. Iona turned around.

At first Iona thought no one was there. Then she realized the door she had heard was not the door to the hallway but the smaller door that led to an adjoining room. Beside this there stood a woman.

She was tall, with features too striking to be comely on a woman. Her best features were her light brown hair and her large grey eyes. She wore an elegant silk gown of deepest blue, the dress not of a servant or relative but of the mistress of the house.

Iona rose on legs that were unsteady, her mind racing from possibility to possibility as down a corridor of locked doors: This was Fell's sister, his cousin, his mistress, his secret wife. Her mind wrestled with each possibility and weighed it against the evidence of her eyes. The awful truth dawned on her.

174

This *was* Fell, got up in woman's clothing.

"You!" she said weakly.

"Yes," said Fell, coming forward and helping her back onto the window seat. "I am sorry to give you such a shock. Would it help you to drink some wine?"

Iona looked at him in the light, and suddenly her mind made the last leap to the truth. Fell was a woman.

Something rose in Iona's throat, but whether it was a shout or a sob or a peal of laughter, neither occupant of the room was to know. Before she could utter it Iona slumped over in a faint.

❦ ❦ ❦ Lady Twixtwain's miracle tonic had as its source a spring in the heart of the Weirdwood—the same spring that provided a measure of flood control for the network of subterranean canals that wound their way to Ylfcwen's palace.

Things were not well with the elf queen. Spies of the Royal Household Agency had caught her in an abandoned ballroom, about to let go of the chandelier and attempt an illicit solo flight. Ylfcwen had been placed under house arrest, confined to her room while her former numerologist and rune caster set about divining the name of her successor. They had even replaced her silver ankle bells with iron anklets that locked with a key.

This the director of the Royal Household Agency put around his neck on a ribbon. It lay upon the front of his robe beside all the other keys, the ones to the lapidary and gemarium, interrogation rooms, and the passages that led Above.

"You may still ring for anything you require," he said through the door, when she was locked into her royal bedchamber.

She tested the bell cord to see if it would indeed be answered. Minutes passed, then an hour. The director had perhaps meant to be sarcastic.

Hours passed in the dark; she did not light any lamps. When the fireflies died she doubted they would replace them. At last the door opened, and her faithful dresser entered bearing a tray; behind her trailed an elf guard in full armor. This struck Ylfcwen as rather excessive; with the weights on her ankles she could barely walk, much less bolt for her freedom.

Without meeting her mistress's eyes, the dresser set the tray on the nightstand and left the room. The door was relocked.

Ylfcwen pounced on the tray. Its contents proved disappointing: a flask of water and a heel of coarse bread—not even goblin bread, thank you, but the stuff they fed the weavers.

With a sigh, Ylfcwen closed her eyes and brought a piece of the bread to her lips. As she did so, the queen thought very hard about marmalade tarts, and from there her thoughts moved rapidly to the secondary larders and other storerooms that honeycombed the lower levels of the palace. The possibility of forgotten provisions for some upcoming festival gave the tasteless bread some savor.

Then she remembered something else that lay forgotten in the storerooms.

An opportunity presented itself more quickly than she had dared hope, in the form of her faithful dresser, who took pity on her mistress and brought her a glass of rootwine and a jasmine cake. Out of pity, she even unlocked her mistress's weights and replaced them with the jeweled anklets. While she was bending to this task, Ylfcwen brought the tray down on the dresser's head.

As Ylfcwen bound her hand and foot with the cords from several wingcases, the queen took pains to make her boundless gratitude clear.

"It will not go too badly with you. After all, you didn't cooperate in the least."

Above her gag, the dresser blinked.

Not wishing this faithful servant to starve, Ylfcwen removed the gag and fed her captive the rootwine and jasmine cake. "I dare say they will find you before long," Ylfcwen added thoughtfully, easing the ring of keys from the dresser's belt.

Ylfcwen did not change into the earth brown clothes that were the required attire for elf royalty Above. She would not be returning, so what were the rules to her? Instead, she donned one of her favorite gowns. She seemed to remember being married in it, once, to whatever-his-name-was, Aethyr's father. It was a gown fit to fly in, fashioned of silk gauze hardly more substantial than breath, to which clung a frost of opal dust and crushed pearl. By some happy unlikelihood it still fit.

Her heart beating swiftly, Ylfcwen let herself out by the hidden door in the closet, behind the shoe rack. She lit a small lamp and stepped down into the cool, slightly damp air of a narrow staircase.

 Grimald was in his father's workshop, making a birthday present for his mother, a small tooled girdle-book that she could tie to her belt while working in the garden, with blank pages so that she could write in it the spells to keep the rusts and blights, worms and rabbits away.

He was vaguely aware that it was growing colder and that he was getting sleepy, but so intent was he on his work that he did not pay it much attention. By the time the punch and hammer fell from his hands, he had lapsed into something between sleep and death.

Looking for her husband, Caitlin found him, his usually ruddy face blue with cold. For one long, terrible moment she could hear no heartbeat in the boy's chest.

Binder came running, unable to make out his wife's words but hearing in her shout an urgency that filled him with dread. Grimald was already stirring and saying he was all right, but he did not protest when he was put to bed hours before the usual time.

"That was no faint," Binder said under his breath.

Caitlin started to answer, but burst into tears instead, giving way at last to exhaustion and panic. For weeks gnawing fears had robbed her of sleep at night. By day she was to be found divining with wax in a basin of water, in a fruitless attempt to see what fate would befall Bram. She saw now why the basin had not answered her; it had been Grimald who was marked for misfortune. Remorse made her heartsick; she felt weak and wanted to retch.

He led her to a chair, strangely calm himself, soothing her.

"Shhh . . . shhh . . . listen. Cait, look at me. It will turn out all right. You'll leave tomorrow, the three of you—I'll put you and the boys on a boat to Chameol. Iiliana will know what to do. I'll close the house and follow as soon as I can."

She nodded, holding fiercely to his hand.

"Oh, Badger . . . I haven't loved him as I should have. First I was mourning Bram, then Rowan—"

He gave her a gentle shake. "Hush. No more of this."

It was only then that they noticed Bram sitting quietly in one corner of the kitchen, his eyes strangely magnified by the lenses of his spectacles.

"Go to bed," said Binder. "I'll be up in a little bit to tuck you in. Go on."

Wordlessly he went, like a clockwork boy.

🌸🌸🌸 The next day dawned cold, with a film of ice on the water pail. Binder had been up all night, first packing, then relieving Caitlin at Grimald's bedside. Caitlin had been to bed for an hour or two at his insistence. At dawn she was in the garden, covering with moss those herbs that would survive the winter, harvesting what would not. She seemed relieved to have a plan of action and eager to have the journey already behind her.

The boys had been told they were going to Chameol, to see their Aunt Iiliana. Each was allowed to take a few of his special things, so long as they were not heavy. Grimald was agonizing over his choice: He wanted to bring his vole's skull but was afraid he might lose it. In the end he decided to leave it behind in favor of the playing pieces for liar's checkers, good for passing time on the voyage.

"I was on a ship before," he said suddenly.

Bram glanced up from his own packing, an uneasy expression on his face. "Were you?"

Grimald stared past Bram, as though at a memory, a shadow just behind him. "And it was a boat, really, made of wicker, like an eel trap. I was just a baby. Mama was with me—" He stopped, frowning.

Behind his spectacles Bram's eyes were strangely bright. "No. Someone else. A woman with hands like paws."

"Yes . . . Her name was—"

"Ordella."

The boys looked at one another, each frightened: Grimald at remembering what common sense told him he could not possibly recall, Bram at his changeling visions. For in his mind had risen, clear as life, the picture of a small, scurrying woman whose smile showed a row of pointed teeth. To her breast she clutched an eel trap containing a baby with yellow eyes, a baby that did not, could not cry.

"You were there, too," whispered Grimald.

Bram nodded. "Yes. She brought you, and took me away."

Suddenly, Grimald knew everything, knew why his skin was ruddy and his hair neither fair nor ink-black but fox-red, knew why his mother sometimes looked at him the way she did, why his parents argued about him, why once, long ago, he had caught his father crying.

And he was running, down the stairs, out of the house, through the herb garden and into the woods, running without seeing, running without feeling his feet on the ground or his heart pounding in his chest, feeling nothing but his ragged breaths and the drumbeat of his blood in his head, beating a chant: *Changeling. Goblin. Changeling.*

The branches of the trees reached out to catch at him, stinging his face. A twig caught him in the eye, but he ran on, tripping over roots, stubbing his toes on fallen branches and stones, running toward nothing, away from everything, as though he could change the truth by running into some other version of it. He would run straight into the Otherworld from which he had come, to which he belonged, to which he had always really belonged.

His foot landed on something slick, and before he realized his misstep he had broken through a glaze of ice and plunged into freezing water. As he fell, his head struck an overhanging rock, and Grimald sank, unconscious, beneath the surface.

🍂🍂🍂 It is always prudent, where there are wolves, to hunt with a companion who can repel an attack should one somehow become unhorsed. When Galt suddenly decided to go hunting in the Weirdwood, he went alone, liking his own company little enough as it was and not wanting anyone else's. He took with him a bow and arrow capable of bringing down a stag but hardly a Direwolf.

As he rode he remembered with discomfort his encounter with the girl tailor. He remembered the wolfish snarl that had come out of her throat and half imagined he was being watched by Direwolves as he rode.

Which he was.

A sentry posted at the first fringe of trees had signaled an alert, which had passed through the ranks back to the lieutenant.

A wolfskinner! snarled the final messenger, a young male.

How foolish of him to venture into the wood, said the lieutenant, wonderingly.

Shall we kill him?

No—for now, watch him well. But show nothing—not your yellow eyes, not your white fangs.

When she heard the news, the matriarch of the Direwolves sang under her breath a song in Old Wolf, a sweet ritual song of revenge.

Now the pack flanked the intruder on three sides, hidden by the brush and bracken. Normally, Galt would have sensed their presence and taken steps to prevent an ambush, but his mind was occupied with other thoughts than hunting.

He was both desperate to see Ulfra again and terrified at the thought of seeing her. For the first time in his life, Galt had not the slightest idea what course of action he should follow. At the end of yet another sleepless night in which he had pondered it all for the hundredth time, Galt had saddled his own horse well before dawn and ridden out without a word to anyone as to where he was bound.

He was quite certain he was losing his mind. What else could explain the irrational thoughts that had beset him, thoughts of attaching himself to the most unsuitable female imaginable? She had bewitched him; that was the only explanation for it. He had given the fur-lined cloak to his housekeeper with instructions to burn it. Whether this was an attempt to win favor with the girl tailor or a mere preface to throwing himself on the same pyre, Galt had no idea.

Night air, unhappy liaisons, too much ale, the moon—all these things had no doubt driven him mad. Perhaps killing a deer would make all right with the world.

So he rode out. The wolves stayed well back, just close enough to keep him in sight.

The horse first? signaled the lieutenant of the left flank to the she-wolf.

Yes. But save the man for me.

Before Galt knew what was happening, the wolves appeared out of nowhere, more than forty of them, assembling on the path as though conjured from mist and shadow. Two wolves seized Galt's mount by her forelegs, while a third dispatched the unfortunate beast with a bite to the neck. With a shriek the horse sank to her knees beneath her rider, dead.

Galt screamed curses at the wolves, but they pressed so close that he had no room to fit an arrow to his bow. Then a wolf lunged at the bow and bit the string clear through. Unhorsed and unarmed, Galt prepared to die and racked his brain for a prayer, any prayer. But all that came to mind were oaths, and those profane.

Stay, said the she-wolf sharply.

The wolves suddenly drew back, flattening their ears in deference and glancing quizzically at the matriarch of the pack.

Don't you smell it? said the she-wolf, stepping up to sniff Galt's beard, his sleeve, his gauntlet. *She has left the mark of Her blood on him. He is Hers alone to kill.*

The left lieutenant stepped forward to smell for himself. *So it is.*

They apologized for the bowstring and the horse, then turned and dissolved back into the wood the way they had come.

It was some time before Galt was able to summon the presence of mind to slide from the saddle and find a stream to slake a throat parched with fear. That, and wash off the blood of his poor mare.

As he bathed, the prayers of his childhood came flooding over him, and he knelt in the cold water, muttering them feverishly, one after the other, wishing he had some offering to leave behind on the bank to mark this spot for future pilgrimages. At last he unbuckled his hunting knife and buried it in the streambed, where its jeweled hilt glittered beneath the swiftly moving water, bright with cold.

Upstream, something else glittered and caught his eye. Galt glanced up and was instantly transfixed by the sight that met his eyes.

A golden barge was just turning the bend in the stream. Its gilded prow burned in the sunshine of the clearing, casting back the bright sparkle of the stream, and its pennants fluttered in the breeze. But none of these rivaled the brilliance of the beautiful navigator.

The streambed was too shallow to be easily negotiated, and Ylfcwen had been obliged to abandon her throne to pole the barge around the corner. The effort had undone her silver hair from its careful arrangement, and the exertion had brought the lavender blood to her cheeks. A single silver droplet of elvin sweat sparkled like a bead of quicksilver below her queenly nose.

The barge made the turn and drifted further downstream before it came to a halt, its keel stuck in the pebbly bottom. For the first time the elf queen noticed the man bending his knee to her on the shore.

"Don't sit there staring," she snapped. "Help me get this thing up onto the bank."

Something in those opal eyes drove every thought but obedience from Galt's brain. Shoulder to shoulder (hers came only to his elbow), they pushed with all their might until the gilded prow of the barge had nosed onto the muddy bank. Then Ylfcwen scrambled back aboard and threw Galt the end of a cable. Together they dragged the boat the rest of the way out of the water.

"Cover it," she panted, and Galt did as he was told, disguising the barge with moss and ferns.

Ylfcwen was looking quite disheveled. There were twigs in her hair, and the hem of her skirt was dragging with the weight of water and mud. Paying Galt no more heed than if he were a dog or a horse, she stripped off the dress; the wet jeweled silk made a strange sound as it was peeled off, a little like corn being husked and a little like ice cracking on a lake.

"Your handkerchief," she said to him, holding out her hand.

183

He surrendered it, and she spread it on the bank so that she could kneel without muddying her knees, and washed the dress out in the water, wrung it out, and draped it over a branch to dry. Then, using the surface of the water as her looking glass, she put her hair to rights.

Elvish fabrics are strong and dry almost instantly; when Ylfcwen went to feel her dress it was dry enough to put on again.

She handed Galt back his handkerchief.

"Hook me." At his blank look she stared at him closely, wondering suddenly if he were simple or mad. "The hook at the top—I can't reach it. Fasten it."

He did so, and only then did he notice the wings, veined and iridescent, beginning to unfurl like new lilies. Their facets, catching the sparkle of the stream, were so like the texture of her gown as to be indistinguishable from it. Ylfcwen kicked off her jeweled ankle weights and floated up to hover above Galt's head, level with the top of a silver birch.

"Keep the weights, if you like," she called down to him. "They will fetch a fine sum. A reward for your trouble."

"I am much obliged to you," he said. At least his mouth formed the words; his throat didn't seem to be working.

She ascended in a lazy spiral, threading her way between the lower branches and finally through a hole in the canopy of the uppermost boughs, startling a bird from its perch. She hovered there, high above the Weirdwood, enjoying her first good aerial view of the world Above in several mortal lifetimes. The countryside was so cunning, with its hedgerows and fields dotted with haystacks. Beyond the fields a town lifted dull red chimneys and white spires to the sky. Far off, the palace glittered, bright banners tugging in the breeze.

Ylfcwen turned her wings this way and that until she caught a balmy current of rising air, and let herself be lofted higher and higher, carried westward, more or less in the direction of the palace.

184

❦ ❦ ❦ By the time Binder found him, Grimald was past saving, past even the saving of the otherworldly arts. Binder hoisted him onto his back—so much lighter than a load of firewood—and carried him back to the house.

They gently laid him out on the kitchen table. Caitlin mutely went about lighting all the candles in the house. This time, she would do the fitting thing and stay up with the body the first night. She moved as though in a trance—unseeing, unhearing, unknowing. From a chair by the hearth, Binder lifted a haggard face to watch her.

"Stop it, Cait." His words came out in a hoarse whisper.

She looked at him blankly and then turned back to the next candle.

"I couldn't for Rowan. I have to now."

As Caitlin lit the candle on the table near where Binder was sitting, he blew it out, and her taper as well.

She began to cry, shuddering with mute sobbing. He took her arm and gave her the chair and brought a blanket and a dose of something that tasted of bitter herbs and gin.

"It won't make me sleep?"

"No."

She sipped it, then half rose from the chair. "Bram . . ."

"It's all right. He's asleep in bed." He looked at her, then kissed her wrists. "I'll look in on him."

Bram was in bed, but not asleep. He was staring at the ceiling above his bed, trying to remember how the map went, over his bed in Ylfcwen's palace. Start at the center: Ylfcwen's palace. Now add the tunnels in gold, and the canals in silver. Then the gemfields and the hothouses and the firefly hatcheries and the pomegranate orchards. And then the wingless monsters, and the blue void.

But an unwanted thought intruded, no matter how hard he concentrated. Maybe you went to the blue void when you died.

185

Maybe Grimald was there now, being tormented by wingless monsters.

He wondered what dying was like. He remembered his long dive when he and Ethold had escaped through the sacred lake, how his lungs had burned for want of air, how easy it had seemed at the time to simply breathe the water, but how some part of him had resisted the water, how some part of him had remembered what air was, and light, and life. And then there had been the beckoning surface, and the light beyond it.

By the time Binder looked in on him, Bram was asleep, twisted in the covers, one leg hanging out of bed. He still had his spectacles on. Binder removed them and put them on the table. Then he untangled the blanket and tucked the boy in.

Grimald's knapsack still lay on the other bed. The pieces to liar's checkers lay scattered on the bed; some lay on the floor. Before leaving the room, Binder picked up the much-prized vole's skull where it lay among the other treasures.

He first went down to the workroom to get a length of bookbinder's ribbon on which to thread the small skull. When he came back into the kitchen, the fire had died down and Caitlin was fast asleep. He took the empty mug from her lap and set it on the shelf.

The fire had kept the body warm. When he lifted Grimald's head to slip the ribbon over it, the boy's neck was warm to the touch. In the glow cast by the coals, Grimald's body seemed a statue on a tomb, still as marble, but for his hair. This had dried in the heat of the room and was standing up in fox-red wisps, the same in death as it had been in life.

Binder lit a taper from the coals and went around the room, relighting candles.

13.

Revelations

◆

Iona sat in her room and thought. She had come out of her swoon to find that her shift had been changed for a warm, soft nightshirt, much like the one Columba had replaced with the bit of diaphanous nonsense. She had been tucked into the great curtained bed. Beside the bed there was a tray on legs, which held a covered dish and a selection of books: some ballads (long banned and very hard to find) and a natural history with colored woodcuts.

She was most of the way through the natural history when she thought to look under the cover of the dish. The silver dome, when lifted, revealed a plate of cold partridge, cheese, and pickles, and a note:

> I know I cannot possibly explain *myself*, but when you are ready, will you at least let me explain my motives?
>
> Your friend,
> Fel

"And well you ought to," Iona muttered, picking up a pickle and going back to a passage on the spinning mechanism of spiders. When she had finished the book, she ate the partridge and then slept a little, until she awakened to a knock at the door.

It was the housekeeper, looking not at all surprised.

"The mistress—Master Fell that was—wishes me to tell yourself that she has gone out and expects to be gone for some hours and most strenuously urges you to make yourself at home in the rest of the house." This speech delivered, the woman craned her neck slightly, as if to peer around the doorjamb. "May I air the bedding?"

🌿 🌿 🌿 Iona dug down to the bottom of her trunk for her most worn-out muslin and her stained workroom smock with the large pockets. In this armor, she ventured downstairs.

By day the rooms were airy and flooded with light. There was no great dining hall, but a smaller salon with a table that might seat eight comfortably. This opened into a modest library whose shelves gaped here and there. The gaps, however, were free of dust; the books had perhaps been recently sold. If the choicest volumes had been pawned, Iona longed to know what they must have been, for the selection that remained was splendid, if small.

She came next to a workroom, much of which was taken up by a massive wooden contraption. A wooden frame slid into place beneath an iron plate held in place between two huge beams. A lever turned a giant screw and lowered the plate until it touched the wooden frame.

Why, she thought, it's like the press I use for my prints. But the plate in place on the bed of the press was like no woodblock she had ever seen. Small, irregular pieces of metal had been fitted together in rows within a wooden frame, with thin pieces of lead between each row. After some study, Iona realized that the individual pieces of metal were runes, carved backward in raised relief.

188

"What do you think?" said a voice at the door.

It was Fell—or Fel, as she had written it—in man's dress again. Iona tried to muster some indignation, but only said, "How is it done?"

"They are cast, actually. First I carve the letter on a steel punch, then strike the punch into soft metal, usually copper or brass. Then I pour hot lead in."

Iona nodded, running her hand over the surface of the strange metal block. "So you can reuse them—you only have to carve them once."

Fel smiled. "Exactly."

"The press must have cost a fortune."

"A small one, anyway: most of your dowry. I hoped you wouldn't mind." Fel had taken off her hat and gloves and now shook out her light brown hair. "Do you mind if I don't change? I confess I've come to prefer this attire."

"Who am I to dictate to my lord and master?" Iona thought she had spoken without sarcasm, but Fel blushed furiously.

"I suppose I have put off this explanation long enough. Here, let's got to the library."

❦ ❦ ❦ "At first, I did it for the most selfish of reasons: money, and my freedom." She smiled. "For me, they were the same. I was the youngest child of a goldsmith, and his only daughter. He died, and my brothers were some of them dicers and all of them bad at business. So there was no dowry for me; nothing for me but to make the best marriage I could.

"And I could not bear it! My father had taught me his trade; I was a skilled metalworker, so I thought that perhaps I could make my own living. But no guild would have me. And I was no beauty: The only offers for my hand were from men my father's age—or older.

"In desperation, I sought out a marriage broker. She suggested that, while I could not pass for a beauty, I might make a

189

credible man. I am overtall, wide of shoulder, slight of hip; my hair is mouse brown; my feet, hands, nose, all unwomanly large. Grievous flaws in the figure of a woman, they are favored in a man." Fel paused in her story, as though struggling to find the words to make her case before a judge.

"Will you believe me, poor deceived Iona, that when I first heard it I thought it a heartless, a reckless scheme? But her arguments were compelling, and so I found myself watching you from that upstairs window. And once I saw you, I knew marriage to the sort of suitors who had courted me would—not *break*; there would be no breaking *you*—but somehow *reduce* you. You, your work, would never have been the same. I couldn't bear to see that happen."

Iona had sat quietly, letting Fel's words wash over her. At last she turned up a face devoid of expression.

"What is your real name, then?"

"Felicity. But my brothers always called me Fel."

Iona smiled wanly. "There was something all along that seemed . . . out of kilter. The way you shunned strong light; you never took your hat off, or your gloves . . ."

"Yes. I had to keep my face in shadow as much as possible, and while my hands are large, my wrists are a woman's." Fel laughed. "The *hardest* thing was not losing my temper with you! My speaking voice is low enough, but when I'm really angry it climbs an octave. Honestly, sometimes you were incredibly—"

"Provoking?"

"Well, yes."

"It's all right. Other people have told me the same thing." She was silent for a moment, running her finger along the brim of the soft hat.

"You might have let me in on it, you know."

"The broker forbade me—if the match should not come off, or if you should confide in a maid, it would have meant an end to the scheme for all the others."

190

"The others!" A smile tugged at the corner of Iona's mouth. "I see. What happens now?"

"Well, in a few weeks, I will meet with an untimely accident . . ."

Iona looked at Fel, uncertain whether she was serious. Then she began to understand.

🌸🌸🌸 Entering the pantry, the unflappable Winsom dropped the sickroom tray in startlement.

Seated at the small table by the window was an elf, her wings furled and folded neatly across her back. She had recently flown: The wings were flushed with violet blood, making them shimmer like opals. The gown she wore, an ethereal confection of silk and crushed pearl, was hardly seemly. Her presence had a strange effect on the objects in the pantry; beside her, the copper jam kettle on the wall took on the appearance of a gong, and the ranged jars of spices seemed offerings at an altar.

Ylfcwen set down the letter (from Winsom's second cousin Elga), now bedribbled with pink stains. At her elbow, the bowl of fruit Winsom had saved to make a plum flummox was sadly depleted. Ylfcwen licked plum juice from her fingers and bent to pick up the medicine bottle that had skittered across the tiles to stop at her feet. She read the label, sniffed the cork, and made a face.

"Good heavens! If *that's* what you're dosing him with, no wonder he's at death's door." She sighed. "I suppose I had better see him."

Winsom gathered enough wits to object. "The doctor said no one was to see him."

"Well, obviously he didn't mean me. I'm royal and I'm a relation. Last I knew, that gave me some kind of rank in the sickroom."

*　　　*　　　*

191

🦎🦎🦎 "Ethold."

Lord Gobeleyn heard his goblin name and opened his eyes.

"Mother. Majesty. I am honored on two counts."

"You look dreadful."

"Do I? I wouldn't know. Winsom is superstitious about mirrors in sickrooms." Speaking was an effort; he had to close his eyes.

"With what that quack is dosing you with, they should fit you for a shroud and be done with it. I wouldn't let him near a hangnail of mine."

"Have you a better plan of treatment?"

"A remedy never known to fail. You will return Below at once."

He searched her features for a clue to her humor and swore softly. "I believe you mean it," he said wonderingly. "Tell me, what has brought about this change of heart?"

She related the story of her house arrest. In the middle of her tale, Ethold fell into a fit of convulsive, silent coughing. She leaned forward, an anxious feeling in the pit of her stomach. Then she realized he was laughing.

"That poor hunter's face! I wish I had seen you in that barge."

"I don't see what's so funny."

"No, you wouldn't." Suddenly all the laughter left his eyes. "It's a pity that you didn't come a few days ago."

"Why is that?"

"It might still have made a difference. But there's no helping it, now. I'm dying."

Cold fear bit at Ylfcwen's heart. "A dramatic gesture, I'll grant you, but completely unnecessary under the circumstances. I am prepared to abdicate so that you can take the crown."

"But I don't want the crown. I've lived Below as the Pretender and I didn't fancy it. I don't imagine I'd like Goblin King any better. Besides, I'm ready to die. I *want* to die."

192

She placed her hands over his mouth in alarm. "Don't say that!"

He removed her hands. "Listen to me. I am tired of living. I've been half alive since Vervain died. The only thing that kept me going was getting Pending away from you and the Royal Household Agency."

"You are not going to die," Ylfcwen said peevishly. "I won't permit it."

"Then I am afraid I will have to disobey you," Ethold said, a wraith of a smile playing over his lips. "But promise me something. There is a boy. He came to town to look for someone. He went down the wrong alley and was fleeced by some thugs. I took him in. His name is Nix."

Ylfcwen discovered that swallowing had become uncomfortable. "Nix," she repeated, and her voice sounded thick and unfamiliar. Was she crying?

"He needs to be taken in hand, or he'll fall in with a bad lot. Take care of him. He won't heed Winsom, but he'll heed you. Mother! Are you paying attention at all?"

"Yes, yes: Won't heed Winsom; a bad lot." Her sleeve of crushed pearl was useless as a handkerchief. The tears rolled down her cheeks unchecked.

"Then promise me you'll look after him."

She promised, and Ethold fell back against the pillows, satisfied. The conversation had sapped him, and the light behind his eyes seemed dimmer.

"I brought something for you," she said. She unwrapped the toy barge and placed it on the coverlet where he could see it.

He smiled and took her hand. When Ylfcwen felt his pulse, the last of her hope slipped away. His pulse was rapid and uneven. It grew weaker beneath her fingers, and after a few minutes it stopped.

Ylfcwen sat and looked at his features; they were peaceful, and for the first time she saw in them a likeness to herself. She tried to rise from her seat on the edge of the bed, but lead seemed to flow in her veins; she couldn't move. The Royal Household Agency published a pamphlet on the Correct Forms of Grief and the Degrees of Mourning. She had been made to commit it to memory as a girl and could remember none of it now, only a rumor of a queen long ago who, out of grief for her dead consort, had torn out her own wings and gone to wander Above.

Well, she was already Above, so there seemed no need to tear out her wings. She had the distinct feeling they were going to come in handy still. She could have used a short flight around the garden to clear her head, but there was that boy to deal with and that person in the pantry to tell. Ylfcwen went to find them, not missing the light silver music of her old ankle weights, for her feet were heavy enough now.

🌿🌿🌿 What woke Caitlin was the sound of the last candle guttering out in its own wax. She sat upright in the chair for some minutes, trying to remember how she had fallen asleep there. Then her eyes fell on the body on the table. Before she could shut them out, the events of the previous day flooded into her mind.

She rose from the chair and went to look in on Bram. Binder had fallen asleep beside him; the two pairs of spectacles lay side by side on the table between the beds.

She went back to the kitchen and forced herself to approach the table. After she made herself take the first look, it wasn't as bad as she'd feared. Grimald's body was as ruddy in death as it had been in life. The fall through the ice had left no mark: There was not a scrape or a bruise on him.

Caitlin went to the chest and took out towels and a length of clean linen for a winding sheet. From the cupboard she took the funeral herbs she would need, beeswax for filling his ears and nostrils, and a seed cake for his mouth. Then she set some water to warm, not the water hauled daily from the stream, but the springwater she kept in a covered pail for compounding her herbal tonics. It did not matter to Grimald whether the water was cold or not. She was only warming it so that her own hands were not frozen as she bathed him.

When the water had warmed enough, Caitlin dipped in the sponge and began to wash him, singing lightly under her breath. She did not sing the proper songs, the ancient ones handed down to be sung during these chores. And she did not sing mournful songs. Instead she sang a cradle tune about the fox in the moon. That was what she had called him when he got a dreamy look on his face: her fox in the moon.

Suddenly she snatched her hand back as if burned: *His eyes were open.*

She let out her breath slowly, willing her heart back to a slow rhythm. She had lifted Grimald's head to wash the back of his neck; the movement had probably caused his eyes to open. Much as she hated to, she should find some coins to put on them. Caitlin reached over to draw the eyelids down again.

The eyes followed the movement of her hand.

Suddenly she remembered the toothache spell she had cast on the mice. Her voice shaking, she began to sing the ancient washing song backwards. It took all her concentration to reverse the notes and syllables, and she almost forgot to breathe as she did it. When she finished the washing song, she began the sheet-winding song. On the second verse, a muscle convulsed in the boy's throat.

At this sign she lifted him from the table and struck him sharply between the shoulder blades. A trickle of dark water escaped his lips, but there was no other response. The eyes, when she looked at them, were fixed and glassy.

Had it been her imagination after all, fatigue, a trick of grief? Perhaps the eyes had moved, not with life, but with some last twitch of liveliness when all other life had fled the body. It was

195

known for bodies to play such tricks, the lungs to draw a sudden disconcerting breath when the body was rolled in the sheet.

After a moment she collected herself and resumed the task of bathing him, passing the sponge over his face, tenderly washing his eyelids. She had not wrung enough water from the sponge; some of it ran down his cheeks and chin, into his ears and parted lips.

He frowned and coughed. His eyes flickered open, and the light of memory was in them, and reason's spark. He had been restored to her, through some miracle, just as he was.

Caitlin found she was weeping and laughing at the same time.

"My little fox! You always did hate water in your ears. . . ."

🦊🦊🦊 Binder remembered Sleeker, and how the otter's wounds had vanished after being washed with springwater. Then Caitlin recalled visitors to the spring, gathering the water in bottles. It was a cure-all, they had told her. Good for the blood and the complexion and the circulation of the feet. Caitlin saw no harm in letting them collect as much as they needed for their remedies. She had even seen it for sale in the town, in bottles marked "Miracle Revivifying Tonic."

But now Caitlin wondered whether it was more than good, pure water. When Grimald was able, they took the boys and set out for the spring.

Two things struck her immediately as they approached the pool. The first was the moss: Beneath a crust of frost it was still green and living. The second was a turtle resting near the water's edge. Its shell had been damaged, perhaps in a tug-of-war between two fox kits. The damage should have killed it, but the edges of the shell showed signs of mending.

They all took sticks and began to break up the ice that covered the pool. Beneath the ice the water was perfectly clear;

they could see to the bottom, which appeared to be covered with moss.

"It's tiled!" said Binder. Sure enough, here and there where the moss was thin, a pattern was visible of squares fitted together.

Caitlin began to dance on the edge in impatience. "And I think I know what's underneath those tiles!"

"Mother," said Bram suddenly, "let me dive. I did before, when I came up from Below. I held my breath a long time, and the water was at least as cold as this."

Binder was unpersuaded and Caitlin was of two minds. In the end it was Grimald who convinced them.

"It's magic, isn't it? I don't think he *can* drown in it. Besides, we can tie a rope around him, and if he gets into trouble, he can pull on it, and we will pull him up."

❧ ❧ ❧ Bram was diving back to the Otherworld, his hand held tight in Ethold's, the dark waters closing around him. The water seemed to shimmer with light, and the light was a kind of music, the tremor of a string that had been plucked. He didn't need to kick; the water drew him down.

It was easy to pull the moss away. The square tiles formed the border of a mosaic; in it, a woman stood by a fountain at the center of a maze. In one hand she held an elder branch. Her other hand pointed to the ground at her feet.

The tile she was pointing to was larger than the rest, and it had a half circle cut out of one edge. Bram wedged his thumb into the space and pulled up the tile.

Beneath the tile there was a metal box, its lid free of rust and embossed with runes. It was too heavy to lift, but the iron ring in its center seemed sound. Bram untied the rope from around his waist and fastened it to the iron box. Hoping his knot would hold, he gave the rope three sharp tugs, and the box began its ascent to the surface. Bram followed it, kicking for all he was worth.

It took all Caitlin's determination not to open the box on the spot. They had to get Bram home to a warm fire, and she wanted to have her tools beside her—if the book disintegrated when she opened it, there would be a better chance of saving a portion of it.

Both boys were bundled into the big chair and given cider as hot as they could drink it. Caitlin brought down her tools—the soft, small brushes and bone paper knife—while Binder spread a cloth over the kitchen table.

The box was set on the cloth and examined. It had no visible hinges or clasp. Caitlin read the runes on the lid: "And they shall all be healed, made visible and made one."

It was hard to read the rest of the runes; while the box was not rusted, it was discolored. Caitlin took a soft cloth and began to rub the remaining runes clean. With the slight pressure a catch slid out from a recess. Caitlin pressed it, and the top panel of the box sprang up, revealing a leather book satchel.

The boys leaped out of the chair and pressed close.

"It's dry!" Caitlin said wonderingly.

Binder reached in and took out the satchel. It was the kind once used to carry sacred books, in the days when reading was forbidden, when books were used to bless crops and launch ships and cure cattle of disease.

"Careful," Caitlin murmured. "It may be protected by some kind of mischief."

Binder shook his head. "No. We found it; we unlocked the box. I think we're home free." He undid the buckle and drew out the book.

The sight of it drove the power of speech from them, and they could only stand and gaze in wonder.

The Book of Healing was bound in boards covered with silver. The cover showed a knot garden with a fountain at its center. The flowers in the garden were worked in pearls and precious stones. On the petals of a rose rested a topaz-and-onyx bee no bigger than a barley grain. The herbs were all accurate. They found feverfew, and harefoot, and sweet balm.

"Open it!" said Bram, his eyes shining.

"Yes," said Grimald. "Open it!"

The pages were pristine and intact. Plant after plant leaped from the pages as if it had been pressed between them and not merely painted: allheal, hedge-maids, pretty mugget, ruffet, stinking goosefoot, wake-robin. The colors of the plants were fresh and intense, and as the pages were turned they seemed to give off a crushed green smell. Beside each plant was a column of strange runes that listed the animal that had dominion over the plant, its mortal and elvish names, and the phase of the moon during which it was most potent.

Binder, looking up, saw Bram reading over his mother's shoulder. Bram had taken off his spectacles to dive; they were in Binder's pocket, forgotten. Binder started to say something, then checked himself as Bram turned to Grimald, eyes bright.

"This one's called goblin's ears!"

14.

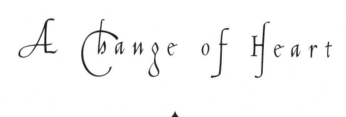

A Change of Heart

◆

Berthold William Alfonse, Crown Prince of Twinmoon, was wed to his highly suitable princess in a ceremony that lasted three days; the toasting, feasting, and general making merry would go on for twenty-one days, a dizzying succession of masked balls, pageants, and almsgiving, during which prodigious amounts of wine and roast meat were made away with and much royal goodwill dispensed to the needy. There were commemorative statues to unveil and almshouses to dedicate. The palace's vast menagerie and gardens would be opened to all and sundry. But no event would draw a larger crowd of gawkers than the ritual burning of the marriage bed.

The special gilded bed in which the newlyweds had spent their wedding night was dragged to the center of the tourney fields and set alight. Fireworks sewn into the mattress exploded and lit up the night sky. With every explosion the crowd roared and toasted the royal couple's babes-to-be. From carts, vendors sold cakes called burn-the-beds: Sweet with orange rind and dense with seeds, they were dipped in ale between toasts.

The prince stood on the balcony of the palace and watched the fireworks. Theirs was a predicament, he had to admit, but they would extricate themselves from it somehow. In public they would, of course, have to keep up appearances, but how they conducted their lives in private was no one's business but their own. After a tasteful interval, they could move to separate bed-chambers. Then she might conduct herself as she pleased, so long as she was discreet.

But he had been unable to make the matter understood to his young bride. Behind him, she sat on the real marriage bed and wept quietly.

"Don't," he said without turning around. "Please don't."

She began to sob in earnest, hot tears falling from her dark spaniel eyes.

He went and sat beside her on the bed and chafed her hand. "Here; dry your eyes. We'll just have to make the best of this. I don't like it any more than you do."

The crying had brought some color into her face, and the tears had stuck her eyelashes together in little clumps that were curiously fetching. She gazed up at him, her face flushed and her girlish bosom heaving. Berthold took pity on her, and kissed her.

She kissed him back, an unpracticed but wholehearted kiss. The feel of her tiny shoulders beneath his hands drove reasonable arguments, separate bedchambers, and tasteful intervals from the prince's mind. For a moment, he ceased to hear the sizzle and bang of fireworks out on the old tournament grounds.

He pushed her gently but firmly away. It had been a lapse, that was all. He would be careful not to forget himself again.

But the princess's eye had in it a gleam that had not been there before, and in the lift of her pretty chin there was a suggestion of pleased stubbornness. She was a lever who had found her fulcrum, and was now confident that she could move her boulder. She poured her husband a glass of wine and drew him toward the window.

"Whatever you think best, Berthold. But may we watch the fireworks just a little while longer, before we retire?"

❦ ❦ ❦ A light veil of mist was falling as the mourners gathered in a remote corner of the graveyard, hard against a hillside and rather more overgrown than the rest. The motley band stood around an open coffin. The keeper of the Turtle and Rose was there, and Trammel, the boy actor, with the rest of the troupe. Winsom was there, with Nix and an odd woman none of the actors knew, the hood of a cloak pulled close around her face.

Lord Gobeleyn had expressed his wish to be buried according to the rites of the theater. One by one the mourners filed by the casket, which in accordance with custom contained a coffin bell, a precaution against interring those who were not yet dead. Each mourner dropped a small offering into the coffin, took up the pen provided and made his mark in ink upon the winding sheet, and finally slapped the bell. When it was Nix's turn, he found affectionate insults scrawled all over the shroud. Nix dropped in his own offering (a handful of sawdust from the fencing dummy and a few cherry pits) and stepped away. He was surprised to feel Winsom slip a hand into his—small, warm, and surprisingly strong.

Lord Gobeleyn was not in fact inside the winding sheet. His place had been taken by a man who had gotten drunk during the prince's wedding and drowned in a fountain. Ylfcwen would rather have given her son a funeral in the elvish style, sent him across the sacred lake in a burning barge, but she had been unable to think of a way to get Ethold's body to the barge's hiding place in the wood. Then Ylfcwen had seen the preparations for the

202

royal marriage-bed burning. She thought he would have liked the joke of it, and the rockets, and the revelry swirling around him.

The coffin was closed and lifted onto the shoulders of the actors, who slid it into place in the crypt where all the past lords of the House of Gobeleyn slept their eternal sleep. As they walked from the hillside, Ylfcwen linked her arm with Nix's.

🌟🌟🌟 Very early on the morning after the burial, the funeral party at the Turtle and Rose began to break up. Trammel, who had raised countless toasts to speed the new ghost to its rest, was loudly protesting the end of the party and cajoling the mourners to raise their glasses a last time.

While he was less conspicuous, Nix was far worse for drink. Winsom brought the carriage around, and, supporting Nix between them, the landlord and Ylfcwen began to lead Nix to the door. They had reached the threshold when Nix gave a sudden shout and clutched at the door frame. Plastered beside the entrance to the tavern was a handbill.

"It's just an old notice—a call from the Valet Royal for manikins," said Winsom. "They stopped looking long ago."

Nix shook his head vehemently. "No, no! The other . . ."

Over his protests, they firmly led him to the carriage and bundled him in.

"*Dog's Muzzle* . . . ," he whispered fervently, gazing up at Ylfcwen with an imploring look.

"Yes, yes, dog's muzzle," said Ylfcwen soothingly, tucking a robe around him before seating herself at the other end of the carriage. Watching him fencing, she had begun to think that Nix would need only a little grooming in order to make a Consort. But she was a queen without a court, and besides, she had promised to find his what's-it—his Ulfra—for him. It was a pity. With that otherworldly coloring and talent for fencing, Nix figured in her daydreams less as a Consort than as an agent of revenge against the director of the Royal Household Agency.

She glanced over at him, sliding her feet farther over to one side. He did not *look* as though he would be sick, but one could never tell, and her new kid slippers had come dear.

❧ ❧ ❧ This was the thing that had caused Nix such agitation: Next to the handbill calling for manikins was an old notice announcing the final performances of *The Dog's Muzzle*. Unlike the original playbills, which had featured the girl tailor in a dog mask, leaning on giant shears, the final version showed her wearing wolf's ears, flogging the character of Gout. The cartoon was captioned with a verse from the play that had become a popular expression around town:

> *Come a day, sir, yes, sir,*
> *The wolf will come and beat on you!*

But later the cream-and-black had blotted the words from Nix's brain, and the cartoon was forgotten.

❧ ❧ ❧ In the space of a few days, their little household had fallen into a comfortable constellation. Ylfcwen had resigned herself to the prospect of having her wings painfully bound to her back, when Winsom remembered the fashion for wing cases. Thus attired, she might move in society accepted as a mortal woman, Lady Gobeleyn, sister of the deceased.

Ylfcwen's wings had been the least of her worries. She lived in dread of Nix leaving her to try his hand with the actors. If Nix left, Winsom would soon follow, and she would be alone. She said her Fates every night and lit a candle against them leaving.

One afternoon, as she strolled along the long, vaulted gallery of mirrors, she had suddenly been seized by an irresistible urge to try out her wings. The effect was rather nice: endless copies of herself reflected back into eternity in the glass. She executed a slow roll and tumble, and her mirror selves did likewise, like the view through a kaleidoscope room. When she had grown a little too dizzy doing this, she flew up to inspect the fresco on the ceiling. As she had suspected, the elves were badly done, their expressions annoyingly insipid, their wings anatomically inaccurate.

A muffled cry had made her glance down. She saw Nix, standing stock still in a shaft of mote-heavy sunlight, as though overtaken where he stood by a shower of molten gold. The sight of his uplifted face, the rapture on it and the wonder, let Ylfcwen know that she had made her first conquest.

🐾 🐾 🐾 Ulfra was alone in the workroom of the Cat's Face. It was their customary closing day, and Tansy was spending it with Lady Twixtwain. Ulfra had begged off—since their last conversation, she had been mildly dreading seeing Lady Twixtwain again, though, if pressed, Ulfra could not have said why.

Things were much upset at the house in Goldenmouth Street; Lady Twixtwain was having new carpets put down, and when the old ones were pulled up, the floors beneath were found to be wormy. So she had the floorers in; the clamor of hammers and scraping of planes on wood seemed to sound throughout the house long after the workmen had gone home. Both Opaline and her owner were in a state of high nervous agitation, but it was the dog who was sent to stay at the Cat's Face. "After all," said Lady Twixtwain, "someone has to make sure the carpenters don't sham the work or raid the wine cellar."

So, because Lady Twixtwain had a horror of slanted floors and tables with wobbly legs, Ulfra was in the workroom trying to figure out where a dress had gone wrong, and Opaline was curled up asleep on the rug near the workroom stove.

"What in heaven," muttered Ulfra, turning the garment around in her lap. It was a mess of muslin pattern, grey wool, pins, chalk lines, and loose basted stitches. It had been abandoned by the frustrated seamstress, and Ulfra had to straighten the garment out before the scheduled fitting the next day.

She had just begun to sort it out when Opaline lifted her head from the carpet and whimpered softly. The next moment, the shop bell rang. Ulfra picked up a stitch ripper and bent over her task; the shop was closed, and besides, it was after hours. Whoever it was would have to come back the next day.

Then she saw Opaline looking at her reproachfully.

"Oh, all right!" she said, setting down the dress. "I needed a stretch anyway."

For a moment she did not recognize him without the wolf-skin cloak. He'd been to a barber; his beard was newly trimmed. He still smelled of the leather (though he no longer wore the breastplate) and more faintly of the wine he had drunk with dinner, and the bayberry lotion with which the barber had anointed him. And there was something else—the faint tang of Otherworld.

"I've come for a shirt," said Galt.

"We're closed," she said.

"I know."

It was damp there, on the step. "You had better come in," she said grudgingly.

She was all business and did her best not to catch his eye as she rolled out bolts of muslin.

"This one isn't cheap, but it's the best in the shop. Is this shirt for every day or a celebration?"

"I hope for a celebration."

"Then I would make it up in this, if you like it. It's brushed, so it has a slight nap on one side."

"I like it very much."

"You haven't felt it."

"I don't need to," he said gently.

Ulfra replaced the bolt in its bin. "You had better take your shirt off so I can try some pattern shirts on you."

As he unbuttoned the shirt, Ulfra wondered at the exquisite workmanship. It was made of humble muslin, but a skilled hand had fashioned those buttonholes. Looking up, she saw that Galt was more than usually florid.

"My sister makes them for me. She used to be a nun."

"She makes a fine buttonhole." He removed the shirt, and she was startled to see an irregular scar, pink and raised, among the grizzled hairs of his chest.

"I didn't always wear a breastplate," he said. "I once wrestled a boar and it caught me with a tusk." He smiled, recalling her words in the courtyard the day he had first seen her. "From the boar's point of view, I suppose it was the least I deserved."

She handed him a pattern shirt made up in inexpensive muslin. "Here, try this one." When he had put it on, she stood back and looked at him with a critical eye.

"That looks well on you. A little less fullness in the sleeves, I think, and the neck should be let out. I don't think it needs any decoration but the tuck work."

Galt considered his reflection in the mirror. "No, I don't think the king's guard will haul me in for breaking the sumptuary laws."

"Are you going to wear it at court?"

"I plan to wear it to a wedding."

His meaning was lost on her. Ulfra placed half a dozen pins in her mouth. Tansy was always scolding her, saying she would swallow a pin one of these days, but she hated wearing a pin-cushion on her wrist. She reached for the sleeve, to mark the spot where she would take it in. His hand came up and covered hers; it surprised her, that his hand was so warm. Suddenly she was overcome by a feeling strong and sharp; it was not fear, though it made her heart race, and it was not pain, though there was at its center a sweet ache.

"Look at me," he whispered. And at last she did, looked full into the depths of his dark eyes, and she saw there the reflection of something so unlikely, so unexpected, that it was wonderful beyond imagining.

Galt reached up and very slowly began to draw the pins from between her lips, for it is a dicey business to kiss someone whose mouth is full of pins.

🐾 🐾 🐾 "Things are all in an uproar," Tansy said. She was standing at the window, watching the passersby in Goldenmouth Street and seeing none of them. "I am sure I don't know what to do."

It was the day after Galt's visit to the Cat's Face, and Tansy and Ulfra had spent much of the night in earnest conversation.

"Now *there's* something to consider," said Lady Twixtwain thoughtfully. "Can two people even *have* an uproar? Wouldn't you ideally have to have at least three or four to do it properly?"

They were standing in Lady Twixtwain's house, in a spacious salon sadly denuded of its elegant furnishings. Beneath their feet the new floors had been sanded and rubbed with beeswax to a glassy sheen. Lady Twixtwain bent down and placed Opaline's ball in the center of the floor. After a second's hesitation, the ball rolled slowly but with gathering speed to one corner of the room. Lady Twixtwain pressed her lips together in a grim smile.

"Ah! I suspected as much, but I did not like to say anything until I had made my little test. But my woes are beside the point. Will she marry him, do you think?"

"Who knows? But what will happen to the Cat's Face, if she does? Our reputation rests on her fame, not mine. What am I, without the prince's girl tailor?" Tansy put a hand to her mouth. "Listen to me! I should be wishing her happy."

208

"She is unschooled in love. When the novelty has worn off, perhaps this attachment will seem less compelling. I think Galt knows that and will not rush her to an answer."

"I fear she will rush him! I hate to think what might have happened, if I had not come home when I did."

Lady Twixtwain laughed at her friend. "Tansy! Listen to yourself!"

Tears welled in the leopard-woman's eyes. "I would not see her hurt, not for anything in the world."

"No, of course not. And if he is half as much in love with her as you suggest, neither would Galt. I will come and have a talk with her, but I can't stay long. I have carpenters to murder."

They found Ulfra filling the window with the half-models of the prince's wedding clothes. The royal commission had specified that the Cat's Face should make all the clothes half-size for an exhibition that would travel the length of the kingdom, raising money for the new almshouses and asylums. Ulfra had painted a woodland scene and posed the half-models around it on wire forms riding wire horses. A wire hawk paused on a gauntlet, ready to chase down a wire pigeon suspended from a string.

"It's marvelous!" said Tansy. "But how in heaven's name did you manage this all by yourself?"

"I'm not sure," Ulfra said, working another costume over its wire form. "I wanted something to do with my hands, I suppose."

Inside they found that the fabric in the bins had been reorganized by color, the floor swept, and the stove polished. A box of spangles, buttons, and beads had been turned out on the counter, where Ulfra had begun to sort them.

Tansy covered her mouth and sank into a chair, and Lady Twixtwain began to laugh.

"If it isn't Ella Cinders, sorting lentils from the ashes!" She seized Ulfra's hands and examined them closely. "Just as I thought. You're coming out in calluses, and there's stoveblack under your nails. Come, young woman," she said, taking her firmly by the elbow, "you and I are going to have a little chat."

❧ ❧ ❧ "Well, do you *want* to marry him?"

"I don't know!" Ulfra said. "I can't leave the Cat's Face, and Tansy."

"Of course, you needn't marry him. A young woman in your position should not underestimate the importance of her independence. Especially if she has brains behind her pretty face."

"He says he will wait and ask me again in a year."

Lady Twixtwain smiled and laid a hand on Ulfra's cheek. "Then he is braver than I gave him credit for. Or more foolish."

But Lady Twixtwain saw something in the girl's eyes that made her think Galt would like Ulfra's answer when at last she gave it.

❧ ❧ ❧ The time came for Master Fell to meet his untimely demise. After much discussion, Felicity and Iona agreed Fell should be killed in an accident with the printing press. That way, no one would question the sealed coffin. They fashioned a body out of bars of lead wrapped in paper and linen and dressed in some of Fell's clothes.

"Are you sure it's heavy enough?" asked Iona.

"I was *pressed* to death!" cried Fel. "How heavy could I *be*?"

Burial took place in the part of the graveyard reserved for the grander tombs and vaults. Niccolaus and Ermingrude stood to one side with Columba and her betrothed, while Iona stepped forward to strew rose petals on the coffin. Another young woman, dressed in the green mourning reserved for relatives, stepped up and emptied a vial of ashes-of-roses over the open grave.

"Who is that?" Columba whispered.

"Some female relative of Fell's," said Ermingrude. "A sister, I think, just come from the nunnery."

210

Behind this conversation stood Lucivia, heavily veiled. She was watching the two mourners with some satisfaction. The match seemed to have been a good one, and she liked to see her newlyweds doing well. She had heard that the young widow planned to carry on the work of Fell's printing shop. Broadsides had appeared in town announcing the opening of a press available "to print small volumes at modest cost with quality rivaling any copyist." Lucivia already had another match planned, between the youngest daughter of a wealthy ship's captain and a young woman with a great gift for music but without prospects for making a prosperous marriage.

🌾 🌾 🌾 Marriage seemed finally to be agreeing with Berthold, a fact that relieved the matchmaker considerably. As the court gossip mill ground it, the crown princess had stood up to her father and said that she intended to accompany the prince to the theater. They had their own private box, and so there could be nothing improper in it. Lucivia had gone herself and had been gratified to see the way the prince let his hand casually rest on the princess's knee. It seemed Berthold had finally realized the benefits of his situation.

🌾 🌾 🌾 The grave diggers stepped forward and tossed the first spadeful of earth onto the lid of the coffin.

"How I like that sound," Fell whispered to Iona behind her handkerchief. "Freedom!"

"Hold it till we get home, can't you? I think Columba suspects."

But Columba had worries of her own. Her affianced husband was a man of business, and he had expressed concern about the cost of her planned bridal attire. To pay a king's ransom for a gown to be worn but a few hours was madness, he said. Did she want them in the poorhouse before the vows were even said?

Had she any idea what an ell of swansdown silk cost? As much as a carriage! She should prevail upon her father to make them a gift of the money, instead. So there were to be no watered-silk gown with pearled bodice, no elfsbreath overskirt with opal finish, no otter-skin gloves, no fur-trimmed traveling cloak. He had already thrown down the gauntlet, saying he thought she might be married in Iona's gown, *made over.*

She quite hated him already.

🌣🌣🌣 There was great excitement in the Binder household as they prepared for a long-postponed visit from Iiliana. The Book of Healing was to be returned to Chameol, and the Binder family was going to accompany Iiliana on the voyage. The Book would be installed in the library at Chameol amid great celebrations.

Everything was ready for the visit. The various interior surfaces of the house had been swept, scoured, or polished. Provisions had been laid in: nestled in the coals of the hearth, an iron kettle of duck, sausage, and beans was beginning to release a mouthwatering aroma. The boys, already keyed to a high pitch of excitement, began to squabble over the pinecone animals they were making to decorate the dinner table.

"Take it back!" said Grimald, twisting his brother's arm.

"No! It *does* look like a skunk. Who ever saw a fox with legs that short?"

Badger looked up from the antlers he was whittling. "You two need to take the edge off your tempers before you cut yourselves. Here—why don't you go down by the stream and gather some moss for the animals to stand on? You can check the fish traps while you're at it."

They went off, after being sternly admonished not to tease the snapping turtle. Binder picked up Grimald's fox and smiled. It *did* look like a skunk.

❦ ❦ ❦ Caitlin despaired of turning her workroom into a bed-chamber befitting a former queen of Chameol. At last she sat down on the bed to catch her breath, casting a critical glance around the room. A linen runner transformed the ink-stained worktable into a washstand for the ewer and basin. The cot where she took her naps had been covered with a feather bed and counterpane borrowed from the Harrier farm. An earthenware pitcher held black branches with small scarlet berries. Not palatial, she thought, but it has a homely charm.

A crown of red hair appeared at the top of the ladder, followed immediately by Iiliana's laughing eyes.

"Careful!" cried Caitlin, as she was caught up in a fierce embrace. "I'm filthy."

"Never mind—I've been two weeks on a ship—I'm no rose myself," said Iiliana, holding Caitlin at arm's length. "My dear, my dear! How it mends my ragged soul to see you!"

Caitlin felt a sudden stab of relief that was as keen as anguish, and had to turn away. "Nice of Badger to tell me you'd arrived! Wasn't he downstairs?"

"I wanted to surprise you. Besides, I had a long letter for him from Elric, and he was instantly engrossed." A former knight of Chameol, Elric was Iiliana's brother and Binder's dearest friend.

"But I can't contain myself another minute," said Iiliana. "Take me to the *Book!*"

The Book of Healing was in the bindery among the roots of the oak with the red door. Powerful enchantments had spared it the ravages of flood, fire, and bookworms; eight-year-old boys, however, were another matter, and Caitlin had not been about to take chances.

Iiliana sat before the Book a long time, turning its pages silently, so that a casual observer might have thought it was a book she knew well. She asked once for more light and took from her pocket a jeweler's glass, which she fitted to her eye in order to examine a detail of one of the marginal paintings. At last she leaned back with a great sigh and sat a long time with her eyes closed. Just as Caitlin was beginning to wonder whether she had fallen asleep, Iiliana's eyes opened. They were full of tears.

"Well," she said in an unsteady voice, wiping them on her sleeve. "I could stand to wash my face, change my linen, and drink a pot of tea."

❦❦❦ "I have to admit, once the excitement wore off I was a little disappointed. I had hoped to find all four books together."

They had taken their tea out into the clearing to enjoy the last rays of light.

Iiliana bit her lip. "What was the rhyme on the cover? They shall be healed and made visible? Maybe we need to heal something before the others will come out of hiding."

"The strange thing is, I don't read that particular rune script well at all, yet I knew what the words meant. I understood what was *written* even when I couldn't make out the *writing*."

"I noticed that, too. The Keepers didn't know who would eventually find the book. Suppose they thought that reading might die out entirely. So they added a charm to help the reader along. We know of charms to keep someone from reading what they aren't meant to see. It only stands to reason that there would be an opposite kind of spell."

❦❦❦ Just then the boys returned from the stream. Bram hung back as Grimald threw himself on Iiliana with a great, triumphant bellow. Her braids pulled down from their circlet and hanging to her waist, Iiliana lifted Grimald's hands from her eyes long enough to glance at Bram.

"Unhand me!" she said to Grimald, who wanted to know whether her ship had encountered whirlpools or sea monsters on the voyage. "Yes, the sea unicorns bored an enormous hole in the bow, and then we were sucked into the whirlpool. We had to take turns plugging the hole and bailing to get afloat again."

It was late when they sat down to supper. Down the middle of the table, the strip of moss had been arranged with ferns and pebbles in a miniature landscape, through which wandered the pinecone animals, one in front of each place. Binder had a badger, Caitlin a doe, Bram the disputed fox/skunk, Grimald an otter, and Iiliana a stag and boar (since the boys could not agree who should make the animal for the guest, they both had). Small rushlights flickered the length of the table, shining on the crockery.

After dinner, Caitlin sat and watched Iiliana as she brushed out her braids, her magnificent copper hair streaming over her shoulders in the flickering rushlight. She kept up a steady stream of jokes with Grimald on her left, quietly winning over Bram on her right.

What if our lots were reversed? Caitlin wondered. What if it were me sitting there, home triumphant from a mission to Twelvemoon, playing aunt to someone else's children? Before she could shut her mind to it, the troublesome thought had crept into her mind: What if she had remained on Chameol, had never married? She could have raised Grimald by herself, on Chameol. And there would never have been Rowan.

But with the thought came a sudden certainty: If she had not lost Rowan, Bram would never have been restored to her.

She drank her cider and caught Binder looking at her. He took her hand and pressed it gently.

"Wishing you were a seer on Chameol?"

"A little. Does it show?"

"A little." In the rushlight his blue eyes gave nothing away.

215

It was well past midnight when they finally went to bed. He was restless beside her, and the darkness between them seemed vast and thick with unspoken questions: Once on Chameol, would she want to remain? If it hadn't been for the boys, would she have left long ago?

But he did not speak then, so she did not have to find answers. She lay awake, listening to his troubled breathing slow and change its pace as he sank into sleep. When sleep came for her, Caitlin dreamed, as she so often did, of visiting Rowan's grave. When she arrived at the spot where they had buried her, she found the moss rolled back and the grave empty. Sitting nearby, washing her tail, was a vixen, the ruling animal of the fabled herb known as cheat-grave, named for its ability to bring people back from death's door.

"Where has she gone?" asked Caitlin.

"To the moon," replied the vixen. "She was really the moon's child. You could not have kept her."

Caitlin tried to curl up in the grave, but it was too small. As she tried in vain to pull in her elbows and knees, the vixen gazed down at her, head cocked to one side.

"*That* won't work," observed the vixen. "You will have to make your bed among the living."

Caitlin awoke and lay in the dark with the dream still vivid in her mind, using all her will not to get up and go through the woods to visit the grave.

Beside her Binder stirred.

"What is it? What's wrong?"

"Nothing. A dream."

"With you, a dream is never nothing." He meant it in jest, but it was a jest with a rueful edge. "I'm sorry." Trying to kiss her in the dark, he missed her mouth and laughed. "I can't see a damned thing! Where *are* you?"

"Right here," she said, and felt her heartbeat quicken.

*   *   *

216

🦇🦇🦇 When Caitlin finally awakened for the second time, it was late morning. She left Binder to sleep and made her way to the kitchen, where she found Iiliana yawning over her tea.

"I hope the boys didn't have you out checking bat nets at dawn."

"They did, but I was awake anyway. I confess I was up all night, poring over the book, half afraid it would disappear before I'd finished reading it, like Ella Cinders's carriage at midnight." Over the rim of her cup, Iiliana's eyes laughed disconcertingly. "You look as though you spent a sleepless night yourself."

Caitlin was maddened to feel herself blush like a new bride. "I never could hide anything from you."

"Forgive me—I can't help teasing. It makes me happy to see you lose sleep for a good cause." Iiliana searched her face. "Or am I wrong?"

Caitlin shook her head. "No. He and I have had our rough patches. I think we smoothed them out a little last night. What's this?"

On the table was a scrap of paper on which was written a short column of letters and numbers:

$$W\ 11$$

$$N\ 23$$

$$E\ 19$$

$$S\ 6$$

"Where did this turn up?" asked Caitlin.

"It fell out of the looking-glass frame when I was washing my face. I wanted to ask you what it meant."

"It's the tailor's riddle I wrote you about. 'Waist, eleven; neck, twenty-three; elbow, nineteen; shoulder, six.' "

"Oh, now I see. When I read it, I took them for the points of the compass."

Caitlin sank slowly into the other chair, a curious expression on her face. "Iiliana . . ."

"What? What did I say?"

"Of *course* they seemed like nonsense. They aren't tailor's measurements at all!"

15.

The Tailor's Riddle

◆

"Upon my soul!" cried Bembo Gill, "if it isn't a pigeon among the cats!"

The unexpected messenger had landed on the sill, met one yellow-eyed feline stare, and had promptly flown to perch on the highest rafter, where it trained on the bookseller a beady eye, as if to say, Now what?

After rummaging in the tangle on the landing, Bembo finally unearthed the stepladder used to retrieve books from the highest shelves. It brought him level with the rafter. There was a capsule affixed to the pigeon's leg.

Master Gill,
If I may beg a favor, would you call on the proprietors of the Cat's Face in Everlasting Lane and tell them that I plan to pay them a

visit tomorrow at noon on an urgent matter of great mutual interest? (Can you come, too? It involves the Books.)

Your servant, C. Binder

Bembo seized the pigeon firmly and made his way back down the ladder. Holding the bird out of reach of the swarming cats, he went to the window.

"I imagine you will find your way home the same way you found me," he said as he released it. It was true, he thought: A pigeon under a spell looks much the same as any other.

🐾🐾🐾 When they set eyes on the leopard-woman, Bram and Grimald stared and stared until Binder spoke to them sharply.

"Close your mouths, both of you, before you catch a fly! Excuse them," he said to Tansy. "They know better."

"Oh, let them look," she replied. "Can you blame them? Besides, I'm used to being stared at. After all, I made my living from it."

Another consequence of her days as a curiosity with Folderol's circus was that Tansy took the extraordinary in stride. She made a curtsey to Iiliana, High Counsel of Chameol and Ambassador to the Thirteen Kingdoms, as though she were any other customer, and nodded to Bembo Gill, not in the least put off by his moth-eaten attire or ragged ear. She heard Caitlin's story of the Book at the bottom of the spring with interest but no great show of surprise; Caitlin might as well have been describing the design of a gown she had seen.

"Let me see if I have this right," said Tansy carefully. "You think they changed *west* to *waist* and *north* to *neck*, in the hope that some apprentice through the years would notice that the measurements were nonsense."

"Yes," said Caitlin. "Only no one did. Even if they did notice the measurements were nonsense, they still had to figure out what they really stood for—points on the compass. Now, my guess

220

is that the numbers stand for paces, or maybe tiles. I don't suppose this is the original floor?"

"I can't say for certain, but it *is* very old. The tile layer we had in to do the new rooms had not seen its like."

The stone tiles were black and smooth, so tightly joined that there was not room to fit an eyelash between them.

"Then I think it would be tiles, not paces. Now, if only we knew where to begin."

"The room isn't square," said Binder, who had been silently counting tiles. "It's longer than it is wide."

"The right wall was moved in to make a closet," said Tansy.

"Then the original center of the room . . . was about here," said Binder, pausing at the spot.

Caitlin kneeled to examine the tile. "No different from the rest."

Bembo Gill began to laugh. "Look up!"

At regular intervals along the ceiling, there were hooks for hanging lamps; the iron of the hook directly overhead had been worked in the shape of a hand pointing down.

Starting with the tile below the hook, Grimald and Bram counted out the tiles: eleven west, twenty-three north, nineteen east, six south. Incised very faintly on the surface of the last tile was a hand pointing up.

Like the tile at the bottom of the spring, this had a thumbhole cut from one edge. It proved to be hinged to the tile next to it and lifted quite easily. They all crowded around to see.

There was an iron strongbox, the twin to the one that had been pulled from the spring in the Weirdwood. Caitlin let out her breath; she had been half expecting to find a tiny staircase spiraling down into the Otherworld.

The box was laid on the worktable. It was not so discolored as the first; the dark, glossy metal seemed untouched by time. The lid bore a different inscription: "That which was destroyed shall be recalled from dreams and longing."

Like the first, it had no latch. Unlike the first, no amount of polishing would open it. Caitlin tried, then Iiliana, and so on around the room.

"I don't seem to have the magic touch either, I'm afraid," said Ulfra, handing the box back to Caitlin.

At these words Bembo jumped as though stuck with a pin. He traded a meaningful glance with Caitlin: He was the only person in the room with a changed shape.

"That just leaves Bembo, I think," she said, handing him the box.

At the bookman's touch, the hidden clasp sprang open, revealing a book satchel like the first. The book he removed from it was bound in plain oak boards.

"It doesn't look like one of the Books of the Keepers," said Caitlin.

"Well, we'll know as soon as I get this clasp undone," said Binder.

"Not one of the Books, but something better!" said Bembo, rubbing his hands together. Caitlin looked at him; he had had just that gleam in his eye once before, when speaking of the love of books that had cost him his true shape. He turned now to Iiliana. "It's nothing less, I'll wager, than the catalog of the lost library of Iule."

"That's done it," said Binder, as the clasp gave way.

It was as simple within as it was without: The pages were closely written in black ink, with no decoration of any kind. It appeared to be a list of books. The pages were ruled, divided into columns for the title, author, and donor of each volume. At the end of each entry some words had been added by a different pen in an ink that was somewhat browner.

"Oak gall," said Binder.

"These runes were written by a second scribe and, if I'm not mistaken, in great haste," said Iiliana.

Caitlin bent over Iiliana's shoulder. "In the hours before the Keepers fled?"

"Maybe they tell where the books were hidden," said Grimald.

"One would think so," said Iiliana. "Unfortunately, I've never seen this particular rune tongue before and I haven't the slightest idea what this says."

"I can read them."

Bram had spoken without meaning to and now, finding them all looking at him, he stared, tongue-tied, at the floor.

"Go on," Bembo urged gently. "You can read them. . . ."

His tongue suddenly loosened, and the words tumbled out in a hurry. "They're elvish. The Chronicles were written in them. I had to do my lessons in them every day. I can still read them." He pointed to the first line. "It says, 'In the name of the blessed sage Thyllyln, who kept and hid you, I bid you appear.' "

His words echoed in the workroom, then faded away, leaving them standing in a charged silence they were afraid to break. Then Iiliana laughed.

"Gracious, I half expected—"

She was interrupted by a cry of surprise from Tansy, who stood pointing at the padded board used for pressing clothes.

"The goose! Everyone, look at the goose!"

Sitting upright on its stand, the tailor's iron had begun to glow and hiss. Soon the glow had spread and deepened until the whole iron was fire red. The hissing rapidly rose to a kettle's screech, and soon the iron was white-hot. The screech grew so loud that the boys covered their ears. Then suddenly it ended in an explosive pop that made them all jump.

When the steam cleared, the goose had vanished. In its place was a book, its cream vellum cover decorated with a chameleon worked in gold leaf.

"The Book of Changing," said Iiliana, reaching for it.

"Careful," said Tansy. "It's still hot."

When it had cooled, they let Bram open it. "After all, you summoned it," said Iiliana.

Twice he reached for it, and both times snatched back his hand at the last minute. "You do it," he whispered to Grimald.

The covers were quite cool now. Grimald undid the metal clasps that held the book shut and turned to the first page.

"It's ruined!" he said, dismayed.

At first glance it seemed that the book had been damaged by water. The runes were meaningless blots of ink, the pictures in the margins random smears of pigment, as though the colors had run in the rain. But as they watched they saw the runes dissolving and reforming before their eyes.

"The famous shifting runes . . . ," said Iiliana.

"Yes, the ones that have driven so many scholars mad," said Caitlin. She turned to Tansy. "Have you got two small mirrors I can borrow?"

Reflected in the second mirror, the runes sat still long enough to be read and the swirls of color in the margins resolved into wonderful illuminations: A serpent with a dog's head chased its tail; a griffin played cuckoo in a raven's nest; monkeys in armor jousted astride unicorns. But most wonderful of all, the illuminations were constantly remaking themselves. As they watched, the dog-headed serpent succeeded in swallowing its tail and disappeared entirely.

At last Caitlin returned the book to its satchel, and Bram read aloud the charm for the next entry in the catalog.

" 'In the name of the blessed sage Gudule, who kept and hid you, I bid you appear.' "

Nothing happened, or for a few minutes it seemed that nothing had happened. Then Ulfra noticed that one of the old pattern books kept at the back of the shop had fallen from its shelf and was hanging suspended from its chain. It was no longer a pattern book, but a volume bound between covers of ivory carved with all manner of fantastic beasts.

"Careful," said Iiliana, as Caitlin reached for the clasps that held the book shut, "If my memory serves me, the Keepers protected this Book with wailing runes."

224

"Don't worry," said Bembo, producing a small vial from one pocket. "Powdered bookworm. I always carry a little with me, just in case. Really!" he said, catching Binder's doubtful look. "You never know when it might come in handy."

The book was dusted with the antidote, and when it was opened, the wailing runes were mostly subdued, though they whispered and muttered among themselves. The Book of Naming was a catalog of the names of things: all the beasts and birds, the stones and gems, the seas and rivers, the winds and stars. The Book had fallen open to "The Creatures of the Air." In addition to remarkably lifelike portraits of goshawks, swallowtails, and mute swans, the artisan had painted dodos, the phoenix, dragons, and a strange creature of mortal form that carried tall, feathered wings folded behind its back. The outer surface of the wings was a glossy black, the inner surface iridescent. Each creature's name was written underneath its picture in four rune tongues: ancient mortal, the elvish tongue that Bram had been translating for them, and two others Iiliana didn't recognize.

"I think this one might be goblin, but it's not one of my rune tongues. And this other one—from the accents, it must surely be Longaevi."

"What is Longaevi?" asked Grimald.

"The language of the Longaevi, the Long-lived Ones," said Iiliana. "The old stories say they were a winged race older than the elves. They got their name because they lived much longer than you or me."

"What happened to them?" asked Grimald.

"No one knows. One cradle tale says they built their houses too near the sun and were banished to the Land of Night. Some people think they fled from the Pentaclists and settled in the far north, beyond where our maps end."

"They weren't in my anatomy book," said Bram. "It just showed elves and goblins."

Unable to contain his exasperation, Grimald punched his brother in the arm. "We swore, no secrets! You never told me!"

Bram rubbed his arm thoughtfully. "It was just an old school-book." He looked up into his mother's face. "Wasn't it?"

Caitlin bent down and gathered Bram to her with one arm, snaring Grimald in the crook of the other, and hugged them so fiercely that they protested.

"I think we should stop," said Iiliana. "I know I'm all out, and Bram can't read all those charms aloud. We can come back tomorrow." She turned to Tansy and Ulfra. "That is, if it won't disturb your work too much?"

"Heavens, who could sew after this?" said Tansy, "Besides, the work will wait."

"But will our ship?" said Binder. "We sail for Chameol the day after tomorrow."

"We'll sail," said Iiliana. "The books have stayed hidden this long; they should be safe a little longer. The Keepers knew what they were about."

It was agreed that they would stay the night in town; Bram would teach Caitlin and Iiliana to sound out the charms so that they could retrieve as many books as possible the following day.

"Here's the thing," mused Tansy. "With all the festivities for the prince's wedding, the inns are full. I'd gladly put you up myself, if only I had enough beds."

"That's all right," said Iiliana. "We have a place to stay." The Knights of Chameol kept safe houses in every village and town throughout the thirteen Moons. Thus, a beleaguered knight might find sleep in the hay over a buttery in Twinmoon, or between fine linen sheets in a nobleman's summer house in Fifth-moon, or upon a pile of sails and nets in a fisherman's shack in Eightmoon, all of them refuge for those engaged in the struggle against the evil necromancer. Now that Myrrhlock had been destroyed, the Knights had been dispersed, but the network of houses remained in place, ready like the Knights against the day when they would be called to serve again. Lately Iiliana had been turning some of the safe houses to new uses.

226

At the corner, they parted from Bembo Gill, who could not be persuaded to sup with them. As Caitlin watched him walk away down the street, she felt a vague foreboding, though she could not have given it a name. At her side, Bram slipped his hand into hers, and she gave it a squeeze.

"Does he have to go? Can't he come with us?"

"No, he had to feed his cats." But the words rang hollow as she said them.

As though he sensed this, Bram ran after Bembo, who heard the rapid approach of footsteps on the paving stones and turned around.

"Here, here! What demon's at your heels?"

"Don't go!" Bram gasped the words, choked by sudden tears.

"I must. I will be going away on a journey, and there is much I have to do to prepare for it." Bembo smiled a fond, sad smile. He no longer seemed a befuddled shopkeeper; now his eyes were sharp and wise, and in their depths Bram saw something ancient and strange that made him shiver.

The bookman reached into his pocket and withdrew a small object wrapped in a handkerchief. "Now, now, no tears! Here is something for your mother. Will you give it to her, with my thanks?" He pressed the handkerchief into Bram's hand.

Bram took the handkerchief and nodded, too heartsore to speak. He clutched it tightly, watching Bembo's retreating back until the bookman turned a corner and was gone. There was a faint buzzing coming from the handkerchief-wrapped something. Carefully Bram undid the loose knot.

It was the bee treatise.

🐝 🐝 🐝 "Madam, there are visitors downstairs to see you."

Lucivia set down her pen and glanced at the clock; it was an unfashionable hour when most people could be expected to be lying down before the theater.

"Visitors? More than one?"

"Two ladies, a gentleman, and two boys. The one lady, she asked me to bring you this, with her compliments."

Lucivia scanned the note, then slid it beneath her blotter.

"I'll be right down. And you can lay out my blue silk with the pearl fringe."

"Madam?" Rose wavered in the doorway.

"Why? Weren't you able to get out that mud stain on the hem?"

"Yes, of course, madam. It's just that, well, that's your court dress, madam."

"Yes, Rose, and I would like you to lay it out, please."

Burning with curiosity, Rose did so, wondering which of the guests was of sufficient rank for her mistress to dress at this uncivil hour, and what the note had said. She would not have been much enlightened to learn that it contained two words ("Surprise . . . Iiliana") and nothing more.

✿✿✿ "My dear!"

Lucivia crossed the room to Iiliana and embraced her. "Poor good Rose was staring at your note so hard that I thought it would spontaneously ignite. This *is* a surprise, and such a happy one!"

"Pardon the hour and inconvenience." Iiliana introduced Caitlin and Binder, without explaining their connection to Chameol. She did not need to; one glance at Caitlin's seer's eyes told Lucivia her entire story. She remembered a ballad that had been popular some seven years ago that told of a seer who had left Chameol to wed a knight and live in the Weirdwood.

"These must be your boys," she said. But that redhead was surely a goblin, Lucivia thought, watching them all agog at such wonders as gilded mirrors, tasseled footstools with clawed bear feet, and an embroidered screen depicting the mining of gems.

The dark one was mortal, but he had the unmistakable stamp of the Otherworld on him. "Rose, I think you might make a bath ready in the blue salon. In the meantime, why don't you show our young gentlemen guests the theater?"

Before his marriage, the prince had made a gift to Lucivia of a model theater, complete with scenes for *The Dog's Muzzle*. In addition to miniature figures of the prince and Gout, there was a little Modesty pursued by a pack of small, flocked wolves, and the girl tailor had a tiny pair of tin shears that snipped. After twenty minutes, a faint howling reached the others from down the hall, followed by the sounds of happy mayhem.

The Books had been locked into Lucivia's strong room for safekeeping, and while Rose was supervising the business of the bath, Lucivia brought a bottle of wine from the cellar and prepared a rarebit and toast over the sitting-room fire. Iiliana saw the royal crest on the wax that sealed the wine bottle and smiled. It was a vintage put up expressly to celebrate the prince's wedding.

"You're looking very well," Iiliana observed. "Matchmaking must agree with you."

"Yes, I suppose it does. The enterprise certainly has surpassed my dearest hopes for success."

"But that's outrageous!" Binder protested when the nature of her matchmaking was explained to him. "How is it any better than the court of Fifthmoon?" The lords and ladies of Fifthmoon lived strictly segregated lives, having next to nothing to do with one another. As a result, the court of Fifthmoon had no babies. "If men are such hopeless creatures, you might as well wall us all in and have done with any pretense."

"It seems to me," said Lucivia, "that the walls are already up. They are the marriage laws. They are invisible walls, it is true, but they are all but insurmountable to a young woman without a dowry. Unless she has a way to earn her living, she must marry it. What is badly needed is a guild for women, where they can learn their own trades." She smiled. "Besides, from my vantage point, I see little risk of mortalkind dying off anytime in the near future."

But Iiliana was not about to let the shuttlecock lie, and she and Binder began to trade rapid volleys. Caitlin sat a little to one side, lulled by the fire and deep in thought, letting the good-natured argument wash over her.

🌿🌿🌿 It was late when at last they retired. Rose had long since bathed the boys and put them to bed. When Caitlin paused to look in on them, they lay at angles in the great canopied bed, each clutching one of the theater's tiny players.

The air of the room was stale and close, and Caitlin crossed the room, dodging stray wolves and bits of scenery, to open the shutters to the night breeze. She stayed there longer than she meant to, enjoying the cool air on her cheek. The runes had rotted her brain, she thought sadly. Time was, she would have been able to tell what was out of kilter. Leave the cloister at your peril, that's what I'll tell the next aspiring seer I meet. Your eyes'll cloud over and your brain will turn to sponge.

The night watchman passed beneath the window, crying his singsong "All's well," but the words sounded tinny and false. No, she thought suddenly, all's *not* well. That's what I felt when Bembo said good-bye. Suddenly she wanted another look at the Books.

The book satchels had been locked in Lucivia's strong room, a small, windowless closet with a iron door where she kept her clients' dowries (as well as her own considerable commissions). Its shelves held fabulous sums of gold and equally fabulous gems. Lucivia had given the key to Iiliana before retiring, and the High Counsel had made her bed on a cot just outside the door.

Iiliana had just unpinned her hair; it streamed down her shoulders like a sheet of flame. She paused with her brush in midair as Caitlin appeared.

230

"I thought you had gone to bed." She gave Caitlin a more searching look and set down the brush. "What's wrong?"

"Perhaps nothing. I'm probably being a silly goose, but I won't be able to sleep unless I have one last peek at the Books."

Iiliana took the key from around her neck and unlocked the massive door. At once a curious sound met their ears, as a child raving in a fever or an old woman delirious with pain. "Something's awakened the runes," said Iiliana. "Here, help me get the door open."

Despite its weight, the door opened easily. As soon as Caitlin drew it from the satchel, the Book of Naming began to wail in earnest.

"What a din," said Iiliana, covering her ears. "Let's hope the king doesn't call out the guard."

"I forgot about the powdered bookworm," said Caitlin, turning the pages until she came to the section titled "The Creatures of the Air." The picture of the Longaevi was just as she remembered it. Then what had caused her such unease? She turned over the leaf.

There, in the margins, the artist had painted the story of a nobleman who loved books so much that he sold his true shape to a pawnbroker. So the man she knew as Bembo Gill was very likely a Longaevi prince, and a prince probably impatient to resume his true form.

"Of course!" Her hands trembled as she unbuckled the other satchel. The book she drew out was not the Book of Changing but a manual on bell ringing.

Iiliana sank onto the cot and clutched her head.

"How could it have happened?" she moaned. "I saw Lucivia lock the door myself. How could anyone have gotten past me?"

"I don't think anyone did," said Caitlin. "I think the books were switched before we ever left the tailor's shop."

"By whom?"

231

Caitlin took a deep breath. "Iiliana—there is something I should have told you about Bembo Gill."

But before she could begin, she saw Binder looming in the doorway, boots in hand, his clothes half buttoned and buckled. "Bram's not in bed."

"But I left them both asleep," said Caitlin.

"Grimald woke up and found him gone."

"Sweet heaven, the window . . ."

Binder swore, stamping his foot down into his boot. "How far is it to Bembo's shop?"

🌸🌸🌸 Bembo opened the shutter and peered down at Bram.

"Got any peppermint whistles? Treacle mousetraps? Larks' tongues?"

Bram could only shake his head.

"That's all right, then," said Bembo, holding open the door.

Bram walked in and sat down on the stool by the ink-stained worktable.

"I'm sorry I can't make you any tea. I sold the kettle this afternoon so that I could feed the cats before I left. Though they will have to fend for themselves, anyway."

"Why did you switch the books?" said Bram, staring at his hands.

"You noticed that, did you? Why didn't you say anything then?"

"I thought you might bring it back when you were done."

"Your mother would have thought to look here eventually. I imagine she's on her way already. If she's noticed you've gone missing, too."

"Why did you take the Book?" Bram looked up, eyes dull with anger and confusion. "I could have memorized the spell for you."

"I wouldn't have let you. Shape changing is not a pretty

thing, and it can be perilous, especially for one like me, who has been held in another shape so long. No, changing one's shape is best done alone, in the dead of night, when little boys are safe abed."

Bram folded his arms tightly and hooked his ankles around the legs of the stool.

"An immovable object, are you?" said Bembo. "Oh, dear. Well, it can't be helped. I've no time to argue." Clutching the Book of Changing with one hand, the bookman mounted the stepladder and unlatched the skylight.

"Where are you going?" Bram called.

"First? The roof."

Bram hesitated for a moment, then scrambled after him.

Bembo held up a finger to test the direction of the wind, nodded, and opened the Book of Changing. In order to read the shifting runes, he had rigged a pair of makeshift spectacles fitted with double lenses cut from his shaving mirror. It made him look like a madman, or a wizard. He began to recite the spell in a strange tongue. It was rough on the ear at first, but grew ever more musical.

Bram had been expecting "Abracadabra!" and an explosion like the one in the tailor's shop, but for a long time Bembo's chanting seemed to have no effect at all. Then Bram noticed something growing out of the neck of Bembo's shirt and out of his cuffs, greenish black, like a statue being covered with ivy.

It was the shape changer's tattoo, growing and changing and remaking itself the way the runes and pictures on the page of the Book did. Before long, every inch of Bembo's skin was covered by the tattoo, and as he chanted, Bram could see that his tongue was tattooed, and even the palms of his hands, and his eyelids. Then Bram couldn't see him anymore; his body was enveloped in a greenish black cloud with an acrid, inky smell that burned Bram's throat and made him hide his eyes in his sleeve.

On and on Bembo chanted. His voice changed and was not

a human voice anymore, as though the words where issuing from a different throat. Bram opened his eyes and saw that the cloud had become a dancing sheet of green flame and that the figure in the center of the flame was no longer Bembo Gill.

The chanting ended abruptly, and the flame snuffed itself out, leaving a little oily, greenish soot around the feet of the creature Bembo had become. Like a man, but not a man, he was wrapped in a strange cloak. He raised his head, and Bram saw a sharp, dark face with brilliant eyes, ancient eyes. Then the creature shook off the cloak, and the wind caught it and spread it, and the cloak was a pair of wings that blotted out the sky.

The wind from the wings as they beat blew Bram's hair back from his face, and the look from the eyes froze him where he was, unable to speak or move or breathe. The creature fixed him with that look, then rose from the roof in a single smooth motion, catching the southerly wind in the broad sail of those enormous wings, rapidly rising higher and higher, until the dark wings disappeared against the cloud-driven, moonless night.

A single word came down from the shadow that guttered against the sky. Even from that height it was so clear that it might have been whispered in Bram's ear: "Farewell."

Bram lay a long time on the roof, crying for wonder first, then for grief, then for Ethold, then for Bembo, until all the tears were gone. His face and hands were filmed with a greenish soot, he wiped them on his shirt, then picked himself up and dusted himself off. After he had done the same for the Book of Changing, he climbed with it back down the ladder and sat down on the stool to wait. It was not long before a carriage rattled in the lane outside. Feet hammered on the stairs, fists rained on the door, voices he knew called his name.

He got up to let them in.

234

EPILOGUE

Three Years Later

✦

If the truth were known, Galt missed sitting in the threepenny seats at the theater. He had never got used to sitting in the box like a nobleman. For that matter, he had not got used to being a nobleman. The prince was now King Berthold, and six months ago he had bestowed on his friend and huntsman the title and lands of Lord Weirdwood. This afforded his wife no little amusement.

"You will have to pay the wolves a rent," she said. "After all, it *is* their wood." Her tone was gently chiding, but she spoke the truth. So the day after he was elevated to the nobility, Galt walked into the Weirdwood and left one of the king's peacocks, smuggled from the palace grounds in a picnic basket. He tethered the bird to a tree and walked back out of the wood.

The Direwolves did not eat the peacock right away, but bit

235

its tether and let it wander through the wood, fattening on acorns.

A few weeks more, said the she-wolf contentedly. She liked peacock, especially when her lieutenant plucked it for her. *Remind me to give them a gift in return, when she has her first youngling.*

❦ ❦ ❦ "How often do I have to pay rent?" Galt asked Ulfra the next night.

They were dressing for the theater, and she paused, holding the two ends of her necklace poised behind her neck.

"Quarterly," she said thoughtfully.

He took the ends of the necklace from her fingers and fastened them deftly, then kissed the nape of her neck. "Sooner or later the gamekeeper at the palace is bound to count the peacocks and come up short."

"Yes, but by then the wolves will be content with a peacock feather and a suckling calf."

He was never quite sure when she was serious. Sometimes he suspected it was that very uncertainty that lent spice to their married life.

❦ ❦ ❦ It was the first performance of a new play celebrating the first birthday of the Princess Ivy-Ysolde, and the theater boxes were full of lords and ladies in their best finery—the finest of it from the workrooms of the Cat's Face, tailors to the king and queen. But none of the patrons were more elegantly turned out than the strange couple in the box two down from Lord and Lady Weirdwood's.

The woman was of indeterminate age—her hair was silver, but her face was remarkably unlined: There was not a crease or wrinkle anywhere upon her translucent skin. Her long black gloves appeared to have been painted on her alabaster arms, and on her white throat a necklace of peerless sapphires smoldered with a deep blue fire. Her gown was heavy brushed silk, the inky blue known as black swan. When she turned to speak to her companion, its expertly draped folds glittered with a black dew of tiny jet beads.

Ulfra leaned over to whisper in Galt's ear.

"Who is that lady? She is very familiar."

Galt had come to think of his encounter with the elf queen as a revelation or a dream. Besides, rouged and dressed in silk, Ylfcwen looked passably mortal. "Lady Gobeleyn. The man I've never set eyes on, but from the way I've heard him described, he must be her young ward, Lord Motley. I know very little about him except that he is supposed to be a wicked hand at cards. Around town they call him Lord Piebald."

It was plain to see how he had gotten the nickname. The hair on his head was snow white, but his closely trimmed beard was coal black. Between these extremes, his eyes were a startling blue—and somehow startlingly familiar. When they met her gaze, those unsettling eyes made Ulfra jump. But it could not be Nix: He was too tall and too old. His clothes were cut in simple good taste, but the jeweled pin that fastened his plain neck cloth could have bought several gowns at the Cat's Face.

The play had started. Ulfra turned her head and watched the brightly lit scene unfold; the rich colors of the costumes; the exaggerated, pink-and-white-painted faces of the actors. She let the laughter wash over her, but the first act passed, and she could not have said what it was about.

After the play the royal couple gave a supper at the small summer palace built for the young queen's use on a quiet bend of the river. There was dancing and music, and at midnight the sleeping princess was brought out to be admired. The king led Galt off to see the aviary, which had a pair of nesting falcons.

"The oddest thing happened yesterday," said Berthold, unlocking the first of the gates to the aviary.

"How so?"

"Well, a madman was brought before me. He had been caught outside the palace gates, and his pockets were crammed with gems, the like of which I've never seen before. The palace guards assumed he had stolen them from the palace, but they were far finer than any gems in *my* crown, and besides, they were all uncut. The man was raving, clear out of his head, going on about how he was the king of the elves, that there was a price on his head, that there had been an uprising in the gemfields, and that a new Pretender was leading a revolt."

"What did you do with him?"

"Waved my hand, granted him amnesty, and told him we would hide him until the danger had passed. He's in the new asylum."

They had come to the second gate, beyond which lay the seven interlocking greenhouse pavilions that formed the Queen's Aviary. The king paused, key in the lock.

"Hear that? Those are the peacocks. You can hear them in the palace, they're that loud. Filomena insisted I move them, when her time was near. She said it sounded like children being murdered in their beds. She didn't think it could be good for the child."

"It doesn't seem to have harmed her."

"No. She is beautiful, isn't she? But, there's another odd thing. One of the peacocks is missing."

🌿🌿🌿 Ulfra was unaccountably restless and wandered out onto a balcony to enjoy the cool night air. Overhead the constellations wheeled their way across the heavens, the wolf star chasing the hind it would never catch. Below, willows on the river's bank bent to listen to the song of the moving water. A climbing vine on the wall gave off a sweet perfume; the smell of it made her heartsore.

Suddenly she smelled something else, so faint it was barely perceptible among the tangled scents from the ballroom behind her—the burning tapers and the mingled perfumes and pomades of the dancers as they exerted themselves. This smell was faint: an after-dinner clove held between the cheek and gum and fresh sawdust from the floor of a fencing salon. It reminded her keenly of the sawdust in the ring of Folderol's ragtag circus.

A man was standing at the other end of the balcony. He stepped forward, and the light of the ballroom fell upon his face. It was Lord Motley. At the sight of him Ulfra turned away, leaning out over the balcony to breathe the air from the river and clear the smell of him from her head.

"Are you all right?" he said with mild alarm.

She did not at first reply, and when she finally found her voice it came out in an urgent whisper.

"I had to do it, I *had* to."

"I know. I did think it was a rotten trick at first, but they were good people. They took good care of me."

"We couldn't live forever, picking pockets and stealing geese, always on the road. I wanted you to stay in one place. And I— I wanted to learn how to read and write and speak like a woman instead of a wolf."

She was overtaken by a sudden storm of tears. For a few minutes he waited to see if she would cry herself out. When she began to cry harder, he drew her away from the balcony, away from the lamplit windows, into the shadows and into his embrace. For a little while they clung to one another, while the river ran by below them. In a willow tree a whippoorwill sang to the moon's broken reflection in the running water.

Little by little her sobs subsided, and at last she stepped away. He offered his handkerchief; she accepted it wordlessly and dried her eyes.

"Don't be shy, have a good honk," he said. "I've got handkerchiefs by the dozen now."

She laughed and blew her nose loudly. "You're so *tall*. All those shirts I sent—they never fit you."

"They did at first. Before I grew."

"So I see. You look as though you've done very well for yourself."

He shrugged. "A run of good luck, that's all."

"Promise me . . . promise me you won't fleece anyone at cards."

"Don't worry." He laughed. "I'm reformed."

"Yes. But you still smell of Wolf, somehow."

He glanced back at the illuminated windows of the ballroom. "I should go and find her." She knew he meant the silver-haired woman in blue. "Ours is a long way home." He clasped her hand. "Good-bye, then."

"Good-bye—" She was about to say his name in Wolf, but she stopped herself. "Good-bye."

She turned back to the river and remained there a long time, until Galt came to find her, her cloak over his arm.

"You're chilly," he said, chafing her bare shoulders.

"Am I? It was so close in there, with everyone dancing."

He wrapped the cloak around her and paused behind her a moment, his chin resting easily on the top of her head as he gazed up at the night sky. "Got your fill of stars?"

She turned to him, laying her cheek on his shoulder to hide the tears in her eyes. "No."

"Well, let's go home to our own piece of heaven."

🌿🌿🌿 Nix quickly rounded up Ylfcwen's cloak and gloves, but it took some time longer for him to round up Ylfcwen. He finally found her in the royal nursery, gazing down at little Ivy-Ysolde where she slept in a curtained cradle. She was beautiful for a mortal child: all porcelain pink and gilt, with dense rose-gold lashes fringing her eyes and soft rose-gold curls on her head. Her small, dimpled fists lay outflung on the coverlet, and her small red mouth was pursed into a tender rosebud.

"Don't even *think* about it," he said, taking Ylfcwen by the elbow and leading her from the room.

240

"I wasn't." She was annoyed at the suggestion, all the more so because she had turned the matter over in her own mind and come to the same conclusion.

❦ ❦ ❦ Out of *W*'s, Iona set down her composing stick, yawned violently, and stretched. Across the shop, Fel looked up from the type for the broadsheet she was inking.

"Tired?"

"Out of sorts." Iona made a face at the shelves of set type, tied within wooden frames. "I *could* put all that away."

"Anything but that! Just make the book shorter. Of course, we can't print it at all unless the paper comes through."

Iona took one of the bundles of type from the shelf and untied it, picking through the lines for *W*'s like a child picking currants out of a pudding. At last she gave a sigh of resignation and began to sort the type into the wooden case before her, rapidly returning each rune to its own pigeonhole.

Fel pulled the first proof of the broadsheet and held it to the light to check the impression.

APPRENTICESHIPS
BY ORDER OF HER ROYAL HIGHNESS QUEEN FILOMENA,
THE QUEEN'S GUILD
HAS BEEN ESTABLISHED TO OFFER APPRENTICESHIPS
TO YOUNG WOMEN IN THE FOLLOWING TRADES:

Apothecary	Pewterer
Bookbinder	Printer
Clock Maker	Silversmith
Cobbler	Tailor
Hatter	Woodblock Engraver

APPLY AT THE QUEEN'S GUILDHALL
NEW GUILD STREET
(OLD JOUSTING FIELDS)

Outside the house where Bembo Gill had kept his shop, there now hung a new shingle. On one side was carved *BOOK-BINDER* and on the other, *APOTHECARY*.

The house had been divided along similar lines. Living quarters took up the left half of the house, and their respective workshops, the right, the bindery on the upper floor and the apothecary below. In the stairwell, rising fumes of distilled herbs mingled with the smells of warm glue and leather. The apothecary shop shared a hearth with the kitchen of the living quarters. It made it handy when one had to watch the progress of both dinner and a batch of herb simples. There had been confusion only once, when they had had the fever remedy for dinner instead of the soup. None of them had had a cold all that winter.

Bram came in from his round of deliveries and set the basket down on the wooden counter beside the scales and the large jar with the picture of the mandrake man on it. Caitlin looked up from the powder she was grinding.

"That was quick. I hope some of them paid?"

He nodded. "Almost everyone, even the asylum, and they *never* pay their bill." He took a small milk can from the basket and poured some of its contents into a pie dish, which he set on the floor. Cats materialized from all the corners of the shop but not so many as there had been in Bembo's day. Excellent mousers, much in demand, their sale kept both boys in shoes.

He poured the rest of the milk into a bowl and broke a piece of bread into it. Then he bent down to pick up the child, not quite two years old, who was playing under the counter.

"She's got into the dried lizards again," he said accusingly, taking a blue-tongued skink away from the baby and balancing her on his hip. "You have to keep an eye on her."

"I was," Caitlin said. "Besides, dried lizards never hurt me, and I cut my teeth on them. They made me wise."

"Says you." He put the baby in her chair and tucked a napkin around her neck.

242

"Try one and see, if you don't believe me."

He only made a face and spooned some bread and milk into the baby, waiting to make sure she wasn't holding it in her cheek, ready to spit it out when he wasn't looking. You had to watch her all the time; she was three-quarters imp, lilie was. He glanced up at the ceiling.

"How's it going up there?"

"I'm not sure. It's been dreadfully quiet. I hope quiet and not too dreadful."

🌿🌿🌿 While his father was checking over the binding, Grimald could do little but stare at the worktable. Outwardly he appeared confident and even a little bored, his inward agonies betrayed only in the sidelong glances at his examiner.

This particular binding was the fruit of three years' study at his father's elbow, learning the bookbinder's craft; if it met with approval, Grimald would begin working in the bindery alongside apprentices from the royal guilds, some of them as old as seventeen.

Grimald's sidelong glances told him nothing. Binder had attention only for the book in his hands. The sewing was sturdy but not too stiff; the book opened invitingly in the hands. The vellum had been stretched neatly over the boards, the excess leather at the corners having been pared thin, but not too thin. The rounding of the spine was skillfully done, too, with light, glancing blows of the hammer that left no marks on the vellum. Finally, Binder fitted a jeweler's glass to his right eye and bent to examine the decorations.

Grimald had chosen the scene of the animals exiling the fox to the moon. All the animals had been worked blind, in deep relief, only their crests and hooves and horns touched with gold. The night sky had been stained a deep purple, and clouds scudded over the face of the moon. The fox was in his tiny boat, with its sail furled, telling the first of a hundred tales to forestall his departure. The fox's tale was represented by a thin scroll issuing from his mouth, with some runes on it. Gathered around the boat to listen to the story were the boar and the wolf and stag from the woods, the badger and rabbit and lark from the meadow, the frog and pike and otter from the lake. The bat hung from an overhead branch beside the whippoorwill and the owl.

Binder removed the lens from his eye, replaced his spectacles, and turned to Grimald.

"Six o'clock. You'll eat breakfast with the other apprentices. It won't be as nice as you're used to, but from now on you'll be treated just as I would treat any of the others. Understood?"

Grimald could only nod. Binder's stern expression relaxed into a smile, and he reached out to clasp the boy warmly to him.

"Well done."

🦊🦊🦊 Back in the apothecary shop, Bram finished giving lilie her bread and milk, sponged the milk from her upper lip, and set her down among the cats. Then he resumed unpacking the basket, which contained a great many bottles of all shapes and sizes. It was his job to wash them out and scrub off the labels and cut new corks for them.

Caitlin watched him. She was proud that he had doggedly stuck with his studies of herbs, even when it meant bottle washing and bill collecting. In the evenings, after the baby was asleep, he would read her large herbal for hours, poring over its pages as though it were a tale of knights' derring-do. He need not have cut the corks or watched the baby, but he was greatly insulted if either task was taken from him. Grimald complained that his brother's nose was "always in a splint."

Caitlin would have been completely content except for two things. She would rest easier once lilie had passed her third birthday, for then she would be older than Rowan had lived to

244

be. But part of her would remain restless as long as the Book of Summoning remained lost. She did her best to be philosophical about it. Yet of all the Books, it was the one most likely to stir up trouble. It might be used to summon hail and drought, floods and locusts, and even waking spirits. In Iiliana's opinion, it was better left undiscovered, and at last she had persuaded Caitlin to the same view. So it was that the three remaining Books were installed in the library at Chameol amid great celebration.

And still, and still . . .

❧ ❧ ❧ It would have eased Caitlin's mind considerably to know that the Book of Summoning had made its way into one of the lower storage rooms of Ylfcwen's former palace, where it lay in a chest with surplus copies of the *Elf Book of Court Etiquette* and sets of the ten-volume Chronicles. It was fifteen years into the reign of the Goblin King of the New Realm before the party dispatched to inventory the storerooms of the corrupt elvish regime discovered some sixty chests of books. They stood a minute debating: One was in favor of cataloging the books and making a report to the Minister of the Inventory. Another suggested burning the lot. But at last the captain in charge sealed the room and placed a green flag on it so that it would be left for a later inventory in a hundred years' time. And so they moved on to the next storeroom.

"Silver wing implements, assorted," said the captain. "Make a note, then down to the mint with them. And wing cases, assorted. Those can go directly to the furnace."